PRAISE FOR LARRY BROOKS

"A master of terror and suspense." —*Publishers Weekly*

"An intoxicating and intelligent tale of corporate corruption . . . entertaining." —*Publishers Weekly*, for *Bait and Switch* (Editor's Choice, 2004)

"*Darkness Bound*'s final scenes burst with the intensity of a first-rate horror film." —*Publishers Weekly*, for *Darkness Bound*

"An addictive thriller." —*Publishers Weekly*, for *Serpent's Dance*

"Crime novelist Raymond Chandler was widely acknowledged in his day as the Poet Laureate of The Dark Side (he looked about as inconspicuous as a tarantula on a slice of angel food cake). He died in 1959 and ever since there have been many pretenders to his throne. Among the best are James M. Cain, Elmore Leonard, Robert B. Parker, James Lee Burke—all masters of the craft, all wordsmiths of the first order, but none of them had Chandler's gifts. After half a century of being on the lookout for a crime fiction writer with a voice that rivals Chandler's, one has finally appeared, quietly chugging his way

up the bestseller lists with *Darkness Bound, Whisper of the Seventh Thunder, Serpent's Dance,* and *Bait and Switch.* His name is Larry Brooks. The guy has a slick tone and a crackling, cynical wit with lots of vivid descriptions (of both interior and exterior landscapes), and the sparkling figures of speech dance off the page and explode in your inner ear. Though as modern as an iPad 5S, he is truly and remarkably Chandleresque. He's dazzling. Check out his new one, *Deadly Faux*—it's sexy, complex, intelligent; a truly delightful novel with more plot twists than a plate of linguine swimming in olive oil."
—James N. Frey, author of *How to Write a Damn Good Novel*

DEADLY
FAUX

DEADLY FAUX

A NOVEL

LARRY BROOKS

TURNER

Turner Publishing Company
200 4th Avenue North • Suite 950 Nashville, TN 37219
445 Park Avenue • 9th Floor New York, NY 10022

www.turnerpublishing.com

Deadly Faux

Cover design: Gina Binkley
Book design: Glen Edelstein
Jacket design: Mike Penticost
Author photo: Robin Damore

Library of Congress Catalog-in-Publishing Data
Brooks, Larry, 1952-
Deadly Faux : a novel / by Larry Brooks.
pages cm
ISBN 978-1-62045-417-6 (pbk.)
1. Undercover operations--Fiction. 2. Criminals--Fiction. 3. Las Vegas (Nev.)--
Fiction. 4. Suspense fiction. I. Title.
PS3602.R64437D43 2013
813'.6--dc23
2013024441

Printed in the United States of America
13 14 15 16 17 18 0 9 8 7 6 5 4 3 2 1

For Laura
My wife, muse, mentor, and object of obsession

PROLOGUE

LAS VEGAS
March, 2009

Phillip Valentine didn't look like a guy who'd just had a bag pulled off his head. His captors seemed to notice, mumbling something about having a certifiable pretty boy in their humble presence.

For someone who survived on four hours of afternoon sleep and a daily regimen of macrobiotics, Maalox, and testosterone injections, the impeccably coiffed Phillip Valentine was always ready for his next close-up. Even now, after a thirty-minute ride with hands bound, head covered, and a gun wedged into an armpit. Each crease—both in his face and in his two-thousand-dollar suit—was perfect, sharp as the steak knife he once used to terminate the employment of a cheating Pai Gow dealer.

Or so the rumor held.

Someone had an unhealthy sense of humor. If they thought they could intimidate him with old-school theatrics they were sorely mistaken. Valentine and his business were untouchable, and every player on either coast knew it. Those who didn't were soon made to comprehend the consequences of their misjudgment.

He had been dragged to his current position, where the bag

had been pulled from his head. He was standing next to a tennis court behind a massive house with Tuscan pretensions, facing a neon-blue swimming pool fed by an illuminated waterfall tumbling over synthetic rock. The type of place his wife used to covet before her tastes turned to cocaine and low–body-fat security personnel.

His hands remained tethered behind him as he evaluated his surroundings.

Suddenly he heard a familiar yet elusive sound, a metallic clank, oddly nostalgic. He pivoted to see a batting cage paralleling the court, at one end of which was a pitching machine. A stocky man in his sixties stood astride a portable rubber home plate in an awkward stance, shorts tight and too short, thick legs black with coarse hair. Sweat flew from his face as he swung the bat, an action which, despite the resultant line drive, lacked any semblance of grace. It reminded Valentine of his golf buddies who, after years of lessons, still swung as if they had stowed a bag of tees in their rectum.

"You a baseball fan, Phillip?"

The guy, who hadn't yet turned to look at Phillip, had East-Coast city hair, shaped and fixed with enough product to lube a small motorcade. Valentine had never seen him before, which, along with the fact that he was all of five-six, made him nervous. The shorter the caricature, the bigger the swinging bat. Phillip Valentine, who was a proud five foot seven himself, knew this all too well.

He remained silent as the guy slashed at another machine-fed pitch.

"Greatest game in the world," said the batter, his eyes on the pitching machine. "You got, what, two girls, right? Twins. Ten or so. Got their mother's looks."

Something twisted in Valentine's stomach.

The next pitch was fouled away, which seemed to piss the little man off. He regrouped quickly, reassuming the stance.

"I got two boys. Nolan and Ryan. You know, after the greatest fucking professional athlete in history."

"Jordan and Gretzky might disagree," Valentine calmly shot back.

"No disrespect," countered the host. "But shit, seven no-hitters? Fifty-seven hundred Ks? Excuse me all to hell, nobody wearing satin shorts or ice skates comes close."

"Who the fuck *are* you?" asked Valentine. "I know everybody in this town."

He sensed a slight movement beyond the cage. A bulky figure sitting in shadow, watching them.

A swing and a miss, followed by a spitting profanity.

"I'm new. And who the fuck I am don't matter. What the fuck I want, *that* matters. You know what I want, smart guy? I'm betting you do."

Valentine did indeed know. He had been fielding offers for his hotel casino from shady operators for years. Lately, the usual suspects had been presenting what appeared to be squeaky-straight deals, easy financing for offshore properties that promised mutually satisfying returns, with a few discreet spiffs on the side. So far he'd heard nothing that interested him.

He knew all that was about to change.

The stocky little host emerged from the cage, pausing to press a button on a remote control hanging next to the entrance, causing the machine to wind down to an eerie, idling silence. He held the netting open as one of the thugs went behind the cage to a guy sitting in what Valentine now realized was a wheelchair. The occupant, about the same age as their host, had distant eyes and was soft about the chin, wearing penny loafers and a Lakers jersey. Baby Huey in NBA knockoffs.

The helpful thug pushed the wheelchair inside the cage. The chubby fellow sitting in it smiled giddily, happy to be there. Clearly, nobody was home.

"Check this out," said the host, holding the remote up so Valentine could see as he cranked the dial. "Ryan threw, what, ninety-nine? Hundred on a good day? Clemens and Randy, too, back in the day. Now you got Strasburg and Verlander, but the jury's out, you know? Those older guys, they got fitter as they aged. And you know what? They got smarter, too. Like you and me, except we got prettier, too."

"Is there a point somewhere on this horizon?"

The host pursed his lips, as if considering options. Or, as if insulted that his guest didn't appreciate his humor.

"Point is, nobody hits a hundred *twenty* mile-an-hour fastball. It hits *you*."

The man in the wheelchair was mumbling the theme from a McDonald's commercial. Two all-beef patties and a sesame-seed fastball.

Valentine closed his eyes, comprehending the point.

The host continued on. "They say you're one tough sum-bitch, which I respect. So in a roundabout sort of way, this is all your fault."

Thug logic, thought Valentine, trying to keep his face stoic.

"Of course it is," he said dryly.

The man's expression went blank as he pressed a button on the remote. A moment later a blur of white flashed from the far end of the cage with an audible buzz. The ball, more like a bullet now, struck the wheelchair-bound man's temple. It sounded like a watermelon hitting the pavement from three stories.

"Jesus!" yelled Valentine, involuntarily jerking backward. The goon caught him, gripping his face to force his gaze back toward home plate. The wheelchair guy's head hung limply to the side, his eyes rolling back to reveal sockets filled with white. His tongue protruded, searching for words from a suddenly dead brain.

The little man leaned close, his voice softer than before, his breath stale bourbon and garlic.

"So far you've turned down four offers to avail yourself of my services. I have one more for you. I suggest you take it."

Another ball exploded from the machine, this one hitting the fallen man's mouth, imploding teeth while nearly severing the wagging tongue. The ball came to a rest a few feet away, stained with spots of blood.

The host, whom Valentine had already cast with Joe Pesci in this emerging cinematic nightmare—stared down at the ball, biting his lip. He hesitated as he gathered his thoughts.

"Skip and I were kids in the old neighborhood. Back in the day. I promised his mother I'd take care of him, and until the day she died I did that. I always do what I say I'm gonna do."

He looked up. "You seeing a point on the horizon now, Phillip?"

"You sick little fuck . . ."

The man with the remote control shrugged.

The next ball crushed an eye socket. The once-cheery fellow in the wheelchair no longer moved.

"Skip's mother expired yesterday. A stroke."

The two men locked gazes.

"I'll send a card," said Valentine.

"No, listen to me, you got it wrong. I cared for him like a baby brother. Fed him, got him laid, paid his medical bills. Even put him in a pricey bullshit school for the learning-impaired. Bastards did nothin'. I figured, his mother dead and me having wiped his ass all these years, he owes me. So this morning over waffles I ask him, you wanna help me make a point today, Skip? An important point? He said sure."

Valentine closed his eyes as the next 120-mile-an-hour knuckleball crushed the dead man's throat.

"Sooner or later," said the man with the bat, "everybody says *sure*."

Valentine, struggled to free his head from the grip, which had tightened to the point of pain.

The host didn't notice, nodding slightly, almost wistfully, his gaze still on the newly dead guy. Then his attention snapped back to his captive guest.

"The point is this, you smug little prick. If I'd do this to someone like Skip here, innocent as a fucking kitten, someone I've loved and protected since I made my first buck . . . if I would do this to him . . ."

He paused, his head cocking like a dog that had just heard its name called.

". . . then imagine what I'd do to someone I don't even

know, and already don't think I like. I mean, if it gets me what I want. You feeling me *now*, Mr. Phillip Pretty Boy Valentine? I think maybe you are. I think maybe you aren't as dumb as you look."

The next inevitable ball impacted Skip's shattered skull with a squishing sound and an ensuing arc of crimson. The host then shut down the machine, commencing an ominous quiet against the soothing backdrop of falling water.

Valentine couldn't breathe.

The thug, sensing this, released his hold on Valentine's head. As a personal touch he added a shove, strong enough to put Valentine on his knees.

"I got your girls. You know this drill—no cops, no press, blah fucking blah. You get to sweat it awhile, then you get to write the happy ending."

He withdrew a photograph from the pocket of his shorts and tossed it to the ground in front of Valentine. It was wrinkled and moist, landing face up.

"Have a nice day."

The stumpy little man walked away, hands pocketed, whistling Skip's McDonald's jingle.

Phillip's twins were smiling directly at the camera, little brunette femme fatales in training, wearing matching UNLV cheerleader outfits. They were sitting next to the pool he was looking at, just on the other side of the batting cage.

"You're dead!" screamed Valentine, but the man wearing the shorts and batting gloves didn't turn back. He just raised a nonchalant hand to wave as he disappeared into the house.

PART
ONE

1

DIVISIVENESS—our two-party system has turned into a frat-house brawl. One nation under God is now just a schoolhouse poem . . . it's more a vitriolic let-them-eat-cake versus all-for-one-and-one-for-all cage match. Meanwhile, the middle is getting whiplash, which is no longer covered by health insurance.
—*Bullshit in America*, by Wolfgang Schmitt

PORTLAND, OREGON

October, 2012

Don't get me started.

No one with a modicum of sense—and please, just shoot me if I ever actually use the word *modicum* in an actual conversation—could blame me for being pissed off about things in general. The airlines want a hundred bucks to change from a flight with a waiting list to another flight that is only half full, and thirty bucks to load your bag. One commuter line wants a hundred dollars for a carry-on. Thank you for flying Trans Sphincter Air. My HMO announced their annual forty-five-percent-rate hike on the day a pro athlete I once admired got busted—again—for beating up a hooker and his wife on the same day, which earlier had brought us the news of a senator tweeting his junk to yet another hooker. The IRS wasn't buying my deduction to The Society for the Prevention of Cruelty to Copywriters, one of which I once was. Reality television hadn't gone away, nor would Britney or Lindsay Lohan or The Donald, who continued resisting a sign-off on the restructuring of his hair.

Grease was no longer The Word. *Bullshit* was.

Far beyond the boundaries of my claustrophobic little world, the Democrats wanted us to forget that half the working population, which was shrinking, is on the public dole. Meanwhile, the Republicans wanted us to overlook the fact that, among all those senators and congressmen and governors with right-leaning tendencies and greasy palms, not to mention dropped drawers in low places, a guy who looked like a blowup doll and with no memory was the best they could come up with for the next Presidential race. That someone could actually be named after a catcher's glove. And because of a book and a movie, half the planet actually believed that Mary Magdalene lived out her days as Mrs. Jesus H. Christ, while the other half—including those with rags on their heads and bombs under their vests—are still quite convinced that God is on their side.

At least Saddam and bin Laden were dead, with no bounty of vestal virgins anywhere on their eternal horizon.

Bring the boys home? Not that simple, Sparky.

What's a thinking man to do, give Newt the vote? I don't think so.

In my case, the answer was sanity itself. In my abundant spare time I wrote a column for a liberal local weekly—I'm no liberal, by the way, but it was the only paper interested—entitled *Bullshit in America.* Somehow calling it out for the consideration of my thinking brothers and sisters made it all the more tolerable. Maybe people would realize they are not alone in their frustration at being jerked around.

There remains no shortage of material.

Then, just when I thought I was safe from the stench of my own indignant cynicism, the next chapter in my heretofore vanilla but suddenly very strange existence was about to be unleashed.

Or, perhaps better said, *unhinged*.

After one dance as an undercover facer for the Feds, a chin for hire, the last thing I ever thought I'd do was once again take up arms as a designated seducer of women at the behest of someone with a badge. A strange destiny indeed for good cheekbones and a few years modeling underwear for the local metropolitan daily.

My name is Wolfgang Schmitt, and I'm here to confirm the rumor that shit really does happen.

MY dear, sweet, institutionalized mother looked at me and said, "I *love* your new show!"

Which, had I been some talking-head movie reviewer on local-access cable—almost got that gig back in the nineties—would have been sort of sweet. But I was a happily unemployed advertising hack who had just come into a buttload of under-the-table federal money—I'll explain *that* later—so my smile was at once forced and sad.

My mother thought I was Chuck Woolery with shorter, cooler hair.

She wasn't the first person in recent memory who thought I looked like a gameshow host, but she was the only one who could attribute that fine opinion to Alzheimer's. Okay, maybe the resemblance was there, but I preferred the occasional George-Clooney-meets-Owen-Wilson comparison I used to get in bars. We were sitting in what had once been a bedroom in a Victorian mansion overlooking the Willamette River—which no one born east of Idaho has ever pronounced correctly—but was now a private nursing facility that charged five grand a month for round-the-clock apathy and food with all the charisma of car wax. The first thing I did with the aforementioned money— earned via the seduction of a billionaire's wayward wife under the threat of being audited to hell and back—was move my mother out of the state-funded hellhole into which I had originally, and naively, deposited her in the hope that someone wearing a starched white uniform would give a shit.

That notion proved to be an airball. This place was about as therapeutic as the funeral home it had once been. But that was about to change. I had an idea, and I had the cash.

"I'm not on television, Mom."

"Oh, did they cancel you? Who do I write to?"

"I'll look it up for you. For now, besides that, you seem happy today."

Maybe if I told her she looked happy, she'd buy it. My mother was constantly smiling, a trait I'd hoped would endear her to the staff until I remembered this was Planet Dementia. She wore a sweatshirt with the words *My Grandma Can Beat Up Your Grandma*—purloined when the woman in the next room died with no relatives willing to pick up her things—over a baby-blue flannel nightgown and fuzzy purple Barney slippers. The sweatshirt and the slippers both hid an excruciating irony—my mother had no grandchildren.

As her only child, that was, of course, my fault.

According to the staff here in hell's little waiting room, from time to time my mother believed she was on a cruise ship. And that she was the cruise director. One day I arrived to find her leading a geriatric line dance in the foyer to the tune of "Achy Breaky Heart," everyone wearing robes and black knee socks. After forty-nine years of living with a man whose favorite word was "goddamn" and whose idea of a family vacation was going clamming in the rain, I didn't have the heart to tell her otherwise. The day my father died, seven lost years earlier, was the first day she forgot who either one of us was.

The universe is funny that way, trading one purgatory for another.

I visited my mother three times a week. We no longer had the past in common, so there wasn't much to discuss, this being a blessing for both of us in many ways. Since I could not impose the needs of my recently broken heart on her motherly sensibilities, I found myself trying to convince her that the captain and crew really liked her, and that, yes, those new folks on *Hollywood Squares* really couldn't hold a candle to Paul Lynde and his dead cronies. Somehow Whoopi Goldberg in the center square just didn't cut it for Mom. The meaninglessness of the banter had given me a chance to look critically at the accommodations, and the closer I looked, the less I liked what I smelled. A faint scent of urine always greeted me upon arrival. Sometimes there was spilled food and what I feared was vomit on her bedding—it wasn't easy to tell the difference—and that blue flannel nightie never seemed to get a day off. The staff assured me that laundry was a daily exercise and that it was taken quite seriously, and oh, by the way, that urine smell was my imagination. This was not true, however, of the crumbs that accumulated on the floor in the corners of her room, luring the occasional undiscerning cockroach.

I don't think they liked me all that much, actually.

The administrator was quick to flash his certificate of compliance from the state board of nursing home auditors, but frankly I didn't appreciate his attitude. He reminded me of that guy who married Liza Minnelli, the one who looked like an exhumed extra from the *Dawn of the Dead* and got another few minutes past his allotted fifteen sound-bite minutes when Michael Jackson died. If someone had told me the guy running my mother's nursing home was a holdover from the old funeral home days, I'd have bought it.

I should have checked her out of here weeks ago.

Then one day Mr. Formaldehyde sought me out to announce that, with deep regret, he was closing the home. I had a month to find my mother a new ship in which to cruise. Something about unreasonable regulatory pressures for sanitary upgrades—his look told me he thought I might have had something to do with that one—and the increasingly hostile and unfair reimbursement policies of those bastard Republicans politicizing Medicare. He casually mentioned he hadn't been able to find a buyer, adding that the building required significant capital improvements and that, frankly, none of it penciled out. Cheaper, he said, to shut the doors. It was at that very moment, as I visualized the aforementioned pencil penetrating the membrane of his inner ear, that a lightbulb with the wattage of a Tom Cruise smile illuminated my near-term investment strategy.

And so, being the good and newly moneyed son that I was, I decided to buy the place.

2

The idea to buy a nursing home wasn't as impulsive as it sounds. Concurrent with my search for the meaning of life—*my* life, that is, which lay before me like a blank page in front of a blocked screenwriter—was the quest for a way to invest my newfound fortune from my recently completed Federal undercover gig. Since every mutual fund I'd been intimate with in my life saw the bottom fall out—not to mention those lovely front-end loads—I was thinking real estate this time. Real estate, I surmised, was at an all-time post-Bush low, and an all-cash offer lent even more leverage. One of my buddies happened to own the largest chain of senior care facilities in the state, and between his trips to NFL games and test drives in the annual new exotic ride, we'd managed to squeeze in a lunch, during which the notion of buying something together had surfaced. Our unified vision was for a small, high-end facility, ten to fifteen beds, with a higher-than-normal nurse-to-patient ratio, and hopefully an improved nurse-to-personality ratio. Even better, RNs that didn't smell like Marlboros. The Ritz of Retirement, the Four Seasons of Senility. A new standard of care in which children with guilt issues could deposit their obsolete parents.

No price is too high where guilt is concerned.

When I got home that afternoon after telling my mother the news, and after stopping at Best Buy to price plasma screens, I indulged in my daily ritual of checking my account balance online. Something about seven digits to the left of the decimal makes even a tough old cynic like me giddy.

Today, however, my account balance was confusing. In fact, my money and the account into which I'd dumped it was missing altogether. A line of red-lettered words told me that no record of this account number existed. Same with my username and password.

I had been swallowed by cyberspace.

Amazing, the narcotic effect a quart of piping-hot adrenaline has on the flesh, which is weak.

The manifestation of emergency hormones is known as *fight or flight*, both of which were on my mind. Except in my case, the people I needed to fight were some four thousand miles away, wearing baggy khakis and flowered shirts to work, saying *"yeah mahn"* to any question asked of them. That left *flight* as the remaining option, but such arrangements would take at least a day, one which I felt my nervous system would not survive.

Another option loomed: my phone.

After forty descents into voicemail hell and an earnest assist from Verizon, all I got was a busy signal and a headache.

When I finally clawed myself from this maelstrom of self-pity, I realized I was late for my dinner date with my new girlfriend. A celebration of a very special occasion indeed.

Happy fucking birthday to me.

3

Is it just me, or do the shitstorms come in threes?

The good news was that the woman sitting across from me was in every way the diametric antithesis of the woman who had recently done a number on my heart. She had resurrected something, and it felt a lot like healing. The bad news was that we were in a pretentious poseur lounge full of women looking for guys who were as rich as I was before lunch, which reminded me of my current financial crisis.

Such distractions served to also remind me that, despite a new infatuation that was as welcome as it was intense, I wasn't over my recently departed fiancée. Until an hour ago I had significant new money in an offshore account, too much time on my hands to watch the interest compound, and a blank canvas to fill with dreams I could now afford. Like facilitating my mother's comfort to the end of her days. But there remained the matter of that gaping, bloodless crater in my soul, as empty as my offshore account.

It would be a great night to take up drinking again.

Carolyn Carr had a style that was sophisticated in contrast to the *I'm-from-like-L.A.* edge of Tracy, my recently incarcerated ex-fiancée. Carolyn was confident rather than flamboyantly needy, her breasts God-given rather than Dow Corning's finest polypropylene. She was a dramatic brunette with midnight eyes that smoldered; Tracy, a chemically augmented blonde with ice-blue eyes that made men squint. Carolyn read Joyce Carol Oates and listened to Rachmaninoff; Tracy read *Cosmo* and still had all her Donna Summer CDs. One was Chivas, the other was Jack on the rocks. If ever there was reason to move on with my life, it was sitting before me in that bar in a black business-bitch suit over a crisp white blouse, sipping an elegant martini and staring as if I were a warm hors d'oeuvre, her smile subtle as she did unspeakable things to an olive with her tongue. Great focus was required, though the fact that my ex was hunkered down in a federal pokey awaiting trial for murder one—part of a backstory I may or may not get around to—no doubt doing her nails, certainly gave me a fresh and healthy perspective.

I hadn't told Carolyn much about Tracy yet, certainly nothing close to the truth that was stranger than fiction. I didn't want to break down right in front of her, though she certainly knew there was a gaping, unexplained hole where my heart used to be.

Not a good thing for a new romantic prospect to see.

We were celebrating my fortieth birthday with a downtown skyscraper bar nightcap after filets at Morton's. Frankly, I was happy to cast off the final mantle of an underachieving youth, a folly to which I'd clung with a foolish passion that hadn't served me for the past decade. Bars had become bleak social intersections, a place to rendezvous rather than hang. My friends had been married long enough to be within shouting distance of their first divorce, which meant a kind of full-circle return to the hopeful illusion of *The Scene*, only with nose hair this time. To them I was a hero, the last bastion of nuptial defiance, a target of vicarious adulation. Especially since I drove a car their domesticated wives would never stomach.

Wives, in particular, regarded me as a kind of plague.

But it was bullshit then, and it was bullshit now. In light of the federally subsidized adventure I had recently survived and the proximity of death that came with it, I was desperate to find something worthwhile to do with what remained of my life. I was hopeful it was sitting right in front of me.

She saw my wheels turning and smiled.

"You're distracted," she said. "Or you're suddenly obsessed with my breasts."

"I've been obsessed with your breasts since the moment I saw them across a crowded gym."

"You have to pee, then."

Damn, that woman was perceptive. This was precisely what I'd wanted her to think.

"Sorry. Happens at this age."

The truth was something else entirely. My money was missing, four thousand miles away in a Cayman Islands financial institution for the covertly inclined, and there wasn't a thing I could do about it, other than sit here on my midlife crisis birthday and look inexplicably distracted in front of the woman I secretly hoped might inhabit my bed, if not my future.

The missing money had been shitstorm number one.

Carolyn, a twenty-nine-year-old corporate attorney I'd met in my spinning class, couldn't relate to my lame attempt at geriatric humor. Her last boyfriend had recently retired from a mediocre career with the San Diego Padres, which said volumes about her understanding of old age.

She said, "Don't get any on those cool shoes."

The Bruno Magli's I was wearing were precisely two hours old, my birthday gift from her. When a woman gives you shoes for your birthday, it's her way of saying you need a fashion tune-up. I took that as a good thing.

I stood to lean in and kiss her cheek, a ritual which had become our custom over the course of four dates thus far. There was a subtle scent of something expensive as my lips made contact, and I allowed myself an extra half-second to savor the utter perfection of the moment. As I drew near I noticed that her eyes had closed, and that she was smiling.

Because of that I walked away full of hope. Sooner or later she would learn that my smart-ass bravado was every bit the bullshit I claimed to detest. That I was, in fact, a guy who listened to the lyrics, a guy who passed a flower shop and wished there was someone I could buy flowers for, a bona fide romantic putz who couldn't buy a membership in the Guy's Club if he tried. Hell, I cried when *House* went off the air. My glib Hugh Laurie act was all a cover.

Maybe, I told myself, she was *the one*.

I waited until the bathroom door closed behind me to whip out my phone. I wanted to see if my Caribbean bank's twenty-four-hour customer service line was back in business. If not, there was the business card of a certain FBI agent residing in my wallet, a man who might just have some explaining to do.

4

The rules of social etiquette in the men's bathroom are as ancient and rigid as anything the Brits could ever imagine for their royal clan. Conversation and eye contact are strictly forbidden. One must spit into the urinal upon approach, preferably in smooth conjunction with the lowering of the fly. One's eyes must remain fixed on the tile squares directly in front of your face, though occasional upward glances are permitted if things take too long. No humming or whistling, though belching and farting are overlooked and in some establishments are encouraged. Even if two men are previously acquainted, they know to leave their abundant wisdom concerning golf and football in the hall.

It's like a wake in there, only with soggy paper towels on the floor.

Those who violate the code fall into two categories: inebriated ex-frat boys—this being the source of the term, *shit for brains*—and inebriated good old boys who couldn't scrape up the tuition. Both species very much like the sound of their own voice.

On this night there were two of the latter, dressed down for guys' night out, though in their case they had the wrong address and the wrong uniform. These two had stopped for a quickie with the uptown talent before heading for the strip joints by the airport. They flanked me in this lineup of urinals, and I found myself the net for a volley of vile observations about an unfortunate woman from the bar. They were early to mid-twenties, one shaved bald with an earring and an inexplicable patch of hair under his lower lip. A barcode was tattooed on the back of his neck—let us assume the artist made sure this guy would scan at the price of cheap hamburger—while the other wore a baseball hat worn at an angle and a sleeveless T-shirt from Hooters. Nothing says *moron* quite like a post-pubescent white guy with the bill of his cap hanging over one ear.

Without a neon beer sign hanging in a window, these bottom feeders were clearly out of water. These were guys who painted faces onto bare, flabby stomachs at football games and spit stale bon mots at the officials such as, "Hey shitstick, make a goddamn call!"

Tonight they felt strongly that the woman from the bar had significant need of an immediate and much-overdue orgasm. They were also of the opinion that she would find their carnal ministrations, rendered in a classically canine posture, quite pleasant indeed.

These, of course, were not their precise words.

"Nice talk," I mumbled as I wiped my hands dry, the exchange still raging between urinals, my phone call forgotten. This froze them with surprise, as if the mere notion of such an opinion was an unthinkable affront to their heritage as scumbags with dicks the size of curly fries.

"Go fuck yourself," one of them suggested, which I found amusing given the fact that he held his diminutive pecker in his hand at the time.

I just shook my head, the smile never leaving my face. I was a *mellow* man, now, quite able to let such moments slide, if not the comments that inspired them.

Until, that is, I returned to the table, where Carolyn had ordered another round of martinis the color of grass clippings. I'd stood in the doorway for a moment, watching her sip her drink, feeling something tugging at my pride. God, she was gorgeous. I could *love* this woman. It was a feeling I didn't think I would ever feel again. Happy birthday to me.

Less than a minute later the intellectual giants from the john returned to their table, which happened to be right next to ours. I hadn't noticed them before, the significance of which I would recall later. Soon, in fact.

Happy birthday, my ass. That would be shitstorm number two.

5

One of the bozos said, "What the fuck are *you* lookin' at?"

Bad idea.

This conversational inevitability occurred within the first minute of their return from the safe haven of the john. An oh-so perceptive Carolyn had asked me what was so funny—I laughed and shook my head when I realized who they were—the residue of my men's lounge smile having lost none of its contrived nonchalance.

"Just a little joke between us Neanderthals," I said. "Two little jokes, in fact."

Barcode boy heard me. He was *supposed* to hear me, just as he was also supposed to see the quick glance I shot his way. That's when he asked the aforementioned question regarding the direction of said casual glance. My response was in keeping with their level of comedic impotence.

Sometimes you've got to dumb it down.

"A piece of shit," I answered, the smile waning. "I'm looking at *two* pieces of shit, in fact."

Not exactly Billy Crystal, I'll grant you.

Now, before one judges me as somewhat uninspired in this moment of confrontation, let it be known that it had suddenly dawned on me that the object of their conjecture at the urinal had, in fact, been Carolyn. They had made reference to her "prissy little man-suit," which hadn't registered at the time, but now rang with all the truth of a DNA report. Everything they said in the bathroom had been for my benefit.

Carolyn was already gathering her purse. "We're out of here," she said, clicking into prognostication mode.

I stood, having trouble tearing my gaze from the twin objects of my rage, eye contact being an essential element of the testosterone dance that leads to a full-contact scrimmage.

One of them, the dipshit hat guy, stood with me. He was an inch or two shy of my six-three, though he outweighed me by thirty pounds, all of it high cholesterol. He was wearing earphones connected to an iPod hanging around his neck, which I thought was strange in a swanky place like this. Somewhere there was a grip missing from the set of *L.A. Ink*.

He pulled the earphones off in a sort of throwing-down kind of way and said, "Maybe your lady friend should stay awhile. Talk about things that *come* in threes."

I closed my eyes as a palpable sensation washed over me, an urgent heat filling my veins. Within seconds my pulse entered a red zone, moments from ruining any façade of cool I had fooled Carolyn into believing I possessed. Somehow I had to move this circus out of the bar and into the parking lot—a cliché, I realize—and allow it to run its hormonally fueled course. Limits had been exceeded, honor had been defiled. My name had been called, and it had happened in front of my date.

Some bullshit needs flushing, regardless of the consequences. Especially in front of your new girlfriend.

It was at that fortunate moment that I felt a firm hand on my arm. Pulling me away from what surely was a bad decision, particularly where the two young men were concerned. But when I opened my eyes, I saw that it wasn't Carolyn saving me—and them, I assure you—from myself. In fact, she was standing a few feet away, positioned between Asswipe Number One and Asswipe Number Two, watching. Smiling slightly, arms folded. Time itself paused. The angels, purported to weep at moments of human epiphany, doubled over in laughter.

The guy with his hand on my arm was a suit, his hair too Brooklyn, his cheap aftershave preceding him. In his other hand was a badge, which he held before me.

"Duncan Stevens," he said. "FBI."

He allowed a moment for my eyes to expand to the size of tennis balls. He motioned to the chair from which I had just risen and added, "Let's have a chat, shall we?"

With that, Carolyn and the poseurs departed the bar.

Together. Having an amiable little chat of their own.

Shitstorm number three had just commenced.

6

My eyes were riveted on the door, but I could sense that Duncan Stevens was watching me with a certain bemusement. A man who already knew the punch line.

Carolyn Carr was leaving the building, my birthday celebration crunching beneath her killer pumps, my future in tow beside two clowns who looked like they ought to be washing her car.

Stevens tapped his forehead and said, "Did you know that you have this little vein, right here? Sort of pulses when you get mad. Like its gonna pop or somethin'."

I narrowed my eyes in a way that told him he had become the reason for said pulsing. It wasn't the first time someone on my shitlist had pointed this out to me.

He added, "She wasn't your type, Wolf."

"You don't know my type. Or my name."

"But I do. I know everything about you." He slapped his

palms on his knees as if the good part was just ahead. "So. You ready to get back to work?"

My jaw, which hadn't quite closed, dropped even further. Given the fact that I had recently completed an uninvited guest appearance on the FBI's roster of undercover freelance moles—a chin for hire, so to speak—the result of which was all that missing money in the Caymans, the context was clear.

His infuriating smile widened.

"What, you think that was a one-shot deal? That you could just sail off into sunset with all that taxpayer money and clip coupons? Dude."

I squinted at Duncan Stevens, who hadn't been one of the federal *dudes* at my disposal last time out. The more I looked at him, the more he looked like someone from whom I once bought a cheap suit.

"Who *are* you?" I asked. "*What* are you?"

"Wanna see my badge again? We can do that."

I would have said no, but I didn't like the smug edge. Like a new boss who knew he could fire you even though he couldn't carry your bag.

"Absolutely," I said, trying to mimic the synthetic grin.

His expression remained fixed, albeit strained, as he withdrew his wallet and flipped it open, a little too close to my eyes. A literal *in-your-face* moment.

I memorized the badge number and nodded.

"Convinced?"

I looked up. Tried to sound impressed. "FBI. Love you guys on TV. Real life, not so much."

"I get that a lot."

Then I said, "So let's have that *chat* . . . about my money."

He squinted, not sure about the smile emerging on his face. "Above my grade, I'm afraid. I can give you a number."

"Why don't you just tell me?"

"Not gonna happen. You have a problem with that, call the one-eight-hundred number."

"What I have a problem with is my no-strings money

suddenly disappearing into digital hell. And your breath. Got a few issues with that, too."

I watched him process. He was either Sean Penn or, other than the breath, he truly had no idea what I was talking about. I wasn't sure which was the preferred scenario.

"I'll look into it," he finally said, his focus returning. He shifted his weight, crossed his legs in an unsuccessful attempt to appear at ease.

My eyes drifted back to the doorway. "Who was she?"

"Special Agent, southeast region. Works in operations, trying to get into the field. This was her coming-out gig. How'd she do, Wolf?"

My eyes went back to that smile that said he knew precisely how she had done. I felt that little forehead vein begin to twitch and decided to leave the unspoken alone.

He took a sip of Carolyn's water and said, "It's ironic, don't you think?"

"I'm too pissed off to think."

"No, you'll like this. We send her out here, without experience, because of, you know, her obvious assets. I mean, how many field agents look like that, know what I'm sayin'? Same deal with you. When we needed a facer, you came through like a champ. Now here we are, we cast a femme fatale, and look at you. You're a fucking puddle. If that isn't irony I don't know what is."

"A phone call would have sufficed."

"We need another chin, Wolf. One with heart."

"Count me out."

"I'm serious. We have a case that requires your particular . . . gifts."

"I don't *have* a particular gift. I was in *advertising*, for shit's sake. That's why I'm depressed and, to be perfectly honest, on the verge of throwing you through that plate-glass window."

Stevens cheated a quick look over his shoulder at the thirty-story panorama of downtown Portland, his expression feigning that he was impressed. In that moment I realized I had miscalculated, that he was quite comfortable with all the jousting. Too comfortable, in fact. Sherlock, my FBI handle on my previous assignment, was serious as an embalmer.

"I don't get it," I said. "Why all the theatrics at my expense? Dinner cost me two bills and some change."

He swallowed audibly and replaced the glass.

"We had to see if you had sack."

I squinted, even though I knew what he meant. It was an odd street term for an FBI agent to use, too on the nose.

"Thought you said you needed heart?"

"Whatever. You'll be going into a high-tension scenario. Most of the time you'll be the only guy in the room who hasn't killed someone. We had to see how you react in the moment, if you can hang. It's a fine line. People will be watching closely when you walk it."

"How can I say no to that?"

"My money had you losing it, maybe throwing *them* through that window. Carolyn—not her real name, by the way—was betting you'd keep your cool, mister unflappable, but still a guy with no sack. Sorry dude, it was never gonna happen. But you let them know you were close to snapping. You showed heart, but with serious balls. You respected the sanctity of the moment, the time and the place. People you'll be dealing with, they're all about respect. And they have a thing about time and place."

"So I passed the audition."

"Flying colors, too."

"She thought I'd wuss out?"

"Carolyn says you're a *lovely guy*. Her words."

"Well, that's true. I'm a lover, not a fighter."

"Both can be faked."

"Why me?"

"Because you fit. The woman we want you to get next to will, how shall I put it, find you to her liking."

"Some women just want a lovely guy."

"Not this one."

"Who is she?"

He shook his head very officially and said, "Later."

"I'm busy later."

"Without that money, I'd say you're broke."

"I thought you didn't know about that?"

"Just saying. You want your money, you should consider this. We can help you with that problem."

"That's blackmail, Duncan."

"No, that's a fact, Wolf. There is, of course, additional compensation, which means it isn't blackmail after all."

"Semantics. But just for grins, let's pretend I'm listening."

"Same as before. You cut your deal with the mark, you collect what you can, you keep it when it's over. And guess what, you'll be serving your country while you're at it."

"Gee, I'm all misty. Tax free?"

He smiled, hoisting Carolyn's water glass in a mock toast. "It never happened."

"What am I supposed to do?"

"What you're so very good at doing. Get close, gather evidence, report back. Stay loose, stay alive."

"What's my cover?"

The smile faded somewhat. "There are two covers, actually. One you'll like, the other you'll have to figure out. Just like last time."

"I didn't like anything about last time. Except the car. The car was good."

Stevens shifted, his eyes casting about the room. He was getting tired of boxing shadows, anxious to land a punch.

"You'll go in as her personal trainer."

I involuntarily snorted. "I'm not a trainer."

"That, too, can be faked."

"And the other?"

"The trainer thing gets you into her world. To everyone else you're the help, which means you're invisible. But she'll know precisely why you're *really* there. So to speak. A cover beneath the cover."

I just stared, the impatience surfacing.

He took his time with it, draining the water glass and placing it gently back on the table, running his finger around the rim. Getting off on making me wait.

He'd look good tumbling through the atmosphere toward the street.

Finally he looked me directly in the eye and without the slightest irony in his voice, said, "You, my hunky fitness friend, are going help this woman murder her husband."

7

In Xanadu did Kubla Khan
A stately pleasure-dome decree.
—"Kubla Khan," by Samuel Taylor Coleridge

LAS VEGAS, NEVADA

Ding-dong, the wicked witch wasn't dead after all. She was roaming the halls of Xanadu, looking for employees to fire.

The rumors about Lynn Valentine were legend. That she was the power behind her husband's iron managerial fist. That she taught Leona Helmsley everything she knew about interpersonal relationships. That she hung out in the casino security center for hours, staring at the monitors in the hope of observing grounds for termination. That she hadn't slept with her husband since their tragic loss a few years earlier, favoring the occasional hunk-of-the-month new hire—purportedly also scouted via security camera—none of whom lasted past their probation. That she took her lovers without regard to gender or age or race, as long as they knew their place, which, rumor held, was on their knees. That she was, in fact, certifiably insane.

Much of the conjecture was true. What wasn't served her in other ways.

Xanadu, the legendary Las Vegas institution of higher indulgence founded by her immigrant grandfather and later put on the map by her father, wasn't the largest hotel-casino on the strip, nor its most famous. It was, perhaps, at least since the dawn of the new century, its most *infamous*, especially since her father was murdered—an unsolved crime—and the rest of the town had adopted a Chamber of Commerce–friendly family approach, which lasted as long as President Obama's approval rating. That was when Phillip Valentine, Lynn's husband and the present general manager of the property, had returned Xanadu to the fundamental values that made Las Vegas the great intoxicant that it was: greed, vice, drugs, and the proximity to power, the more dangerous the better. In fact, it was Xanadu that was credited to returning Las Vegas as a whole to its sinful roots, with only a handful of roller coasters remaining. Sure, tourists still roamed the shopping mall at Caesar's and slept on the cheap at Circus Circus. New vacation money checked into the Bellagio and Aria, serious players quietly sipped well drinks downtown while Hollywood's young blood partied at The Cosmopolitan and married at a local chapel on the strip. But for old schoolers and players in the know, it was Xanadu that quietly and seductively ruled the neon night.

In Las Vegas, everyone who mattered knew that Xanadu stood for excess. For sin. If you knew who to ask, and if you could produce the requisite tariff—often a bartered favor—virtually anything and everything was available for the asking. On any given night the tables were filled with serious personalities, any one of whom might be an arms dealer, a narcotics czar, or, perhaps more intriguingly dangerous, a Washington lobbyist looking to cut loose. The cocktail lounges and opulent guest suites—some of which were themed—were filled with those whose capacity for pleasure defied both reason and limits. Rules were unspoken and inviolate. The whole thing ran like a clock, albeit one strapped to the underside of a ticking bomb. Nobody wanted any part of the social and political shrapnel that would materialize should that bomb go off.

Phillip Valentine was the man you asked. But everyone knew that Lynn Valentine was the woman to whom you answered.

The mistress of the manor that was Xanadu, the grand bitch-queen of her world, stood with her arms crossed, eyes fixed on a flat screen video monitor in a darkened room. While the casino's thirty-million-dollar video surveillance system boasted a control room reminiscent of the Kennedy Space Center, the adjoining executive security suite had but one monitor and a single controlling data station from which any of the hotel's three hundred digital cameras—half of which were covertly integrated into the otherwise innocent electronic accoutrements of selected guest suites—could be accessed. At the controls sat a man in his early seventies, Chad Merrill, a former head of security who these days had carte blanche to the property as a consultant. He was paid by Phillip Valentine to keep an eye on the very people who were there to protect him, but he owed his allegiance to the woman standing behind him now.

Lynn Valentine had exclusively worn black for the past three years, ever since her world crumbled. It was a color well-suited to dark hooded eyes and pampered auburn hair that changed shade and shape on a regular basis. Her suits were tailored and severe, worn with the most feminine of heels and bright silk blouses, always adorned with tastefully understated jewelry selected at will from the shops in the hotel's promenade, always returned the next day. She was a woman whose beauty was born more of presence than of blessing, an aura of power and a certain veneer that only cash can imbue. She was in her late forties, and the decades of cosmetic detail had become a sort of self-fulfilling aesthetic destiny. Lynn Valentine was a woman of wealth and taste, the personification of class and privilege, all the more alluring for her worldly experience and the confidence that comes from knowing she could have you maimed at any time.

That, too, was part of the rumor mill.

Lynn Valentine and Chad Merrill sat motionless, their eyes riveted on the screen. Lynn's hand clutched a thick silver cross worn on a thin chain around her neck, always visible no matter what she was wearing.

On the screen a woman of indeterminate age was leaning over a bathroom sink in the one of the suites, her elbows resting on the granite counter, her forehead pressed against the faucet, held there by the man behind her. She wore the standard Nuevo French maid uniform of a casino cocktail waitress, the short black skirt pulled up toward her waist, her fishnet pantyhose torn wide at the crack of her ass. A short man with perfect hair stood behind her, administering a stern quarterly performance review, his suit pants around his ankles, his trademark Dolce & Gabbana silk necktie in a picture-perfect knot. A Bluetooth telephone headset cradled one ear. He was forced to stand on his tiptoes to pound home his point, which he did with staccato enthusiasm, his eyes never wavering from his own image in the mirror before him. It was, quite clearly, the true object of his affection in this encounter.

"Who is she?" asked Lynn, her soft voice the texture of flowing crème de menthe.

"New girl," answered Chad. "Works the Kubla Lounge. You can't see her face until . . ."

His voice faded, waiting to see if Lynn had a response—she didn't—then added, "Tell me what you want me to do with her."

It wasn't the first video of this genre he had shown her. Phillip Valentine thought he knew which suites in his hotel had video bugs and which didn't. Chad Merrill had provided him with that information the year before, when the system had been installed at Lynn Valentine's request. But Phillip Valentine didn't know everything in that regard. Thus far her investment—in the technology and in Chad Merrill—had acquitted itself nicely.

A strange smile emerged on Lynn Valentine's face, the kind that knows how a story will end long before the characters get the script.

"Nothing. For now."

Lynn had only to ask. Frequent five-figure gestures of her

appreciation were only part of the legacy of Merrill's allegiance. She put a hand on his shoulder, feeling how the years had stripped him of a once-powerful ability to personally enforce the Xanadu corporate agenda, which he had done for her grandfather and father-in-law.

"Let them play."

They watched a moment more, then, in a quiet voice, Merrill said, "It's not right."

She patted his shoulder and leaned down, her lips close enough so that she only had to whisper.

"Always remember, my friend, there *is* a God. And She is definitely taking notes."

She kissed him on the top of his balding head and left the room before the face of the cocktail waitress could be seen.

Who the woman in the video was, and what would happen to her, held no interest whatsoever for Lynn Valentine. It was her husband's fate that obsessed her now. And that had nothing at all do with cocktail waitresses and performance reviews.

It had nothing to do with God, either.

8

It was a long night. No one expects to spend their fortieth birthday alone. There's something about the number, a corner being rounded, the end of the road suddenly in sight. I'd long since passed the time when I needed to fill the other pillow with an available pretty face, though that pillow had accumulated quite a résumé in its day. Fact was, I'd switched teams, gone over to the other side. The pretty poster boy for all things single and male was now certifiably lonely and in search of *meaning*. Having the money—back when I had it, which was yesterday—was great, I kid you not. Reserving a table for one to spend some of it, however, simply sucked. And God knows a round of golf and beers with the guys and courtside seats and anything else my married friends envied my ability to indulge in at will didn't come close to numbing the dull ache of the truth.

Wolfgang Schmitt—moi—was on a quest. He was

campaigning for relevance in a world that hadn't, until lately, taken him seriously.

Carolyn hadn't exactly broken my heart. The thing was already held together with scar tissue and duct tape as it was. What she had broken, at least for a night, was my spirit. Which was why, in spite of her betrayal, I was surprisingly okay. Because my spirit suddenly had another option.

The FBI wanted me back. It was a chance to do something that mattered. To make a mark, to take down a few bad guys. A chance to belong to something more substantial than the local country club.

And just possibly, get my money back.

When I glanced at the clock hours into the dark, I realized it was no longer my birthday. It was time to move on. The back forty had already started ticking away.

ON the morning after my little chat with Duncan Stevens, which coincided nicely with the sudden dissolution of my relationship with Carolyn Carr, I drove my very impractical SL55 AMG to Seattle, three hours north, to see a man about a job. The man was Sherman Wissbaum, the FBI agent whom I had dubbed *Sherlock* during my last federal adventure—you, too, would happily embrace such a cliché moniker in lieu of a name like Sherman Wissbaum—and the job in question was the one presently being rammed down my throat by Duncan Stevens.

Duncan Stevens smelled like a lie. But it was the same scent as my suddenly elusive Cayman funds, which meant I was still in the dance. Sherlock was necessary to verify the story. Besides, I wanted to look him in the eye when I told him my money, the very funds he'd personally promised would be mine until the end of all time, was in digital hock. All the professorial tutoring in Quantico could not hide the duplicity of an agent lying through his Crest Whitestrips choppers.

I called his office en route, leaving a cheery voicemail to the effect that I would be waiting in a booth with a lunch menu and a list of questions. Just to be safe, I added that I had a reporter from the *Washington Post* with me who was just dying to meet him. Upon arrival I killed a few hours haunting the Seattle waterfront, watching tattooed butchers with comedic gifts toss dead fish and rusty bromides, much to the delight of an appreciative audience of tourists who had no idea what they were witnessing.

I couldn't wait for lunch. Not only was I famished, I had a few dead fish of my own to throw around.

THE Cheesecake Factory is to food what Al Pacino is to a meaty script: the best choice in town, at least if you don't mind a little overacting. Its Taj Mahal décor and Disneyland sensibility might put off those who prefer their meals on thin china with portions the size of postage, but it was my favorite place. The people I knew who looked down their very stuffy noses at this choice were the same people who would happily mortgage their children to drive my Bavarian car, so go figure. One man's pretension is another's best revenge.

I eat alone a lot of the time.

I took a booth with a clean line of sight on the door, ordered a passion iced tea, and waited for Sherlock to appear.

Which he did, ten minutes after noon. He saw me immediately, nodding a greeting as he plowed past a headset wearing host and arrived at the table with an extended hand.

"Where's the press?" he said as we shook.

"On Grand Cayman, looking for my money."

He ignored the comment, which confused me. The server arrived immediately, destroying my momentum as she took his drink order.

Coffee. Boring.

"Wolf, good to see you," he said, his smile full of shit.

The man's first name fit his image well. *Sherman*—the kid on the team who washed the towels, a little pudgy, freckles, got pounded a lot. The adult Sherman still had a bad haircut and that sycophantic energy, all dressed up in a designer suit with a shiny badge and backed up by a forty caliber Smith & Wesson in his shorts.

He raised an eyebrow and said, "You should know I passed up sandwiches with a deputy director from Quantico for this."

"Because we're pals," I replied.

"Because we're not. You wouldn't waste my time unless it was important. You okay?"

"You tell me."

"She looks like Jessica Biel, by the way. The deputy director, I mean."

I had to smile. Maybe in another life we could have been pals. Sherman Wissbaum would make a terrific wingman.

"You know an agent named Duncan Stevens?" I asked.

"No," he said, a little too quickly.

"You're aware the FBI is inviting me to another party."

He looked deep into me and said, "No."

"Shouldn't you be?"

"It's a large organization."

"And I'm one of that organization's dirty little secrets. Strictly off the grid, as you once put it. Which means, it's a small database. I'm betting you know."

A ghost of concern settled into the creases around his eyes, which now looked away. My stomach began to knot up, the remedy to which would arrive momentarily disguised as a plate of worldclass chicken piccata.

"You mentioned money," he said.

I told him about my sudden inability to access my Cayman account. When the food arrived I was well into Carolyn Carr teeing me up for Duncan Stevens, which I seasoned with a dash of suspicion, cynicism, and doubt, long my condiments of choice. Sherlock hung on every word—he was one of the few breathing folks on the planet who knew my façade was an act. Or perhaps it was the other way around, maintaining solid eye contact except for those special moments during which his pesto linguine required stirring.

"So," I said, dabbing a napkin to the corner of my mouth, "should I be worried, or should I be packing?"

Sherlock spoke with a full mouth. "It's possible that someone in another field office has your file. I'll check it out."

I was ready for that one. I withdrew a folded piece of paper from my shirt pocket and slid it across the table. I took a bite of bread as I watched him study it.

"What's this?"

"Duncan Stevens' badge number."

His look alternated between the paper and me, a smile emerging with a slight nod. I took it to mean he approved, but when he tapped his chin with a finger, I realized he was referring instead to a stealth string of angel hair that was dangling from my lip.

"I'll get back to you," he said, the smile suddenly and ominously gone. "Don't talk to him until you hear from me."

"See, we are pals."

"Which is why you're buying." He signaled the server for the paperwork. As he got up, he read my expression and added, "I'm not the millionaire at this table, Wolf. You are."

9

Halfway back to Portland I was stopped by a Washington State trooper driving an unmarked car. I was doing 71 in a 65 zone—I'd actually slowed down in the hope of finding a roadside Dairy Queen—which put me on the prosecutorial bubble. After what seemed like ten minutes sitting on the shoulder while his computer ran my plates, I watched him approach in the rearview, saw his eyes scanning my jet-black Benz like a kid at an auto show.

"Nice ride," was how he greeted me.

"Thanks. License and registration, right?" I figured a little preemptive ass-kissing was a solid opening.

"Not necessary. Just a warning, Mister Schmitt. Keep it under seventy if you can. Which, I gotta say, probably isn't easy in this baby. Runs, what . . . eighty, ninety grand?"

I smiled, just another schmo from the auto show. This was the strangest conversation I'd ever had with a sworn officer of the law. And lately I'd had some whoppers.

"One-sixty and change."

He whistled. "You, like, a doctor or something?"

"Or something."

He walked the length of the car, running his fingertips over the paint, the way a woman peruses a clearance rack. He wore a grin that told me this wasn't about my rate of speed.

"Under seventy," I repeated. "Got it. Can I go?"

"Yeah, that's it."

But that wasn't *it*. Suddenly he leaned down to rest his forearms on the door. As if he wanted to check out the interior. If I'd have hit the power-window button—a temptation—his head would have cracked the retractable hardtop with enough force to send that little grin into next week.

"There *is* one more thing," he said, a smile emerging.

I stared, decided against the window visual.

"Special Agent Sherlock sends his regards."

Now the emerging smile was mine.

The trooper continued. "Says your friend with the badge is the genuine article, but to proceed with caution. Wants to be kept in the loop, but on the Q.T. Something about interagency politics. You know what that's about?"

"I believe I do. You?"

"Not a clue."

"That's good," I said, shifting into spook mode. "For you, I mean. What you don't know can't hurt you . . . yada yada."

He didn't like that one, but swallowed it.

"Under seventy, Mr. Schmitt."

I nodded. Then my grin snapped into a piercing stare. "This never happened. We clear on that, officer?"

The guy looked like I'd just described his wife's latest pelvic wax job in great detail.

"Yes sir."

I nodded again, just once, then tapped the Benz into gear before peeling out, spraying enough gravel to make my point.

I crack myself up sometimes. In fact, I was still chuckling as the speedometer passed ninety.

Okay. Sherlock had my back. What I didn't know was if he had my money, too.

THE little exercise with the state trooper cost me ten minutes, which turned out to impact the next step in my effort to cover my ass. I'd planned on stopping by my old place of employment to see my friend Blaine, who knew more password codes and shady characters on the take than a snitch on *Law and Order*. By day Blaine headed the ad agency's Information Technology group—Geek Central by any standard—something I'd always thought might be some court mandated application of the guy's talent for computer hacking. Rumor had it he'd once broken the firewall of a certain software billionaire and later testified at the murder trial for his dead wife, but that rumor remained unconfirmed among the agency's most ardent gossips. The only person in Oregon who could confirm it was me, but that, once again, was another story altogether. Besides, I was no longer employed there, having departed my position as an account executive–turned–copy master to pursue more lucrative opportunities in the field of covert domestic intelligence, where much less overt brownnosing was required.

Shit certainly does happen.

But alas, I arrived at five fifteen, and Blaine Borgia—yes, *that* Borgia, his great-to-the-fifth-power Aunt Lucretia having set the family precedent for scandalous avocation—was a regular five o'clock guy. So I left a package on his chair with a note telling him to check his voicemail, where I'd narrated the favor I was asking of him, which I knew he'd embrace with a dark passion. Like most tech-heads in a creatively driven business, Blaine hated everything about advertising. He was there to play with the million-dollar server network he'd been assigned to manage, something he could do in his sleep. If the partners ever found out he was running a significant internet commerce operation out of his laptop—he was selling a software program called "Hacking for Dummies"—they'd gag on their half-caff no-room caramel macchiatos.

The package contained Carolyn Carr's wine glass from the previous evening. The one Duncan Stevens had used to toast our mutual understanding. If anyone could arrange an off-the-record fingerprint scan, it was Blaine Borgia.

It wasn't that I didn't trust Special Agent Sherlock. It was more like I didn't trust *anyone*.

10

Speaking of Blaine Borgia, one of the perks of swapping dark e-mail humor with a technical prodigy is the availability of jury-rigged digital appliances. Blaine was constantly setting me up with cool stuff, such as the iPad that still eluded my ability to fully comprehend. He'd rigged mine to speak to the computer in my house that controlled the security system—something to do with clouds—the lights and even the heat, so that I could jack the temperature to something bearable before I turned onto my street. The thing even raised my garage door from a range of up to a half mile out, a benefit which could change the entire American way of life given half a chance and a shitload of venture capital.

Raising my garage door was my sole intention on this night. The initial readout, however, indicated that the house security system had been disabled, the heat was already on, as was the stereo. The only thing it didn't tell me was which iTunes playlist was running, and who was inside waiting for me.

There was no car in the driveway. A soft light burned in the bedroom window above the garage, flickering slightly. The intruder was either watching television or I was witness to the initial flames of an impending fire.

Both would turn out to be the case.

The front door was unlocked. None of the lower-level lights were on. A glance at the security panel validated my iPad—the system had been manually disabled forty minutes earlier. Willie Nelson crooned softly from my newly acquired home theater system with three-thousand-dollar speakers the size of baseballs.

Someone knew the code, not to mention my taste in music. Which in turn meant I knew the intruder. That fact narrowed the field extensively. As in, it could only be one person.

My home was a two-story townhouse, really more of an apartment without common walls. My golf clubs were stored in the entry closet, leaving just enough room for an overcoat and an umbrella. Opening the door quietly, I extracted my trusty nine-iron, a weapon that had destroyed more fairways than criminals, but there was always the Annual Off The Books Covert Agent Golf Tournament and Buffet to turn that around.

I knew which stairs creaked, so I climbed accordingly and peeked around the corner toward my bedroom door, which emitted a soft yellow light. A faint voice issued forth.

"Hello?"

A pleasant and familiar timbre.

I lowered the nine-iron and went to the door. The plasma was on—HGTV to drown out Willie, which again confirmed who was here—and each nightstand had two illuminated candles which had heretofore resided on my kitchen table.

Sitting on my perfectly made bed was the pseudonymous Carolyn Carr. Other than a pair of earrings that resembled scale models of a chandelier—I had once admitted to her that I had a little *thing* for earrings—she was dressed for what could have passed as an employment interview.

"Working on your short game?" she asked.

She leaned back onto one elbow, centerfold style. Her other hand stroked the hand-me-down bedspread as if it might purr. It was obvious she'd never done this before.

I shook my head and turned away. This was the last thing I expected from this woman, and the second to last thing I wanted. Only a naked Sherman Wissbaum in my bed would have been worse. She had been to my house once—I would have to be content with the assumption she had memorized my security codes—and the closest thing we'd had to sexual intimacy over the course of our handful of dates was a back-scratch under my wool sweater in a darkened movie theater. Woman had nails like a weed eater.

"We should talk," she said, still patting the bed, infusing the word *talk* with a sticky double entendre.

Right. Clearly, this was what she had in mind.

What we needed was to square off.

"Downstairs," I said softly, already turning to take my disbelief and my nine-iron away. I added, "Whoever the hell you are."

"Renee," I barely heard her say.

Whatever.

11

It was with some regret that I returned the nine-iron to its berth.

I sat in the dark on my living-room couch, considering my options. It took the newly christened Renee several minutes to appear, long enough for me to entertain the notion that she wasn't coming down, that this was a test of carnal will. Or some such battle-of-the-genders bullshit. During those minutes there was no thought of Duncan Stevens or my guardian Sherlock, or even of the memory of the last time my chin had been put into the employ of the taxpayers for the purpose of pursuing justice. There was only Carolyn, who was now Renee, the memory of the handful of evenings we had spent cultivating hope, of the way she smiled and closed her eyes when I kissed her cheek in public, raising her chin just so, the way her eyes narrowed when she stared at me. She was just trying to figure me out, she'd say, plumbing the depths of what she called my "untapped madness."

No woman had ever called it that before.

The time had arrived to tap into it.

SHE finally appeared, wearing the same outfit sans earrings and carrying a very lawyerly briefcase. She took a seat in the chair facing the couch, avoiding all eye contact.

I'd be damned if I would break this ice. Normally I abhor the little games that propel relationships into dysfunction, but tonight was different.

"Well, *that* didn't happen," she said, barely audible.

"Not sure which of us should be more insulted," I replied.

She allowed a moment for the arrow to sink in, then began.

"Everything I can possibly say to you is an inadequate cliché. I'm sorry. I never meant to hurt you. What started as a job became real for me. It wasn't supposed to, but it did, and I didn't know how to get out of it. I was praying you'd forgive me, find a way to go on together. You have no reason to believe me now. Another time, another place, I think we'd have had a shot."

She paused when she saw my hand, which was raised in a thumb-to-fingers flapping motion, which every henpecked male person on the planet knows means *blah blah blah*.

"Cliché doesn't do it justice," I said.

She choked back her preferred response and said, "I thought . . . I mean, just wanted to, you know, *hold* you. Maybe then . . ."

My hand flapped once more. "Pardon me while I gag."

Her head snapped around, a sudden fire in her eyes. "You feel *nothing*?"

She had no idea.

"Oh, I feel plenty, Carolyn or Renee or whoever the fuck you are. All of it bad. It's called pain, okay? Is that what you want to hear? Okay, yeah, it hurts. Which means I cared about you, about us. There it is. But hear this—nobody shits on me like that. Nobody."

She looked away, brought her hand back to her mouth. The sudden quiet was oppressive.

"This is the part where you depart the premises," I said.

"No can do, Wolf."

"Sure you can. It's what women *do*. It's in your DNA."

"Cynic."

"That's *my* DNA."

"Smug prick, too."

Guess I had her fooled after all.

She squirmed in the chair, as if a secret was burning a hole in her willpower. The confident seductress from upstairs had left the building.

She looked back, wiping her eyes.

"You're not gonna like this."

"I already don't like it."

"I'm your handle when you go under."

"I'm going to Australia?"

"Under*cover*, asshole. You'll need a pipeline, maybe a lifeline. You're looking at her."

I whistled without sound. Than added, "Tell Duncan Meathead I'd prefer a more experienced agent."

"You get what you get. The very fact of my lack of field experience makes me easy to hide. No one can make me. I'll be in plain sight. And I'm already in."

"What, posing as my girlfriend, I suppose? Please."

"Girlfriend, yes. Yours, no."

"The answer is *no* either way," I said.

She nodded. Something darker entered the frame, and she didn't seem happy about it.

"Duncan can untangle your money. Get the state department involved. But you have to play it his way. That's the deal."

"Thanks, but I have other resources."

Her eyes were sad. "Actually, you don't. This is Duncan's case. He has the keys to the kingdom on this."

A familiar heat returned to my cheeks. At the moment I couldn't discern the messenger from the message, and for the sake of all parties involved, I sincerely wanted her to leave.

"Let me prove myself, Wolf."

She reached down for the briefcase she'd brought with her from upstairs. She opened it and withdrew a picture printed on paper rather than photo stock, and tossed it onto the coffee table in front of me. From the look of it, the FBI needed a new color printer.

I switched on the reading lamp next to the couch and leaned over. It was a candid shot of a woman standing next to a blackjack table in a casino, speaking to what I had to assume from the ex-con-in-Armani look was a pit boss. Only this pit boss had an aura of submission about him, as if he was getting reamed by a superior. The woman was dressed for an evening out, a black gown with a wispy black shawl, her hair pulled back severely, with earrings startlingly similar to the ones Carolyn had worn upstairs. She wasn't especially beautiful, but she was obviously rich and thus radiated power, which made her alluring in a manner most men don't like to admit to themselves. Like a network news anchor, all polish and cool and one helluva lot smarter than you are.

"Our client," I said, leaning back on the cushions.

"Lynn Valentine. By some estimations, the most powerful woman in Las Vegas."

"Next to Celine Dion," I offered. "And don't forget Lady Luck. I hear she's a bitch on wheels."

"Sweetheart, Lynn Valentine makes Lady Luck look like Mother Teresa on Easter morning."

"Ah, but can she sing?"

She ignored the comment as we stared at the picture on the coffee table for a few more seconds than was necessary.

"So," she said, "do I leave? Or do we talk business?"

I pursed my lips, feeling the cold hand of inevitability wrapping itself around my cojones.

"I just want my money," I said.

It was a lie, but this woman no longer had a ticket to the VIP room.

Renee smiled. The hurt lover who had been stuck between a rock and a federal hard place was gone. My handle was in the room, and it was time to open the case file on Lynn Valentine.

12

My new federal undercover handle had more photographs across the coffee table by the time I returned from the kitchen with a glass of ice water, which was all I was offering. She quickly launched into a well-rehearsed verbal white paper on the case, one with more holes than a John Edwards denial. When I tried to interrupt—I needed a notepad to keep track of my questions—she just flashed an open palm and a grimace to silence me.

She assured me it was all very simple. Really.

Lynn Valentine and her husband ran a hotel-casino in Las Vegas called Xanadu. A place where I had lost several hundred dollars on my last visit, though that was neither here nor there. I lose money in *all* the casinos. Xanadu was older and more seriously retro than the mega-casinos now dominating the strip, but it had a certain dark panache to it. The place reeked of sin. Renee explained that the hotel-casino had been a three-generation family business belonging most recently to Lynn's father, now deceased, but somehow the son-in-law, Phillip Valentine, managed to ingratiate himself into the will as an equal heir and partner.

I attempted to inject a simple question here, but to no avail. Renee was on a roll.

The federal government had never been able to prove a connection between the ownership of the casino and organized crime, other than the fact that known mafia figures were regulars on the premises. Xanadu was no different than other Las Vegas casinos in this regard, though at Xanadu well-adorned thugs and their foreign guests were the VIPs, while anyone looking for a Ben Affleck sighting would be better off at the Palms or the Hard Rock. The long-standing relationship between the gambling industry and certain dubious East-Coast factions had long ago managed to submerge itself beneath the regulatory radar, making the presence of known crime figures at the craps tables a flagrant, in-your-face irony that had no consequences. On a given night one could find the mayor doubling down next to a heroin importer from Venezuela, and nobody would find this odd. Hell, chances were good that later on they'd trade business cards in the lounge over blue-cheese martinis and a lap dance.

I began to interrupt, but another poised palm called for silence. All would be revealed in good time.

The Valentines, however, were nearing the line of regulatory indiscretion. What historically had been an open set of books to the gaming commission was, under Phillip Valentine's regime, the subject of some legal thumb wrestling, with recent warrants and depositions and even a grand-jury inquiry. So far the casino had managed to dodge the federal bullet, but in the process they had pissed off the wrong suits. They perhaps needed a slight push to cross that line, at which time the Feds would be there with handcuffs and unmarked vans.

Renee volunteered that she didn't know what specific infractions of legal subtlety were on the table, assuring me that it wasn't remotely germane—big word for an operations gal from Little Rock—to my assignment.

My role, as Duncan Stevens had so ably described, would be to use my fabled chin to get close to Lynn Valentine, plant some state-of-the-spy-art electronic bugs and listen to the subtext of a few thinly veiled conversations. The sudden advent of Lynn Valentine's desire to murder her husband was the opportunity the Feds had been looking for. By nailing her on a conspiracy to commit murder rap—*nail* and *frame* being synonymous here—they could bargain her sentence in return for names and recollections useful to federal organized crime investigators.

Justice, you see, is always negotiable.

Somehow, listening to Renee explain it, it did seem simple enough. This was a sting, pure and simple. Like she said.

At this point she produced a picture of a little man in a tailored suit, walking through a doorway flanked by two guys the Packers should never have waived. This, of course, was Phillip Valentine, who in some ways was actually prettier than his wife. Phillip Valentine might well be able to kick your ass, but you could be damned sure some guy the size of a bus had his back.

Napoleon had been a great general, but chances are he was a shitty husband. This, I assumed until closer proximity was achieved, was at the heart of Lynn Valentine's quest.

Renee sat back and sipped her ice water, her face tense.

Thin as it was, she had nothing to add to her briefing.

Now it was my turn.

13

"Where to start?" I said, eyes wide with anticipation.

"Allow me to preempt you," she replied. "The less you know going in, the better. In context to your cover—as a personal trainer or as a professional assassin, take your pick—you would have no knowledge of and no interest in the relationship between the Valentines and organized crime. You're there to plant bugs, and to lead her down a road of incrimination. That's all you know, all you need to know. Any more than that puts the operation, and you, in jeopardy."

"Thanks for your heartfelt concern," I said.

"You *are* the operation, Wolf."

Her deep brown eyes were ever so sincere. She obviously cared for me deeply. Just as obviously, she was parroting an answer that had been spoon-fed to her by Duncan Stevens or some other bland suit.

"So it's a coincidence that Lynn Valentine wants to off her

husband at this particular time, right when you guys need a hook."

"We've been waiting for a way to get someone inside for months. That time is now."

"So how do you, speaking on behalf of the FBI, know all this?"

"You have no need for that information."

"You sound like you work at the DMV."

Renee just stared. Thought it might make her smile, but she was getting good at this.

"You say you're already on the inside. So my question is this: why not just plant the bugs yourself?"

A trace of impatience colored her expression.

"Because the idea is to incriminate Lynn Valentine for a capital crime. And to exploit a rift between her and her husband. I'm already under a different cover. Lynn Valentine is looking for a contract killer."

She paused for effect.

"It's my job to bring her one."

I had to bite my lip at the sincerity she brought to the monologue.

"We add a little hormonal chemistry to the mix—and by the way, there is no doubt that Lynn Valentine will want a piece of you—and we have the perfect opportunity."

"A piece of *me*?"

Renee grinned slightly. "Occupational hazard, Wolf."

I nodded slowly. Her gaze had a dare in it, encouraging me to continue to try to stump her. Which would be my pleasure.

"How do I prove my killer credentials?"

"Been there, done that, from what I hear. And quite well."

Our eyes locked, waiting for one of us to make the next move.

I drew a deep breath. I wanted to watch when I told her my story, see if she blinked.

"A few months ago I was a honorable man in a dishonorable business."

"What was that?"

"Advertising. Then a woman who worked for me offers up a job working for a reclusive but paranoid billionaire. Guy wanted me to seduce his wife."

I saw the fog descend and paused. She really didn't know.

"She worked for you, and then she offered *you* a job?"

"She was a plant. Just like you. Turns out this billionaire wanted someone to help get him out of a prenup from hell."

"Doesn't sound like you."

"It wasn't. I said no. And it wasn't easy. Then guess what— the FBI shows up, asks me to do them a favor, be their eyes and ears. A month later a bunch of folks are dead and I'm a secret witness for the federal government."

"Happy ending?"

"The billionaire got off, scott free."

Clever of me. The billionaire's name was Scott. I watched closely, looking for a tell. But she didn't flinch.

"So here we are. With me wondering how the hell am I supposed to be credible as a contract killer?"

"Leave that to us. Before you leave you'll know just how many people have succumbed to your lethal charms, and just how they were dispatched. In case anyone wants to know. You'll be very pleased. So will they."

"Why not just use a federal pretty boy?"

"Because the people at Xanadu are understandably paranoid, and as a result they have a security screening process that rivals anything in Washington."

"They screen their assassins? That's interesting."

"They screen their *personal trainers*, you ass. Which means fingerprints and extensive background checks."

"So use a CIA recruit. Someone off the books. I hear Daniel Craig is available."

I wasn't completely sure that her emerging grin was for me, or because of me.

"Don't you read? They don't like us, we don't like them. Politics versus procedure. Older than the Vietnam Memorial.

And Craig is both British and much too short."

I commenced a pensive stare toward the ceiling.

"Question. I'm a bad dude, right? A professional killer."

"Not in the way you think. I can tell you this—Lynn Valentine is looking for something specific. Not just a bullet in the back of a man's head. That, you can buy on the street."

"I'm an expert, then. A specialist."

"Precisely."

"In what, may I ask?"

Renee's smile widened into something slightly frightening.

"I'll let Lynn Valentine tell you that herself."

I stroked my legendary chin, wondering what that might mean.

"Whatever. If organized crime is involved, then they know who all the contract killers are out there. They have conventions and shit. A secret handshake. Which means, they'll know I'm not a card-carrying member."

Renee thought a moment. A moment too long, in my opinion.

"Leave that to us. Lynn Valentine will be convinced you operate at the very highest and most discreet levels of your profession. An international player, with a paper trail that keeps you out of jail but drops enough clues in case anyone checks. Maybe ex–special forces gone freelance."

"You people can muck around with my paper trail? That's unconstitutional."

"Write your congressman."

This was getting to be fun. With each passing moment you could see Renee growing more confident in her role.

"And Lynn Valentine will be convinced of all this by you."

Renee just blinked. The sound of a neighbor's garage door could be heard over the grind of our respective wheels turning.

"Dangerous stuff," I finally said.

"You'll be covered the entire time."

"I have questions about that."

"Me, as well as other assets."

"Is that what you are? An asset?"

Her eyes closed and her head turned away. "We'll have time to work that out."

"What about my money?"

"Free and clear. As soon as Lynn Valentine sings."

"Is that a condition of sale?"

"You'll have to ask Duncan Stevens about that."

Or Sherman Wissbaum. Whichever came first.

Another long moment of awkwardness ensued. The unspoken hung like a piñata. And me without my nine-iron.

"That's it then," she said, beginning to gather the photos.

"Can you leave some of those?"

"Not a chance, *bucko*."

Those were the last words we exchanged before she got to the door. I couldn't let it go with bucko.

"I have more questions," I said.

"Someone will be in touch. Be ready to fly."

She shot me a complex smile before turning to go, one chock-full of apologies and regret and sadness and hope. A certifiable psychological stew. I watched her walk to the sidewalk, then down the street, all without a glance over her shoulder. A moment later a set of headlights popped on from a car I hadn't noticed upon my arrival, parked a hundred yards away.

I hoped Duncan Stevens had been listening in. If nothing else, he'd be ready with some answers the next time we met.

As I closed the door, I realized I hadn't asked Renee one final question, one that linked to an earlier point of discussion. I wanted to know how—as a federal employee who was already undercover in close proximity to the mark—was she going to avoid having her own fingerprints run by the very same paranoid Valentine clan that was most certainly going to run mine? A girl can wear gloves only so much of the time.

The verdict was still not in. And neither was I.

14

And then . . . nothing.

Four days passed. If you think it's easy living under the black cloud of an impending federal scam, one in which you are the designated trapeze artist without a net, think again. The only person with whom I could talk about it was my mother, who smiled sweetly as she listened and finally asked, "Will I see you at Bingo tonight?"

Such anxiety did, however, lend my daily health-club workouts a new and special meaning. I joined one of those national chains, the kind that makes you bring your own towels, the kind that fills up every January with resolution-happy civilians wearing black socks with their new Christmas Nikes, then empties out again come February. I found myself observing the trainers, none of whom were over the age of twenty-five, recent PE majors with killer abs and hilarious tattoos. I wondered why these Stepford students never talked to anyone on the property who wasn't paying their $35-an-hour tab, thus allowing an entire regiment of grunting, overweight fifty-something men to violate the protocol of form and function on every machine in the place. Some of these guys looked like they were having carnal relations with a mechanical bull.

Men. You gotta love us. If you can stomach us.

I was watching one such Neanderthal from the safe proximity of a treadmill, when I sensed someone firing up the machine next to me. Since the gym was fairly deserted at this mid-afternoon hour, such an intrusion of space was something one notices, like a stranger plopping into the seat next to you in a deserted movie theater.

The stranger was Sherman Wissbaum.

Our eyes met. He smiled gamely, then went about the business of punching in the requisite workout settings. I was jogging slowly, but Sherlock opted for a brisk walk up a steep incline.

I said, "You should really warm up your Achilles tendons before trying that."

He didn't look at me. "You a trainer all of a sudden?"

Made me wonder what he knew.

"Just a know-it-all. Is this a coincidence?"

"I live in Seattle, Wolf. You *think* it's a coincidence?"

"You have my number."

"It's bugged. This is better. Ambient noise up the ass."

"You Feds sure do think of everything."

I noticed that he'd brought his iPhone into the gym with him. Which reminded me of an opinion I held dear: phones in gyms should be banished. And hats. Hats worn backwards. Handkerchiefs tied around the skull, those guys should be tossed out. Especially skulls with little or no hair. Somehow I'd missed the memo that said testicles and hats were compatible accessories.

"Keep your eyes forward as we talk," he said, doing just that. "Seen your new girlfriend lately?"

I tried not to grin as I jogged, eyes dutifully forward.

"Not in four days. You?"

"Rumor has it she's in Vegas."

"No shit."

"Actually, it's about to hit the fan. You ready?"

"How can I be ready? I was supposed to get a copy of my résumé as a contract killer, but that hasn't happened. I can't find her, I can't find you, my money is missing, my mother's on a cruise to the Twilight Zone . . . so no, Sherman, I'm not ready."

The grade was already too steep for Sherlock's milky-white Achilles tendons, so he punched in a lower setting.

"You'll get the call. Go home and pack."

"I better do some wash."

"This is a fucking can of worms, Wolf. Interagency bullshit of the first order."

"Do I get my own jet again?"

He chuckled to himself, feigning great interest in the readout of his calorie expenditure thus far.

"The agents on this case, Duncan Stevens and his people, are off the books. They're a rogue splinter, zealots with their own agenda. They can't nail these scumbags working inside the lines, so they're doing their own thing."

"Funny about that last part. Eerily familiar."

He shook his head. Got him.

"It's illegal. And it won't hold up in court. Not if the Valentines get good representation, which they will."

"But they'd know that, wouldn't they? I think they would. Am I missing something here?"

He became serious for a moment and said, "Yeah. They'd know it."

"So what's the scam?"

"That's what we want you to help us find out."

I punched in a higher rate of speed, which produced more convenient ambient noise.

"Time out. Why not just pull their plug? I mean, if you know what Stevens is up to, then you've got enough for your Internal Affairs people to have a picnic."

Sherlock made a sarcastic face, as if this wasn't such a bad idea. Of course they'd considered all these options.

"It's not quite that simple."

"So, am I going after the thugs, the killer wife, or your kooky rogue agents?"

He punched in a new setting that slowed his machine to a stop.

"Ready for this, Wolf? You're going after *all* of them."

Without another word Sherlock hopped off the machine and headed toward the locker room, a slight limp from a decade-earlier shootout still evident. He flicked a quick come-hither flick of the head, so after a moment I followed.

Inside the locker room he pretended he didn't know me—this is de rigueur in locker rooms worldwide—and I tried to pass the time while I waited for what would come next. Sherlock undressed—not pretty—then slipped into a flowered Tommy Bahama swimsuit and headed my way with a towel.

He avoided my eyes as he passed.

"Whirlpool," he said. "Leave your gym bag on the floor."

*   *   *

I could see why he chose the whirlpool for the next part.

The ambient noise here was something from a Boeing test site.

As I slipped into the hot water I said, "Do you really think someone's observing this little scene from *The Bourne Identity*?"

"Do you really think I'd play casual where your life is concerned, Wolf?"

His look was intense and challenging. It was time to bag the Last Comic Standing routine and listen up.

"There's a phone in your bag, one of those cool new Droids. We've already programmed it with your mobile number, so keep your old phone turned off. It's still good, by the way, if the Droid is off. But use ours."

"All the real spies have smartphones. Some even have brilliant phones."

"You'll love this one. It picks up everything within fifteen feet. Even when it's turned off."

Now *that's* an app. I nodded with genuine appreciation.

"We'll be with you twenty-four seven. Off the grid, but nearby. Just tell me what you want, a meeting, whatever, and I'll get word back to you. When we meet, if we meet, it'll be someplace crowded, lots of ambient background. Be cryptic when you speak, since the rooms are likely bugged. Can you handle that?"

"How will . . . ?"

"You want to listen or ask dumbass questions you know I'm already going to cover?"

"Did you know the tags are still on your suit?"

He closed his eyes a moment, drew a deep breath.

"We've got someone on the inside. Better you don't know who it is. We'll know when you get there, we'll know how they've set you up. You play the role, follow whatever scenario you are given. Don't deviate, don't cross any lines, until you clear it with me first. Copy that?"

I was getting dizzy nodding.

"Keep the Droid with you. It'll pass any screening they throw at it."

"I'll sleep with it. I snore, by the way."

"How are your martial arts these days?"

"Right up there with my feng shui. Are you shitting me?"

"People will expect you to be a badass. You're a killer, Wolf. You may be tested on that one."

"You mean, like, a practice homicide?"

"Hope that sense of humor of yours holds up. Not sure it'll serve you, though."

"I'm actually better at the talk than I am at the walk."

Which was true of most self-proclaimed badasses, actually. If half the battle was in the posturing, then I was golden.

"Just watch your pretty little ass."

"You're not paying me enough for this shit."

His eyes lit up. "That reminds me. Your money's fine. The

whole thing is a firewall under the control of Duncan Stevens' people."

I remembered the expression on Stevens face when I mentioned the money. Maybe he *was* Sean Penn after all.

"Which means . . . ?"

"They've digitally inserted themselves between your computer and your phones and your Cayman bank. They can hack into the receiving end, place a block on any incoming call they want, by area code or specific number."

"They can do that?"

"They have your government's best technology at their disposal."

I made a mental note to check this out with Blaine.

"So, the heat's off. I don't need to do this. I can just use another computer, call them from out of state."

Sherlock looked away, uncomfortable.

"It's not that easy."

I read between those lines. It was Sherlock, not Duncan Stevens, who was now holding my money hostage against my participation. And from the look on his face, he knew I had figured it out.

"You bastard," I said, in case he hadn't.

"Look, it's out of my hands. I'm sorry. Just get this done. You'll come out okay. Word."

You can't help but smile when a chubby white guy with orchids on his swimsuit goes street.

A chubby fellow waddled out of the sauna—fat guys believe this burns calories—and departed before either of us spoke.

"So, I ask again, are you up for this, Wolf?"

I thought a moment. I still wasn't up for it.

"If the mark pays me, I get the same deal as before?"

That would be good old American under the table, tax-free cash. Keep it offshore and don't buy anything stupid for a while. Same drill.

"I'm thinking Euros. That's what all the international players are trading in these days."

I nodded. Two swimmers were doing laps in the adjacent pool, and I wondered if there was any technology on earth that might permit them to listen in while they did flip turns.

"If people start dying, I'm out of there."

"Fair enough. Just keep the Droid close. You'll do fine, just like last time."

"I'm glad you think my ass is pretty, Sherman."

He shook his head. "Everything you need to know is in the Bag."

We touched fists, just like the big boys on ESPN.

Like a prostate exam from hell, I was about to be digitally inserted into the hot, smelly rectum of American greed and lust: Las Vegas, Nevada.

15

Las Vegas

Leonard Valentine had been in his grave less than a week before his grieving daughter had commissioned an extensive remodeling of his hotel. The upper floor, the nineteenth, had been divided into four lavish penthouse suites, each with a rooftop veranda, renting for six grand a night when they weren't being comped to the rich and anonymous. The eighteenth floor was private and under twenty-four-hour armed guard, accessible only by private elevator. This was the mailing address of the Valentine family, twelve thousand square feet of private residence arranged into three distinct living spaces to accommodate the family's very unique needs. Phillip had the northern view, down the strip toward Caesars and the Stratosphere, while Lynn's suite overlooked the Luxor and the MGM Grand and the upstart theme hotels that were bleeding the city dry beneath the shadows of fake monuments and faux antiquity.

The Valentines hadn't shared a bedroom, much less a bed,

in over three years. What they did share were secrets too dark and painful to speak aloud.

Between these very separate quarters were other bedrooms, including suites for the house and security staff. Nestled safely among them was the bedroom of Caitlin Valentine, the thirteen-year-old daughter both parents worshipped in their own way. Her father, Phillip, advocated homeschooling and supervised play, while Lynn insisted on public schooling and normal social exposure. Phillip was a stickler for discipline, Lynn spoiled her daughter at every turn. When their parental styles collided, invariably it was Lynn Valentine who prevailed.

As a concession to Phillip, Caitlin had her own car and driver to take her to and from school. To support a façade of normality she was enrolled in every conceivable extracurricular activity the Las Vegas public school system could dream up. She was a popular girl and a good student, but she had her mother's fire, which meant she was as feared among her peers as she was sought after. One of her eighth-grade term papers had been entitled, "How to Keep the Riff-Raff Back of House," for which she had received an "A" and a vice-principal's request to have the parents call the school at their earliest convenience.

The bedroom adjacent to Caitlin's remained unoccupied and locked. No one other than Lynn had been inside the room for the past twelve hundred days.

AN attractive young woman knocked softly on Caitlin Valentine's bedroom door, under the watchful eye of a security guard seated across the hall. The two avoided eye contact, due to a fallout from a distinctly sexual encounter at last year's holiday staff party that, should it ever surface, would cost both their jobs. As usual she was in her business-school best, with the dark-rimmed glasses worn by actresses trying to tone down God's gifts. But despite the pinstripes and the very proper heels, the woman remained a bona fide bomb. That, and the fact that she had Lynn Valentine's trust and affection, made her the most despised name on the employee roster by both genders.

The woman everyone knew as Nicole—*Sticky Nicole* behind her back—waited a moment, then gently pushed the door open and slipped inside.

Lynn Valentine reclined on the bed next to her sleeping daughter, cradling the girl's head and shoulders while stroking her hair. Caitlin already had her mother's dark glamour, hooded eyes, and bee-sting lips, with thick chocolate hair worn straight and long. What she didn't share was her mother's sense of gloom, and her smile was both radiant and generous. Caitlin was an icon of fresh hope within Xanadu's wicked embrace, and the house staff loved her like surrogate parents.

Nicole approached the bed quietly, kneeling as she smiled at her boss. She, too, reached out and stroked Caitlin's hair, but only once. All around them hand-painted walls depicted the hills from *The Sound of Music,* which tonight were alive with the neon glow of the Strip.

The two women locked eyes, and their voices were low.

"He arrives the day after tomorrow," said the younger woman.

Lynn nodded, staring into the acrylic Austrian terrain. "Are we ready for this?"

"Completely."

"You're sure he's safe?"

"As safe as he is dangerous. Gorgeous, too."

Lynn nodded, though not convincingly. From the outset she had been skeptical of her assistant's assurances, though her doubt was outweighed by her desire.

"I love you for this. I owe you huge."

"It's my pleasure."

"When this is over . . ."

Nicole offered a sympathetic smile as she reached out to touch Lynn's face. Two women sharing a moment, their silence belying the complexity of it all.

"We'll think of something," she said.

Seconds passed. Three years of pain had etched their legacy into Lynn Valentine's eyes, which glistened now with a new hope, black and deep.

"I want him to suffer," she said, her voice even softer, her eyes misting, as they always did when the topic surfaced.

Nicole knew Lynn wasn't referring to the man who would soon arrive at Xanadu. The object of this particular intention was her husband.

"He's very good at what he does."

Lynn nodded. She had never asked for names, and Nicole had never offered. Lynn only knew that her assistant had certain connections, *friends* as she put it, that could make her vengeful dream a cold reality.

"He goes by Wolf. Ironic, don't you think?"

Lynn looked down at her daughter, watching the gentle rise and fall of her chest.

"Wolf," she said, her voice barely audible. "An endangered species. Smart. Fast. Deadly."

Her eyes locked onto Nicole's.

"Perfect," she added with a whisper.

THE woman Wolfgang Schmitt had first known as Carolyn, then later as Renee, and who now masqueraded as Lynn Valentine's personal assistant under the name of Nicole, nodded as she rose to her feet. Then she quietly slipped out of the room, leaving her boss to ponder the implications of what was about to occur.

SEVENTEEN stories below, in the private security suite accessible only to the Valentines and the senior security staff, Chad Merrill leaned back in his chair, hands folded over his abdomen, watching the two women on the monitor before him.

After a moment he withdrew a mobile phone from his pocket and punched in a number. He knew that here in this room, the acoustic and digital aesthetics of which he had designed himself, his words were secure.

He smiled, waiting for his call to be answered.

16

PORTLAND

Viva Las Vegas, my ass.

The last time I hit the road at the behest of God and country, it was all private jets and escargot and women in leather pants. This time it was Carl's Jr. and a rental from Alamo.

The call arrived midevening after Sherlock's hot tub tutorial—I could hear slot machines in the background, I shit you not—a guy who sounded like Gilbert Gottfried telling me that my employment at Xanadu was to begin day after next, and that a car would pick me up within the hour. Enough time to batten down the hatches and arrange for my neighbor to feed my fish for a couple of weeks. A strange schedule, this, but after all, we weren't in the real world here. This was Vegas, baby, and all bets were off.

I called Sherman in Seattle right away with the news. No one answered, and he had instructed me not to leave a message. He also promised he'd call back as soon as he could, which in this case was ten minutes. He told me it was a go, that someone would contact me when I was in position. He assured me I would be under surveillance the entire time, and all I needed to do was summon help through the Droid and manage to stay alive the few seconds it would take for someone to break the door down and rescue me. He also told me that they could not get the warrants necessary to plant any bugs on the premises, but that the transcripts of anything picked up by the covert Droid phone transmissions would be admissible evidence, since they could be corroborated by a credible witness acting under the auspices of an authorized criminal investigation.

The bug, it turned out, would be me.

Fact was, I was eager to get on the road. Everything in my life was suddenly riding on this. Not just the money, which was a significant bullet point. Especially with the closing date on my new nursing home venture looming large. And certainly not because of any chance of patching things up with Special Agent Renee Whatever. That chance had long since evaporated.

No, what was riding on this was *me*.

THE car arrived as promised, this being my first clue that the lap of luxury would tonight be sat upon by someone other than me. It was a cab, driven by a guy named Sunil. As expected he took me to the airport, where, based on past experience, a private jet should have been warming up on the tarmac. Renee would be waiting inside to accompany me, dressed to kill as she provided more titillating details as to what was expected of me as a highly sought-after contract killer.

Didn't happen.

Instead I was taken to the rooftop level of the short-term lot—being Portland, it was, of course, raining hard enough to peel the serial numbers off the airplanes—where we stopped next to the only car in sight.

"What is this?" I asked of Sunil.

"I assumed you knew."

"Humor me."

"Your ride, sir."

"Sorry, my ride has wings and bitter women serving chips."

The driver consulted a slip of paper on the seat next to him.

"Short-term, top floor, Ford Taurus. That's what they said, that's where we are. Have a nice evening."

"Who are *they*, may I ask?"

"No idea. Dispatch came in via fax, with a Visa pre-pay."

"Whose Visa, if I may be so bold?"

"Why, yours, sir. There was no tip, by the way."

"You got that *right*, Sparky."

Waiting in the Taurus was a rental agreement from Alamo in the name of someone named Darren Dalton, a Nevada state map, and a carton of Fig Newton cookies. The latter was a signature move of Renee's, who, in an earlier life as Carolyn the ruthless lawyer girlfriend, was well aware of my tastes in carbohydrates.

There was no phony résumé, no backstory for me to memorize. And until that happened, I would remain my own boss.

Assumption is the mother of all screwups. Whoever had put this little logistical comedy together didn't know me all that well, and despite the covert logic in traveling incognito along the highways of the Western states, I had no intention of passing the next twenty-four hours behind the wheel of a rented Taurus as one Darren Dalton. Who, for all I knew, might be lying dead in a nearby ditch. Duncan Stevens and his band of vigilante agents could kiss my imposter ass on that issue.

I checked my watch. If I hurried I could make the US Airways 11:30 red-eye I'd planned on, with the honey-roasted peanuts for lunch. And if things turned out like I hoped, there would be plenty of cash to cover it when the smoke cleared.

I grabbed the Fig Newtons and hurried into the terminal.

WHAT, I asked myself, was I thinking?

An impenetrable blackness surrounded the airplane as it

hurtled through a smooth void toward Nevada. The lights had been dimmed shortly after takeoff and the cabin was less than half occupied. Nothing moved, including the air. On any other night the monotonous drone of the engines would have lulled me into a tortuous sleep, followed by waking to an inevitable cramp in my neck and breath that would melt naugahyde.

But not tonight.

Tonight I was *thinking*. About the fraudulent résumé that had been promised but hadn't as yet materialized. Wondering how many people had I killed, and how. What was the so-called *specialty* that Renee preferred to leave to Lynn Valentine's revelation, and why all the drama attached to it?

Lying was hard, but not knowing *what* to lie about— priceless.

I was thinking about Sherlock, about the sincere look on his face when he'd given me his word that I'd come out of this with my posterior intact. I believed him. He had been there for me last time, in circumstances that could have easily forced him to choose between his word and his career. No matter that the guy couldn't box his way out of a sandwich bag. For some inexplicable reason I was willing to go the distance with him. *For* him, in fact. Something about making a small difference in a war against bad guys that didn't deserve a fair fight.

I was also thinking about the money, truth be told. Not about the score at hand or the accessibility of my elusive foreign portfolio, but about the much lyricized point of it all.

The seat next to me was empty. It, and the quiet still life of the airplane in which I was riding, reminded me just how alone I was, with no real understanding as to why. I had just left town indefinitely, and the only call I'd made was to arrange feeding times for my angelfish. I had dishonored time itself, both in terms of my relationships and my vaporized career in advertising. Each had been highlighted by campaigns that in the final analysis were fun and persuasive but meant nothing at all. They dealt in consumables, which, like the Fig Newtons in my lap, were tasty but ultimately less than filling. The only woman

I had ever truly loved was in prison awaiting trial for murder, and I had played a major role in putting her there.

What a catch I was.

And speaking of money, let us not forget that a seven-figure closing date on the nursing home loomed just weeks away.

Nobody, especially me, likes losing their escrow deposit.

That acidic thought brought me back to my mother.

As the lights of Las Vegas appeared on the horizon, I pictured Mom sleeping in a hospital-castoff bed, completely unaware of her son's efforts to buy the place out from under the dull apathy with which it was currently being managed, to turn it into a vessel of the mind that would allow her to sail blissfully away. One with clean sheets and adventurous cuisine. I was amazed at the depth of my need to impact her remaining days, given the shadowed childhood I had somehow survived, the cold father I had buried with dry eyes, and the scent of alcohol and vomit on my mother's lips that to this day remained a visceral memory.

Heavy stuff. Questions without answers, intersections without signs. Best any of us can do is keep our eyes forward and our minds on the task at hand. If there's one handy, I highly recommend the in-flight magazines to pass the time. Because the airplane is going down whether you like it or not, be it a soft landing on a long runaway or a haymaker into the side of a mountain.

In either case, all that awaits when we arrive is baggage.

The contents of which, by the way, is of our own packing.

Me, I prefer to travel light.

PART
TWO

17

LAS VEGAS

Six Weeks Earlier

The casino floor at Xanadu had a certain social hierarchy to it, one enforced with stiff smiles and table limits that clarified the issue. The general gaming area was the strip's eighth biggest if you believed the Chamber of Commerce, but there was no shop in town that offered the discreet player as many ways to cloak themselves in anonymity. Tonight a Japanese businessman was the sole occupant of a baccarat pit stanchioned off from the public area, allowing a three-deep crowd of civilians—tourists, local regulars, and anyone else who wasn't known to be among the Valentines' special guests—to observe. He was betting thirty grand a hand, and was down a half million after two markers. Next to him, her chair a respectful foot behind, was an Asian beauty who calculated the worth of each hand in real estate and bling. From the look on her face, not to mention the eight-karat yellow diamond on her finger, Mister Fortune Cookie had some explaining to do.

Phillip Valentine watched without expression, hands clasped behind his back, nervously twirling a gold pinkie ring given to him a few years ago by Mike Tyson after Phillip had introduced the champ to a certain dealer he fancied. Valentine knew tonight's guest well, and had already arranged for a special post-midnight soiree in his suite, including two African-American "models"—the man was very specific: "I want look like Beyonce"—and twenty thousand dollars' worth of high-quality cocaine, which was for his wife, who liked to watch.

Both condiments were a mere phone call away.

Valentine's bodyguard remained at arm's length, a full head taller and in an eternal state of agitation. The man knew how quickly the illusion could shatter, and he was being paid handsomely to keep his boss dry when it did. He put a finger to his earpiece, listened carefully, then stooped to whisper into Phillip Valentine's ear.

There was trouble in paradise. Their presence was required posthaste in the security control center.

CHAD Merrill didn't look up when Phillip and the bodyguard entered the executive security suite. He could see their reflection in the monitor before him, could tell from the boss's worried expression that expedience was appropriate.

He hit a button that summoned an image to the screen. It showed a large black man sitting in a chair next to a door. At first glance he appeared to be asleep—not a good career move for a security guard at Xanadu—but a little study made it quickly apparent that he was unconscious. Drool hung from his lip, one eye partially open.

"Jesus," mumbled Valentine, "that's Marlon. Get somebody up there."

"Five minutes ago," said Merrill. "He's fine. Has no idea what happened."

"Does anybody?"

"I'm afraid so."

Merrill tapped the requisite keys that would summon a new image to the screen.

Valentine leaned in, staring at a new image.

A young girl appeared to be sleeping peacefully on a bed. The lighting was surreal, a computer-rendered transformation of a combined infrared and natural-light signal.

"She looks fine."

"She is fine," said Merrill. "Look closer."

Merrill zoomed the image tighter. A square of white was now visible on the girl's chest, something that didn't belong.

Valentine put his hand on Merrill's shoulder. "What the hell . . . ?"

"She's *good*, Phillip. This is a recording, what I saw when I got here. Lynn's with her now. But you need to see this."

"Is she awake?"

"No. She has no idea. Look closely."

Another keystroke. The image zoomed tight on the white square. It was a piece of paper fixed to the girl's nightie with a safety pin. On it was a handwritten message:

PV—Sam Boyd lot, midnight, alone

PV was Phillip Valentine. *Sam Boyd lot* referred to the parking lot at Sam Boyd Stadium, where the UNLV Rebels played football. The rest of it required no interpretation.

Merrill sensed that Phillip Valentine was not breathing. His body was rigid, eyes fixed on the screen. And because Merrill knew more than anyone about recent Valentine family history, a dark volume which illuminated the context of these video clips, he understood the man's terror completely.

The sleeping girl was Phillip Valentine's daughter. The guard sitting outside her door, and the proximity of video surveillance on both of them, had everything to do with the reason Phillip Valentine's heart was suddenly frozen with fear.

18

Phillip Valentine had to threaten termination to convince his bodyguard to remain behind. After what nearly became a physical exchange of opinions—the natural order of resolution for both men—the bodyguard had insisted that his boss wear a wire, or at least a transponder so they could track his location. But Valentine knew he would be searched, and the presence of covert electronics in a discreet body cavity would do nothing other than piss off the man who had summoned him.

Valentine knew all too well who it was. Enough to avoid agitating the man at all costs.

HIS name was Lou Mancuso, and those who knew him spoke it with only the most reverent of tones. He ran his myriad affairs, business and otherwise, from a modest house in Queens, though he owned four luxurious homes in sunnier climates around the world. The Feds had been unsuccessfully trying to nail him for over a decade on everything from racketeering to murder, and he was on a first-name basis with the detectives who tracked and recorded his every deed and word. The authorities and the press believed he had inherited a significant portion of the Gotti empire, though anyone in an antagonistic position to corroborate this notion had long since disappeared.

Lou Mancuso and Phillip Valentine had met four times. The first was several years earlier at a rented mansion in the hills with a pool, tennis court, and batting cage. What followed were the darkest days of Phillip Valentine's life, what Mancuso still referred to as "a regretful time of negotiation and concession." Their second face-to-face was shortly thereafter, upon Valentine's subsequent agreement to bring Mancuso into the business as a very silent, off-the-books partner. In return for a monthly management fee of one-point-five million dollars, plus complete access to the facility in whatever manner and for whatever reason Mancuso saw fit, Xanadu would be assured a steady stream of global high rollers with an unthinkable appetite—and budget—for vice. Mancuso would also provide a perfectly legal and seemingly bottomless well of capital for expansion and the occasional emergency, as well as the perfectly illegal elimination of anyone and anything who stood in the way of Xanadu's best interests. This included rival "organized families," as he put it, plus the Feds, local cops, and anyone else with a beef. Lou Mancuso's genius was that the problems of his partners just went away, no questions asked.

The money was all under the table, a private transaction between individuals, easily hidden within the books. Which meant the Nevada Gaming Commission couldn't touch them. Indeed, it would take Phillip Valentine filing an official grievance to initiate action, which, given their recent history, wasn't likely.

Phillip was still a father, which took precedence over everything now.

After three years in bed together, both parties had delivered. They had an *understanding*, one that Lou Mancuso constantly reminded Phillip Valentine was in their best mutual interests to maintain. To keep everyone happy, Mancuso had been generous with profits and perks across the board.

The next time they met was to clarify the role of Xanadu's new Director of Casino Operations, one of Mancuso's top lieutenants with a squeaky-clean résumé. Bradley Pascarella would be Mancuso's eyes and ears, who, along with a small staff of yes-men with large guns, would personally attend to the needs of the boss's friends and associates during their frequent stays at Xanadu. He would also manage the arrival of large sums of cash from unnamed sources, unloaded from unmarked airplanes in unmarked suitcases, which entered the casino smelling of blood and departed having been completely and thoroughly laundered. Mancuso himself had stayed at the hotel only once—their fourth and final meeting prior to tonight—buying out the entire inventory of rooms to accommodate a sort of annual meeting for the criminally inclined. Phillip had been forced to cancel the reservations of over three hundred tourists to make it happen, personally dumping them into neighboring properties, and had not received so much as a thank-you note. In fact, he was told by Pascarella that it would be a good idea to take the weekend off. He ran into Mancuso at the airport as Phillip was leaving town, their private jets parked wing to wing at the executive terminal.

Tonight, when Phillip Valentine drove into the empty stadium lot, he saw a single car with its lights on, the door wide open. He pulled up next to it and got out. The car's engine was already running.

No one else was there. The car was for him.

It was a luxury rental from Hertz. When Valentine closed the door, a robotic female GPS voice greeted him by name, then immediately issued a command to drive forward and turn right onto Tropicana. From there it gave him directions to the executive tarmac adjacent to McCarran. It then instructed him to stop within one hundred feet of a sleek black helicopter, the rotors of which were already turning, engine purring like an anxious Ferrari.

The voice signed off: "Thank you for flying with us tonight, Mister Valentine. Have a pleasant evening."

Mancuso fancied himself a bit of a comedian.

A pilot was standing next to the open rear hatch. Phillip had seen the guy around the hotel—he had the face of a small rodent—so there was no mistaking the invitation.

After a digital pat down using a wand sensor that looked like a small tennis racket, Valentine climbed into the rear passenger compartment, the sole passenger tonight.

A shovel was lying on the floor.

THE chopper lifted off quickly, banking west over the Luxor and then south to avoid McCarran traffic, circumventing Henderson heading due east. Within minutes the lights of the Las Vegas metroplex grew sparse, and not long thereafter they disappeared altogether.

Phillip Valentine was being flown into blackness. The perfect metaphor, he thought, for his life with Lou Mancuso.

19

80 MILES NORTHEAST OF LAS VEGAS

A single sparkle of light shone from a carpet of seamless black on a moonless night. The helicopter homed in on it, hitting the landing lights from a hundred feet up to illuminate a flat area, revealing a nearby vehicle. The rotors shut down immediately upon landing.

This was going to take awhile.

The pilot opened the door and motioned toward a black Hummer, its high beam headlights and off-road spotlights in full glory. They were in a small canyon about the size of a football field, slopes of jagged rock rising on all sides, the shadows creating a surreal theatricality.

"Bring the shovel," said the pilot.

"*You* bring the shovel," said Valentine, already in full, crunching stride toward the Hummer.

The doors on both sides of the vehicle flew open. The first man out was Lou Mancuso, wearing an oversized down coat over slacks and wingtips, his coarse helmet hair perfectly waved. Valentine had to bite down on his lower lip to keep from laughing out loud. Close behind were two huge men, one white, one black, both much younger, both with shaved heads. Judging from the way they pocketed their hands to shrug off the chill, they wished they were somewhere else. A gym, most likely.

"Thanks for coming out," said Mancuso, a smirk in full evidence as he shook Valentine's hand. The two monsters flanking him didn't offer the same, so Valentine pretended to ignore them. There was so much to laugh at, which was why he still bit at his lip under the guise of a nervous tic.

He had a feeling the humor would go away soon.

"We shopping real estate?" asked Phillip, panning the surroundings with his hand. Mancuso thought this was hilarious, and at his cue so did the bodyguards.

"In a way, yeah."

He nodded to the pilot, who was standing behind. The man handed Valentine the shovel he'd brought from the helicopter.

"Over here."

Mancuso turned and began walking toward the Hummer. One of the goons took his elbow and urged Valentine to follow.

They moved as a silent unit, stopping ten yards in front of the headlights, where Mancuso marked an X in the sand with his size eight Bragano dress shoe.

"You dig, I'll talk. You have questions, you be sure and let me know. We good on that, Phillip?"

There were no other options currently available to Phillip Valentine other than being good with that. He narrowed his eyes and plunged the shovel into the dirt. It was surprisingly soft, sand and gravel loosely packed from the occasional rains that swept through the desert at this time of year.

One of the bodyguards had gone back to the Hummer to fetch a portable folding seat, the kind used by retirees at golf tournaments. He plunged the stand into the dirt and opened the seat, holding it while Mancuso sat down.

"Mind if I smoke?"

He was already unwrapping a huge cigar. As he dug, Valentine wondered if there was any limit to the extent of the man's caricature.

Between the first flaming puffs he said, "We been doing good, you and me. Ya think?"

"Terrific. How big a hole you want?"

Mancuso shook out the match he'd used on the cigar. "Four by four is fine. I mean, business is good, the Gaming Commission loves you. How's your daughter, by the way?"

Valentine stopped, leaned his weight on the shovel. Parts of the hole were already a foot deep, and his shirt was soaked with effort. He squinted at the man who seemed to be amused with his own capacity for cruelty. He was grinning as he lovingly gave head to the cigar.

"You're thinking," said Mancuso, "that you could put that shovel into my chest before they could get to us. You're thinking it might be worth a shot. Am I right about that, Phillip?"

Valentine's voice was a whisper. "You might be."

"I recommend you keep digging. There's a rifle pointed at your head at this very moment, and I promise he's faster than you are."

Mancuso nodded cheerfully at the Hummer to punctuate the recommendation. One of the thugs had a rifle propped on an open door, pointing right at him.

Mancuso motioned with the cigar to get back to work. But Valentine had something else to say.

"Ah, but that's the point here, isn't it? Me in the hole? Which means I have nothing to lose if you're wrong about who's faster than who. Either way, I get dead. Might be worth a shot."

Mancuso's grin took on a darker hue.

"Oh, you're wrong about that. Besides, if he shoots you now, one of us has to dig this fucking hole, right? It's about utilization of resources. So do us both a favor, okay? Let this play out. See if you're still a smart ass."

Valentine went back to his task. He dug furiously, anxious to get it over with. He spoke without looking up.

"I'm not buying it, Lou. Even you aren't this unoriginal. You get this from that Scorsese movie? I bet you did."

Mancuso again thought Valentine was a laugh riot. He shot a quick glance at a bodyguard to share the moment.

"Actually," he said, his gaze returning to Valentine, "I kind of like it out here. Quiet, you know? Like the moon. You could bury anything."

"You wouldn't be out here freezing your ass if you didn't want something from me."

"Maybe I just like this kind of shit. You called me a *sick little fuck* once upon a time. Maybe you were right." After a pause he added, "to be honest, this is some bad disgusting shit you're gonna see."

Valentine paused to wipe sweat from his face with his shirt sleeve. He'd wondered if that comment would return to haunt him, and here it was. He used the moment to map the surrounding players, in case a move presented itself.

He plunged the shovel back into ground, extracted a spade full of dirt and tossed it toward Mancuso's feet.

"You pissed, Phillip?"

"Impatient."

"Really? Me too, actually. So here it is. Bradley brought you a proposal for a new property in the Bahamas. You turned it down. He brought it to you again, said you told him to go fuck himself. That's not professional. I sent you a memo, suggesting we consider this. You ignored me. That's just plain stupid."

"It was a bad business model."

"Blowing me off is a bad business model. I'm sending you another memo, Phillip. You're standing in it."

Valentine stopped again, but Mancuso barked, "Dig!" He paused before adding, "You're almost there."

"I ran the numbers," said Valentine, trying to sound contrite. "Nothing about your proposal works on paper."

"It's not about the fucking paper, Phillip. It's about laundering money that's too hot for Nevada. It's about the offshore market, guys who can't get through customs. The next frontier, Phillip, it's called global-fucking-ization."

In that moment Valentine realized that Lou Mancuso wanted to conquer the entire world. And that he would crawl into bed with anyone if that's what it required.

Valentine said, "I can't afford it. It's too rich for me."

"Sure you can. I told you I'll cut my monthly in half for two years. That's a hundred twenty million. Half your nut."

"Here's a better idea. *You* build it."

"Don't insult my intelligence. People who do that don't live long enough to find out just how fucking smart I am. Guy like me can't get permits or tax breaks. I can't get near this conversation. But *you* can. This thing's gotta have *your* name on it. I try to make it work for you, put some serious capital in your pocket, and you disrespect me."

"No disrespect," said Valentine. "It's just a bad deal. That's what partners do, they stop the other from shooting themselves in the head."

Mancuso worked the cigar for a moment, squinting as smoke rose into his eyes. It occurred to Phillip that perhaps he'd just pitched the wrong analogy.

"I want that casino, Phillip. I *need* that casino."

"It'll put Xanadu in jeopardy. I can't do that. You don't *want* me to do that. Use someone else."

Suddenly the shovel encountered something solid. Something metal and hollow.

And then it hit him. He wasn't digging his own grave at all. He was digging up someone else's.

One of the bodyguards stepped close to shine a flashlight into the hole, now three feet deep. The object he'd struck was dark brown. He used the spade to clear the dirt away, quickly revealing the round top of what he now recognized as an industrial waste barrel. The black rubber plug was still in place, the rim lined with sealed semicircular flanges, each of which had a slit for use in prying it back up.

Mancuso nodded at the thug, who produced a screwdriver from his back pocket. He tossed the tool into the hole. A clanging sound, sickeningly hollow, rang out as it landed.

"Listen to me," said Mancuso. "I like you. You're a ballsy, arrogant little prick. A guy who takes no shit. But here's the reality, Phillip, and I want you to consider it carefully. I've got your testicles in my pocket. I get no pleasure from this, like I said, it's disgusting. It's just business. Like before. I make your life safe, but I can crush you at any moment. You know that. Which is why you'll do the Bahamas."

His eyes burned into Valentine with what, in another moment, might be mistaken as empathy. Then he added a tag that made Phillip shiver.

"You're just like me. You survive."

He nodded to the thug as he got up and walked toward the helicopter. Lou Mancuso would not be driving back to town tonight. Valentine wondered what this might mean for him.

"Pop the lid," said the goon. He produced a handgun from behind his back to add substance to the request.

Valentine knelt on the barrel as he pried the flanges up with the screwdriver, one by one. It took him two minutes to lift them all, after which he stepped off and straddled it.

He looked up at the bodyguard, who issued a nod to proceed.

The lid came up without resistance, accompanied by a slight rushing of air. A pungent chemical scent made Phillip wince.

The bodyguard shined the light inside.

Valentine looked down. He inhaled sharply, frozen in place as he began sinking to his knees, as if in slow motion, his mouth gaping wide.

Then he closed his eyes.

Moments later his scream pierced the cold Nevada night, the cry of an animal trapped by something it didn't understand.

Inside the barrel was a young girl's body, naked and embalmed, folded into a fetal position. Only the angle of the head was unnatural, cocked back as if gazing up at the lid in a posture of eternal hope.

The eyes were open and dry. Vacant. They stared up at the

man who had been her father. The girl was still, and forever, only ten years old.

The body buried here in the netherworld of the Nevada desert was that of Kerry Valentine, the daughter Phillip and Lynn Valentine lost three years ago when he'd tried to resist Lou Mancuso's initial tender of partnership. When he'd paid the price of Lou Mancuso's indignant rage.

Her twin sister, Caitlin, who had survived when that resistance waned, was now thirteen. Lou Mancuso knew that Phillip Valentine would do anything to protect her now.

He was, in fact, counting on it.

20

There's this thing about being single and forty. It's that feeling of waking up and wondering if *this* might be the day. The day you might meet *her*. And it's a great reason to get out of bed. But because you know your day will in all likelihood be just like the one before it—it's gonna suck—you're pretty sure it won't happen. What you need, what resurrects this feeling and magnifies it into something you can feel in your gut, is a change of scenery.

Like, say, Hawaii. Or a class reunion. Maybe a spring break weekend in Fort Lauderdale. But *not* Las Vegas. The chances of meeting The One in Sin City are like finding the perfect nanny for your kids in a strip bar.

Such thoughts were in the back of my mind as a taxi brought me to meet my fate behind the modest façade of the Xanadu Hotel and Casino. Like any red-blooded American male desperate for a little debauchery, I'd been to Vegas before, though not since they'd shit-canned the ill-fated family marketing approach of the 1990s and returned to an unabashed promotion of sin. *What happens in Vegas stays in Vegas.* Along with your money and, if you had a good time, your self-respect.

Thanks to Special Agent Wissbaum, I had the former covered. As the taxi turned into the Xanadu lot and I caught my first glimpse of the place, it was the latter that was causing my stomach to flip like the Dixie Chicks' career.

THE place was a throw-back in a city that had reinvented itself. The obligatory street signage, nondescript next to the Aria and the Bellagio, was more apropos to a suburban mall than the ten-story neon behemoths of its neighbors. Positioned well off the strip on what was best described as a flag lot, the hotel itself was both pristine and unremarkable, more like a nineteen-story stucco château. There were no tennis courts, no outdoor pool. Looking at it you could sense antiquity, despite a well-intentioned coat of paint and a landscaped boulevard inspired by the grand casino in Monte Carlo. The valets were dressed like jokers from the decks of cards within, and you could smell six decades' worth of Phillip Morris's best before you hit the door.

The familiar sound of the slots was deafening, as I entered, a bag in each hand. Like they were piping it in over the house sound system. The color pallet was whorehouse red, the walls dripping with tasseled curtains and the just-replaced carpet a blend of crimson and black. As if someone had spilled a million cups of coffee all at once. It took a moment to locate the registration desk, which was occupied by a recent graduate of the John Gotti School of Obvious Criminal Affiliation. A bad Robin Thicke haircut and a slick suit, an expression suited to an IRS auditor with jock itch.

I was in a bad mood, I guess.

It occurred to me then and there that an important detail had been left unspoken. My name. I had no choice but to use my own, given no alternative and the urgent need to get my ass into a shower. The young man consulted his computer, resulting in a troubled expression.

"We were not expecting you until tomorrow, Mr. Schmitt."

"Hey, shit happens." I smiled so this would go down easy.

Without reciprocating the man picked up a telephone and, after turning away, spoke softly so that I couldn't hear. Then he nodded—why do people do that on the phone?—and hung up, simultaneously opening a drawer to withdraw a plastic key card. He punched a three-digit number into a device, through which he swiped the card to program it for my room.

I was in. Let the shitstorm commence.

He waved off my Visa, saying it would not be necessary, and without my having to sign a thing he handed over a little folder containing my plastic key card.

"That's it?"

He pursed his lips and nodded slightly. As if I'd just snatched the last tater tot. "That's it."

I pocketed the key and turned, stooping to retrieve my bag. When I straightened back up there was a man standing before me, eyes squinted, jaw clenched. You could see striations of muscle twitching just below his ears, one of which contained an earpiece attached to a small coiled cord that disappeared around the back of his collar. Both hands were pocketed, one of which he withdrew and extended to me.

He was short and wiry, nearly bald, a very fit sixty, every year an adventure. His suit was as perfectly tailored as the desk jockey's, in startling contrast to a face that had seen everything Las Vegas had to offer. A character actor, someone who proudly owned every tough-guy DVD ever made.

We shook hands. The guy was trying to break every bone in mine.

"I'm Chad Merrill," he said. "Welcome to Xanadu."

21

"Wolf Schmitt," I said, squeezing back with all I had.

"I know who you are," said Chad Merrill, pausing long enough for a little smirk to surface. "And I know why you're here." He released my hand and turned. "You're a day early."

A flick of his head instructed me to follow him.

I didn't like his tone. Or, frankly, his mug. Took me about a tenth of a second to read both. But other than his being an asshole I didn't understand precisely what the smirk was about, what he knew and what he didn't. Clearly, he wanted me to ask myself that question, the first volley in a little man's game of who's on top.

As he turned I said, "So, you my new boss?"

From somewhere behind me, a resonant Lou Rawls voice answered, "Something like that."

The man who stepped forward was startlingly huge, something close to six-nine, with an earpiece identical to

Merrill's. I was looking up at well over three hundred pounds of bald angry black man whose fingertips reached down to my suitcase without the necessity of bending at the waist. An attribute every leg-breaker should cultivate.

I followed them through rows of tables full of overdressed players—even at this late hour, or early hour, depending on your point of view—noticing how the dealers avoided eye contact while the pit bosses proactively didn't. About halfway across the vast space I glanced behind to see how Too Tall and my suitcase were faring, but both were suddenly and inexplicably gone.

Merrill headed toward an unmarked door next to the Cashier cage, using a magnetic key attached to a chain connected to his belt. Or his dick, for all I knew. He held it open, and as I entered a sterile hallway I asked, "Mind if I ask where my suitcase is?"

"We'll bring it up. This way, please."

Down the hall, through another door requiring a key, into the back room of the cashier department—stacks of money and chips rested on tables like freshly laundered dishes—and then into an elevator no bigger than an apartment coat closet. Close enough to smell Chad Merrill's cheap aftershave. Again he used the high-tech key, and without the necessity of pressing a floor button—there were none—we began our ascent.

"Old spice," I said.

"Pardon me?"

"Your aftershave. My dad wore that shit."

He nodded without looking at me. "Don't press your luck, Wolf." He'd added the name with a touch of sarcasm.

"Roger that, Chad." As did Wolf.

Seconds later the elevator door slid open to what seemed to be another world, just one level above the casino floor. The ambiance here was positively Tuscan, as if the elevator had moved a block south and opened into the executive suite at the Bellagio. But as we walked down a dimly lit Travertine hallway, I quickly discerned this wasn't where the suits sipped java and swapped lies. Large windows along the hall opened into vast dark spaces that would make NASA envious, enough electronic gear to start a new television network.

Welcome to hotel security. I now knew where my suitcase had gone. And, who Chad Merrill was in the Xanadu kingdom.

He was the guy with the big ax.

We went into a windowless room quickly recognizable as a medical exam suite: padded table covered in tissue, stirrups—I swear to God—a small counter upon which waited a box of rubber gloves, and an overhead cabinet full of God knows what. Merrill tapped the counter and said, "Put the contents of your pockets here. And your watch."

I just stared at him. After a moment I squinted.

"Please," he added, his smile strained.

Fifty-five cents, a good-luck doubloon supposedly salvaged from a pirate shipwreck, a stray paper clip, my recently issued room key, my specially rigged Droid phone. And my Omega Titanium Seamaster, to which I'd treated myself upon surviving my last assignment on behalf of the federal government. James Bond had one, so what could go wrong.

When I was done Merrill opened the cabinet and withdrew a plastic bag, into which he placed my possessions. The silence was surreal, the explanation as clear as it was unspoken.

I think he really liked the watch, too.

"Take off your clothes," he said, avoiding eye contact.

"I don't think so."

Now he looked at me. "Policy."

"You strip-search personal trainers? You're fucking with me."

"I say what I mean. You would do well to remember that."

He eyes went to my computer bag as he held out his hand.

"You want my iPad?"

"Any reason I shouldn't?"

"Other than the porn, no."

My entire business plan for the nursing home was on that computer. Harmless, unless one considered that I was supposed to be a personal trainer, which might cause questions.

He opened the door, the smile history. Knowing he was leaving would make this a little easier. Until, that is, he paused to offer a final thought.

"It's not a strip search, Wolf. It's a body cavity search." Then he smiled again. "Have a nice day."

Welcome to Las freaking Vegas.

22

Shortly after Chad Merrill's departure from the exam room a young fellow who looked like a busboy came for my clothes, which he explained would be inspected and scanned for microelectronics.

"Do all newbies get this treatment?" I asked.

He ignored me completely and left before I could muster my next question. This was not good.

Ten minutes later the clothes were returned, thankfully not by the busboy, who I prayed would not be my proctologist for the evening. That honor went to a woman I guessed to be in her sixties, who had precious little to say besides, "lean over the table, please," and moments later, the dreaded word, "push." Prior to that I heard the snap of a rubber glove and the squishing of K-Y Jelly being expelled from the tube.

This, too, was not good.

Permit me to omit the details. Let's just say there were no

microelectronics to be found in my lower colon that evening, the fact of which made everyone involved quite happy.

Except, perhaps, Chad Merrill. I had a feeling he'd have liked nothing more than to crawl up my ass and learn the truth.

THE room sucked. Third floor, nice view of the loading dock and a row of dumpsters. The aroma of Lysol and a bedspread that reeked of whatever those CSI folks were always looking for here with those infrared light scanners.

To my great surprise and even greater pleasure, my iPad, the FBI-model Droid phone, and my suitcase had all preceded me, presumably having passed muster. Two points for Sherman Wissbaum.

It took me less than two minutes to unpack.

I had no idea what to do next, how to contact Caroline—pardon me, that would now be Renee—or how to begin my pseudo-employment as Lynn Valentine's personal trainer. Given my arrival a day early, I made a mental note to ask Renee why in Steve Wynn's name I was expected to drive here instead of fly, though I assumed there would be no immediate need for such answers. It was just a few hours before dawn and the Las Vegas night was young, so I decided to venture downstairs and see just how deep into the shit I'd fallen.

Just beneath the deepest layer of it is a place called hell. I had the distinct feeling that's precisely where I was.

I'M still waiting for someone to explain the physics of the game of blackjack. Supposedly the house has a two percent edge, more if the player violates the basic principles of the game, like splitting face cards or doubling on two eights. Why, then, do they seem to take your money nine out of ten hands? Vegas math, baby. As elusive as a pit boss with a personality.

I'd been playing cards at a lively table for about twenty minutes before it hit me: there were no schmucks here at Xanadu, nobody hitting a thirteen with the dealer showing a six, nobody hitting sixteens and then swearing at the celestial inequity of it all. Do that here at Xanadu, you get enough attitude to melt the ice in your White Russian. Do it twice and some guy with a grip like a python on steroids will suggest you try another table, maybe one at the casino next door. Or Laughlin. This was serious blackjack, played by serious gamers with no time for conventioneers or anyone who had ever bought a bus pass.

I was about two bills down when the dealer, a guy with one of those moustaches rolled in salad dressing and bent into a Snidely Whiplash twirl, leaned over to me and said, "Pretty lady in the bar wants to buy you a drink."

No one had approached our table or spoken to the dealer since I'd arrived, other than cheesy table talk. Unless the guy had a surgically implanted earphone, he'd been biding his time before conveying the message. The former was entirely possible, I supposed, since his facial hair could pick up an NBA broadcast from another time zone.

"If I'd have been killing you," I said, tossing in another loser, "would you have told me earlier? Before I went cold?"

He continued to deal the cards as he answered. These guys were robots, very comfortable on autopilot.

"Absolutely," he said. "I'm all about the customer. Fact is, this is the last time you'll get to play here, so I thought I'd let you enjoy yourself."

"Yeah, that was a real kick in the pants."

"At least until Mrs. Valentine fires you."

My quizzical expression, framed with a head cocked at an angle, begged for an explanation.

"Employees aren't allowed at the tables here at Xanadu," he said with a very official tone.

I looked down at my cards, wondering how he knew I was on the payroll. Or why he was smirking like Chad Merrill.

Twin queens. I laid them down, sliding them under my bet,

mustering a smirk of my own. The dealer was showing a seven, and after finishing the table, flipped over a nine. Sweet. And then, very slowly, with his eyes locked directly on me instead of the cards, he finished us off with a five.

One of the other players muttered the word "asshole" as he threw his cards in, the accuracy of which seemed to amuse our dealer.

I pushed my chair back in preparation to leave. "Suppose you want a tip, too," I said.

He leaned forward and said, "Here's one for you . . . don't unpack." He waited for this to sink in, then added, "bar's over there."

I turned to where his eyes had pointed with a quick nod. The bar was thirty yards away, elevated a few steps to afford a view of the debauchery, with arched columns and elaborate drapery. Sitting at a table near the cement balustrade railing, sipping a drink as she observed the casino floor, me in particular, was my recently departed soon-to-be girlfriend and current covert employer, the lovely and fraudulent Caroline, for a brief time known as Renee, now probably known in this zip code as someone else entirely.

Which fit. After several weeks of dating, which included my pouring out my heart in various and sundry ways, I had absolutely no idea who she was.

For starters, she was now a flaming blonde.

23

"Love the hair," I said as I sat down, noticing how contrived her handshake seemed. "And the glasses. Very Sarah Palin." Actually, she looked more like a supermodel in a movie trying to dress down for her day job, just to blend in.

Glasses on a smokin' hot woman: priceless.

"Cut the schtick," she replied through a plastic smile. "You're on the clock. And guess what, I'm your boss."

"That mean I get my two hundred dollars back, Renee?"

"My name is Nicole. Welcome to Xanadu."

"Still? That's cool. You look more . . . *Britney* now."

She demurely held up her hand for me to stop. The debriefing was underway.

"I'm Lynn Valentine's assistant and close personal friend. More important, I'm the reason you're here."

"A friend of a friend thing," I offered.

"Let's just say you've been very carefully screened. Lynn has my word on that."

"Lucky Lynn. I have questions. A few dozen, for starters. Can we talk?"

"Not here."

"So why'd you call me over? I was about to get hot."

"To tell you to be in the gym at seven in the morning to begin your employment. In some cute little shorts. And a tank top, I think. I'll send one up with our logo. She'll like that."

"I thought you casino types were barely in bed at seven in the morning."

"Mrs. Valentine requires only four hours of sleep a night."

"Lucky Lynn again. What else does my client require?"

"Discretion. And your respect. Who knows what else."

"She'll have to earn the last two."

"Not true. She's paying handsomely for whatever she wants from you."

I shifted in my chair, wanting to protest but holding back. None of the cocktail waitresses were coming anywhere near us, which I had a feeling was not coincidence. Carolyn-Renee-Nicole touched her drink to her lips, a trace of amusement in evidence.

"You said I'd get a dossier before I got here."

"Already in your room. I suggest you memorize it."

"You also said that Mrs. Valentine hired me because I'm a specialist, I assume in something other than pilates."

"I did say that."

"So I'm thinking it might be a good idea on my part to know what the hell that means. You know, like, beforehand."

"I suggest you ask her."

"But if you recruited me, then you'd know."

"Better if she tells you."

"Wonderful. I'll slip in the question between the bocci ball and the elliptical machine."

She giggled, a ghost of our past, back when she thought I was cute. Back when I thought she was Carolyn.

"But you see, you'd know, too. It might never be acknowledged. Just assumed."

"I usually like to confirm things like that. Women are something men should never take for granted."

She nodded at me approvingly. Then she picked up her purse from the floor and rose to her feet before I could respond.

This meeting was over.

"Let just say that, in a world full of personal trainers, your employer is looking for someone who takes their time with their work. Who wants their client to really *feel the burn*. Emphasis on *feel* and *burn*. Someone who favors intensity over brevity, who knows how to make the experience last. Clear enough for you, Wolf?"

Our eyes locked, mine wide with surprise, hers much too smug. I casually ran my hand over the outside of my sportcoat at the lapel, feeling the presence of the magic Droid phone in my vest pocket. Unless Chad Merrill had somehow disabled the thing, Sherman Wissbaum was squirming as much as I was.

Nicole tossed her business card on the table and departed, the pace and swagger of her walk exposing the fact that she was fully aware of every eye in the place on her exquisite executive posterior.

That much, at least, hadn't changed.

TWO things in my room *had* changed, though. The massive air conditioning units just outside my window had kicked in with a vengeance, sounding like an F-18 in a wind tunnel. This was the room to which folks with a one-night-free coupon were sent upon check-in, with a killer view of the HVAC. More important, my bed had been turned down by housekeeping—only in Las Vegas could this happen at five in the morning—exposing the corner of a manila envelope containing my dossier and, in case anyone asked, some very normal lists of employee rules and hotel features.

As they say on the book jackets, I read it all in one sitting.

Turns out Nicole was one thorough little undercover rogue agent. Smart, too. My cover was virtually bulletproof, and there was precious little for me to lie about. Even my real name, in the certain event that someone would look, had an airtight backstory.

The approach was simple. By design, Lynn Valentine knew next to nothing about me, only what "Nicole" had told her. Steps had been taken to lead any prying eyes—Chad Merrill came to mind—toward the intended conclusion: I was a freelance personal trainer with a penchant for attractive women clients with money. A résumé now on file in the hotel's HR office would corroborate this. If someone chose to make a call to the lone reference shown there, a manager at a small but prestigious Portland health club catering to attractive women clients with money, he would happily say I was the best darn trainer they'd ever had. What the résumé didn't say, of course, was that, in return for this endorsement, his recent conviction for dealing steroids to high-school jocks would be expunged from his record. The rest of my résumé was accurate, the story being that my personal trainer activities were a sideline cultivated over the years of masquerading as an advertising guy.

That much was easy. Nobody outside of Lynn Valentine's staff would be paying much attention to the latest pretty boy in her eternal procession of personal assistants. Hell, I wasn't even a real employee, just a temporary contractor. Based on history, as soon as Lynn Valentine grew hungry for fresh meat, I'd be gone. The band of rogue agents who had placed me here were counting on it.

Another issue altogether, however, was my alter ego as a professional hitter with a knack for lingering death. Nicole was counting on the very stealth nature of my covert identity to explain why so little information about me was available. By definition I was invisible to the mob, one of the criteria for my being hired. They, too, might want to know who I was. And thanks to the cooperation of the Department of Defense—the FBI had pissed all the other government departments off— anyone with the means to inquire would find that once upon a time I had been a highly trained covert operative whose activities were still highly confidential. If they told you they'd have to kill you. I liked that about the new me.

My name would, however, conveniently come up in connection with a recent multiple murder investigation in California, all of it quite legit. Of course, there was no way anyone coming across that information could know I had been operating at the behest of a combined FBI-IRS coalition. Nicole had also summarized four actual unsolved deaths involving shady characters any self-respecting hood would know had been the object of contract killings, even though three of them had been attributed to accidental or natural causes. The fourth victim had simply disappeared. For my short-term purposes here, I needed only to know enough to recognize a cagey attempt to steer a conversation in that direction, and to deflect it with enough style and innuendo to foster a shadow of suspicion.

How that might happen was entirely up to me.

I read it all several times, until the morning traffic reports were starting to appear on the tube.

The final words on the document were handwritten: "Flush this."

I was only too happy to oblige.

I spent the day sleeping, long past noon. Then I put on my walking shoes and took off, figuring that the less time I spent hanging around Xanadu with no purpose—I was, after all, a day early—the better. Two movies, a long walk through two malls, and dinner at a killer buffet at the Hard Rock Hotel & Casino, and it was time to return, hopeful that the other shoe hadn't fallen in my absence.

It hadn't. The room still smelled like hell.

24

I've always loved the smell of spandex in the morning.

The fitness center at the Xanadu Hotel and Casino was as still as a disco at seven in the morning. Most gyms across the globe are bustling with pre-workday exercisers at this hour, but I quickly realized the patrons of this establishment were upstairs puking, or perhaps still trying to find their way back to their room.

The fifteenth-floor gym was surprisingly cutting edge. Someone had turned an interior designer loose on the place, resulting in mauve walls and a deep blue carpet, a scheme not unlike the casino itself. Enya sang—or whatever she does—through ceiling speakers, evoking a strange yearning to do some yoga. A circuit of monolithic weight machines framed the fabricated skyline of New York, New York, through floor-to-ceiling windows. It all looked strangely contrived in morning sunlight, something few Xanadu guests had ever beheld, at least while sober. Along another wall were racks of dumbbells and articulated barbells, all gleaming chrome, these with a view of the MGM Grand and, beyond, the airport. The other half of the room housed various aerobic torture machines, recumbent bikes and treadmills and the latest in elliptical trainers. Everything was spanking new.

I was happy and slightly surprised to see that there were no ashtrays in sight.

Precisely one person was here this morning, pedaling away while reading the *Las Vegas Times Sun*. She didn't look up as I approached, but I didn't buy it. She saw me. She was Lynn Valentine, in the black-spandex-clad flesh.

My first thought was of Olivia Newton-John in a three-decades-old music video they still play on the *Where Are They Now?* shows.

"Mrs. Valentine, I presume?"

Not exactly Mamet, I grant you, but it was all I had. I had never been an assassin before and I was nervous as hell.

"It's after seven." She didn't look up from her paper, sort of a Meryl Streep in *The Devil Wears Prada* thing.

A glance at my Omega told me my tardiness was greatly exaggerated. In fact, I had lingered at the door for two minutes just to make sure I walked in at precisely the appointed hour.

"Mine says seven," I said, hoping she'd look up at the wall clock to see that I was correct. She didn't. "So does yours."

When she did look up her eyes were compelling. "In this building my diamond watch trumps your cheap-ass watch."

Cheap-ass? It was worth six grand. Probably what her band would run you at Tiffany's.

I smiled, hoping it would piss her off. She'd been reading the sports section, which I found sort of interesting in a *go figure* sort of way.

"Then I guess you are Mrs. Valentine. Wolf Schmitt."

I extended my hand. A ghost of a grin teased at the corners of her mouth as she took it, her grip firm. Ridiculously so. She did a quick and perhaps involuntarily visual up-and-down as we shook much too vigorously.

"You come highly recommended," she said.

"I love what I do."

"One would have to, I think."

Awkward moment. There was enough hidden agenda and contextual innuendo in the room, not to mention crackling sexual tension, to script an episode of *General Hospital*. Neither of us knew what our next line would be.

Hers, when it came to her, was a whopper.

"You have a great ass," she said, staring straight into my eye. "I like that in a trainer."

With a completely straight face I said, "I like that in a client, too, to be honest."

Her expression told me that folks didn't lip off to her all that often. Another awkward moment came and went, during which I nodded and pursed my lips as if I'd just been asked if I'd like the steak or the chicken.

"Is this my little test?" I asked.

"Pardon me?"

"I was told you'd test me. How am I doin'?"

Now she also pursed her lips and indulged in another up-and-down, this one not so quick.

"I just hope your balls are as big as your mouth."

If her ensuing smile wasn't full of mischievous glee, the conspiratorial kind intended to let me know this was more a recreational joust than a bona fide power struggle, I would have hit the door. Some abuse you just can't stomach, even for a million dollars. Such attacks, I would learn, were sort of a hobby for her. She liked to stick things into people, see how they reacted.

For the record so did I, but in an altogether different context.

25

"Let's begin with the rules," I said.

Her eyebrows formed a geometrically perfect arch that rivaled anything to be found in St. Louis. Lynn Valentine was pretty enough, but it was a victory of style over substance. Like some of the girls you see working at the Nordstrom cosmetics counter. It's all wrapping paper.

"This is your gym," I went on, "but it's my workout. Forget everything you've read or been told about physical conditioning. Half of it is bullshit and the half that isn't is too intense for the average person to handle. I've been assured you are anything but average, so we're good to go on that count. You do what I say, how I say it, the way I say it, and you'll get everything you seek to achieve as fast as the physics of the human body will allow. There are no off days, there are no excuses. I take this seriously, and I expect the same from you. If that's not the case, tell me now and I'll find you someone who'll kiss your ass precisely the way you like it kissed."

All time and motion froze for a moment. It occurred to me that this little charade was laughable, given that there was no one else in the room. Both of us knew my presence had nothing whatsoever to do with sit-ups. I tried not to glance up at the tiny security camera affixed to the ceiling in the corner, for which my soliloquy had been staged. I hoped Chad Merrill was enjoying his popcorn down in the security suite.

I also hoped—along with wondering why things pop into our heads when they do—that my mother was resting peacefully today, a notion that made this little *Twilight Zone* moment easier to accept.

Somewhere out there Sherman Wissbaum was on the receiving end of the magic Droid resting on the floor nearby, hopefully impressed with my improv.

"When you hear my goals," she said, gracefully dismounting from the Lifecycle, "you'll realize just how serious I am. Deadly serious, in fact."

She didn't smile as she put her hand on my stomach. I could feel the warmth of it through my Lycra sleeveless shirt by Under Armour. I had taken Nicole's advice, gone for the beefcake.

"I want abs like these," she said, her palm now moving in tiny circles over the area of my navel. Her other hand went to my arm, a fingernail tracing the little groove between my lower deltoid and upper biceps, an artful etching borne from two decades of dumbbell curls.

"And cuts . . . like these," she said, her voice lower now.

Back home this was known as foreplay.

"So," I interrupted, my voice betrayed a sudden nervousness, "you want to lose a few pounds."

"About two hundred pounds, actually."

She pulled her hand away. And then, to my horror, touched it to my cheek, her eyes fixed on mine, playing me. Her palm was moist, she'd been here awhile.

"Mostly," she said softly, "I'm after the burn."

Clearly this was a woman who liked to fuck with people's heads.

My expression told her I got it. For a moment there you could have driven a Hyundai down my throat.

This little dance was like sign language. Everything we said was a metaphor for something else. Two something elses, in this case. One of which weighed a hundred eighty-five pounds.

The next few seconds passed quietly. The fact that we were speaking in tongues told me she was sensitive to the probability that someone was listening in. Contradicted by the fact that she seemed to relish pushing the boundaries of double entendre.

"We should talk," I finally said. "There isn't a trainer in the business that doesn't need to understand his client's goals beforehand. Especially in this case."

"I think you know what I want."

Heat assaulted my cheeks. She grabbed a towel and began wiping the sweat from her throat. A ballet dancer's neck, all grace and tendons.

"It's about the pain," she said, not looking at me.

"Come again?"

She looked up. "The pain. I'm talking about the process, Wolf. That's what I want. I want pain."

I was speechless. Which made her smile.

"My workouts, Wolf. No pain, no gain? That's what I want."

If this was another test, I wasn't rolling over.

"Try to keep up," she added. I'd known her all of one minute and she wasn't the slightest bit hesitant to unleash her inner bitch.

I paused for effect. "It's about technique, in context to goals. That's what I do. I'm a technique guy. Especially when it comes to pain."

She leaned close, her lips brushing against my ear, her words more breathe and tone. Soft enough to escape the digital ears that surrounded us.

"I want you to kill my husband. I trust you have a technique for that, too."

I paused long enough to blink emphatically. And to ask myself if the Droid had the digital ears to pick that one up.

"You do cut right to it."

"I do."

Time and space froze again, or maybe it was just my heart seizing for a moment. She had the look of a woman who'd just won the whole enchilada in divorce court from a cheating millionaire. A woman who didn't have time for much foreplay.

"We need to talk," I said, my tone inflexible.

She nodded approvingly. "Meet me in the spa." She motioned toward the elaborate entry to the day spa area, a stone archway worthy of a cathedral. "It's quite loud in there. And hot."

She started in that direction. I was dying to tell her those lumpy leg warmers went out of fashion two decades ago, along with Jennifer Beals' career until *The L Word* came out on cable. But instead I said, "I didn't bring a suit."

I heard her mumble the word "perfect" as she disappeared through the door.

Wonderful. I would begin my work with Lynn Valentine in my jockey shorts, with my trusty Droid phone on the sidelines, neutered by the ambient sound of water jets.

This, Sherman Wissbaum would most certainly assure me if he were here, was why I got the big bucks.

26

This wasn't a spa, it was a Hugh Hefner wet dream. Literally. What some might call a hot tub—this would be like calling the Eiffel Tower a pole—was more like a small swimming pool fed by six fountains, three on either side, each separated by marble steps that allowed access to the scalding water from any angle. The water ejaculated from the gaping mouths of lions carved into three-by-three travertine monoliths, each lined with hand-carved designs that, upon closer examination, appeared to be snakes. Six massive Grecian columns rose symmetrically from each pedestal to a domed ceiling depicting what appeared to be cherubs playing soccer on a field of impossibly fluffy clouds. At one end of the pool was an elevated platform, upon which was a creamy marble statue depicting a man with Arnold's pre-governator body making love to a blindfolded woman with Pamela Anderson's breasts. More fantasy for Hefner. There was no mistaking their posture as simply an impassioned father-daughter embrace after a nice family shower, given the proximity of Arnold's hands and protrusion of Pamela's tongue toward her partner's nipples.

This was Michelangelo after too many beers.

Vapor rose from the bubbling water like evil smoke. The air smelled of Eucalyptus with a hint of chlorine, causing the eyes to mist slightly and the mind to wander.

And it was, as Lynn Valentine had promised, appropriately loud in here.

I sat on the edge of one of the six fountain pedestals, already sweating beneath the gym clothes I hoped wouldn't have to come off. The locker room, also over-the-top in a Grecian porno sort of way, had been empty, which I had concluded was no coincidence. Lynn Valentine could shut down her gym any time she chose. Today would be a great day for that.

Enough time passed to inspire the notion that I had been played. Enough time to allow all manner of second thoughts and doubts to creep in, colliding with the mental image of my online bank account and all those zeros, both the missing and the forthcoming. I regretted skipping breakfast, not having anticipated the effect of all this drama on my personal plumbing.

I was about to get up and conduct a search of the premises when I noticed a flash of peripheral motion coming from the pool. From the waterfall, actually, which emerged from beneath Arnold and Pamela's marble feet. Something was there, a silhouette in shadow, and it was alive.

As I squinted through the blue vapor a graceful hand protruded from the midst of the cascading water. The nails were perfectly French manicured and familiar, and there was a certain sarcasm attached to the way the forefinger beckoned me. Odd as it seemed at the time, and as odd as it sounds here, Lynn Valentine had been waiting behind the waterfall since I got here.

I had no real options.

"Sorry, Sherman," I said quietly as I set the bugged Droid phone down on the marble surface upon which I was sitting. Leaving my gym shorts on—no jockey shorts for Lynn Valentine's pleasure today—I ditched the tank top, slipped into the velvety warm water, and waded toward the waterfall. I hesitated a few inches from the smooth wall of liquid, which had an almost frozen look to it, without the slightest blemish in its vertical surface despite the fact that it was tumbling down. As if it, too, had been carved from marble.

The hand appeared again, grabbing my forearm and pulling me into another world.

*   *   *

I opened my eyes to discover that I was in what was best described as a hot tub within the larger landscape of the spa, curtained off from the larger expanse of the pool by the cascading wall of water. We were directly beneath the happy statue, with our own ceiling depicting a fresco of the same two marble models doing the nasty on the same fluffy clouds that the cherubs had used for recess. To the side of the tub was a sitting space employing a marble ottoman, upon which one could presumably engage in one's own version of that dance.

Lynn was reclining at the back of the tub, her arms wide on either side, a smile on her face as she watched me take it all in. Wet hair made her look younger, almost mortal. More beautiful than she had out in the gym with her John McEnroe headband. She spoke with a startlingly loud voice, which I realized was required to be heard over the ambient roar of the water and the frenzy of bubbles. I wondered if Sherman might pick up traces of what was about to unfold.

"Welcome to my world," she said.

I glanced up, just to make sure my eyes weren't deceiving me. One of the cherubs was on her little hands and knees—enough said.

She pulled me closer, just as she had to yank me into this space. Our shoulders touched, which meant far less audio was required to continue our conversation. Even with the heated water I could feel the warmth of her body on my skin.

"You like," she asked, her face hopeful.

"Oh yeah."

"Some of the most powerful men in the world have been right here, with some of the most beautiful women in the world. I find that exciting, don't you?"

"Depends on how often you change the water."

"No one can see us, no one can hear us."

I pictured the Droid on the edge of the pool, Sherman Wissbaum listening to the sound of water smacking water.

"We need to talk about *that*, too," I said. "I don't sleep with my clients. Even when they are as beautiful as you, which they never are. Mostly they look like Dick Cheney."

"We'll see. And thank you for the bullshit. For now, you need to know that we've got forty million dollars of digital surveillance technology in this building, and this is the only place out of its reach."

"Unless the walls start talking."

"They know better. They work for me, too."

Conversation, I'd always believed, was like poker. The good players look for things, certain *tells* that reveal the machinations of the opponent's mind. Lynn Valentine, with her subtle reminders that she was powerful and dangerous, had just revealed that she was insecure, which is the second cousin to vulnerability. A crack in the otherwise chilly porcelain veneer.

Good to know.

"You wanted to talk," she said, turning toward me, putting her arm over my shoulder. More double-entendre, defensible because of the proximity required for complete privacy. "Here we are."

Our lips were inches apart, our eyes locked. Frankly, it was the best damn job interview I'd ever had.

"Tell me what else I need to know," I said.

27

The most frightening thing about Lynn Valentine's story was the way she told it. There was blackmail and extortion, a cheating bastard of a husband, the very real possibility of the fall of her empire, the prospect of a criminal investigation, and, at the center of it all, a dead daughter, all belonging to her. Enough to bring any woman, from Judge Judy to Oprah, to her knees. And yet her eyes remained as cold as a CPA on tax day, her voice even and well-rehearsed. She displayed all the emotion of someone reading an evisceration textbook to a group of first-year taxidermy students.

I remained speechless, and expressionless, until she had finished. Any questions I might have had were keenly anticipated and addressed. During the entire time our sweaty faces remained just inches apart, close enough to sense the warmth of her breath, with only the slightest variance from the most solemn of eye contact. We were like lovers, intimate but without passion. In other words, like a married couple, behind whose eyes were thoughts of someone else.

I almost felt sorry for her. Until she got to the punch line, the one where she wanted her husband to die in slow and horrible agony, the more unthinkable the better.

How that might happen, it turned out, was completely up to me.

LYNN and Phillip Valentine had the closest thing to an arranged marriage since Jane Austen began writing Merchant Ivory films. Lynn's family had founded Xanadu, Phillip's had run it and made it as successful as it was notorious. Some dark arrangement between the two fathers—something about secrets best kept buried—had brought their children together in rather unholy matrimony (the ceremony was held in a tent in the hotel parking lot) and with the assistance of a little sexual chemistry lubricated with a combined fortune in excess of half a billion dollars, things went swimmingly. At least at first.

Bottom line was—and I was reading between Lynn's very carefully selected words to come to this uncomfortable conclusion—that both of their respective inheritances depended on them staying married. Lawyers with pre-paid retainers would ensure the integrity of the marriage contract long after the two old geezers had gone to their respective makers—one was a fallen Baptist, the other a dedicated heathen—which they had.

My guess was that Phillip's father had the goods on Lynn's father—buried bodies, paper trails, political payoffs—applying leverage that would ensure his son's good fortune long into perpetuity, a word which the man had no doubt never once used in his life.

None of which really mattered, at least where I was concerned, other than serving as context. Phillip and Lynn got married, they had children, they grew to despise each other, they devised a way to coexist—based on what I knew about marriage, it all sounded normal to me—and they began leading separate lives.

And then the lights went out. The man with his hand on the switch was some guy named Lou Mancuso.

IT was at this point that some obscure trace of humanity surfaced in the stoic façade that was Lynn Valentine. As she explained Lou Mancuso's attempt to insert himself into Xanadu's affairs, it emerged from somewhere beneath a deeply buried agony and a much more nimble rage, manifesting as a glaze over her eyes and a barely perceptible wavering of her voice.

"We can do this later, if you'd like."

She closed her eyes, shaking her head just once.

"He took my daughters," she said, as if to short-circuit any further attempt at compassion. "When Phillip continued to resist . . ."—she had to draw a long, slow breath here—". . . he killed Kerry. As a negotiating ploy. Sent us pictures of her head wrapped in a plastic bag. Said if we didn't cut a deal to front the operation for him, he'd kill Caitlin, too."

I had a brain full of questions and the good sense not to ask any. Besides, the answers were all intuitive. The Valentines couldn't involve the authorities without jeopardizing the safety of their daughters, a dilemma that only got worse when Kerry Valentine was killed. Mancuso was no doubt beyond the reach of anything Phillip and Lynn could send at him, insulated by layer upon layer of corporate shells and lieutenants who would die before anyone got close to the boss. In this world the players took care of such business on their own, and from Mancuso's point of view that's all it ever was: business.

The ghost of her pain vanished almost as quickly as it had shown itself. What remained was nothing short of chilling in the steely intensity of its resolve. She refused to look at me, as if the slightest personal connection might impinge on the darkness she was summoning between us.

"That was three years ago. Business has never been better. Not a day goes by when I don't think about how to make him pay for what he did."

"Him?"

She paused, her eyes cold. "My husband."

I whistled involuntarily at the sheer Mephistophelian architecture of it all.

"You still have a lot to lose," I said.

"I don't care about the business. I care about . . . revenge."

"Some might call it justice."

"Semantics."

I shrugged. Inside I was squirming from the proximity to evil. On the outside, I was just wet.

"You want to savor it, be my guest. It's all semantics, anyhow. For me, either one makes a messy job easier."

She grinned darkly at me. "So you don't kill just anyone. How noble of you."

"Oh, I do. But I prefer making things right. Especially for people who can pay. But that's just me."

She took the liberty of running her fingertip over my lower lip. "I was hoping you rather enjoyed your work."

I pulled away.

"Sometimes I do, sometimes I don't."

"But you won't sleep with your clients."

"Nothing personal."

Her eyes scanned my bare chest. "Neither are my hormones."

I nodded a touché, then allowed a few moments to pass. I was scanning for options, hoping to find a bone I could throw to my federal friends. Having sex with the man who would kill her husband would be a sweet exclamation point for her.

"This Mancuso guy, he still a threat?"

"No. With Phillip gone, Mancuso will get it all. Caitlin will be safe, we'll have money. And I'll be . . . done."

She paused to dunk her head. When she emerged, I sensed the candy store had closed.

"That's all you need to know. I've said too much."

I felt another meaningful moment was in order. A chance for me to do a little Machiavellian positioning of my own. I needed to cultivate an attraction, a basis for further intimacy.

"I do what I do for the money."

"Of course you do, Wolf. One million dollars, to the account of your choice. Another when it's done. Work that out with Nicole, I don't want to know."

Two million dollars. I tried not to flinch. Or smile.

"There's more to discuss. I need his habits, vulnerabilities, quirks. I need a timetable, some parameters."

"We meet in the gym every morning at seven."

"With cameras and covert microphones."

Suddenly, in defiance of my previous guidelines, she spun and put her arms around my neck. Before I could move she had her mouth over mine, pinning me against the edge of the tub as she slid over me. Where, I had a feeling, she liked it best.

"Then we'll have to find somewhere we can talk, won't we."

The kiss was much more subtle than the approach. Nothing urgent, despite the pose. More playful than meaningful.

"And where would that be?" I asked, truly curious.

"The only place in the building besides right here that I can be certain Chad Merrill isn't listening."

Her tongue continued to work after the words ceased.

"That would be my bed," she finished.

What the hell. With a move I wished had been captured on tape, I reversed our position so that I was now the dominant player. From her complete and total lack of resistance, I think she liked this, too.

"A dirty job," I said through the kiss, which was picking up momentum.

"When it's done right," she whispered back.

28

Men can rationalize anything. Sometimes it makes as much sense as our belief that golf is exercise and light beer is healthier, but we try. My thinking in the spa with Lynn Valentine was that if I didn't throw her a bone—admittedly not the best analogy in this case—or at least send a message that I was as interested in her as her money, she'd go all business on me and clam up. I was here for no other reason than to get the woman to talk, and I could think of no better way to do it than by sticking my tongue into her mouth first.

But that's as far as it went. I reclaimed my enigmatic status by departing the spa with a sob story about professional ethics and a promise to shag her to the point of delirium when I had earned my pay.

On the way out of the gym I noticed an older gentleman standing outside the door to the women's dressing room. He didn't look away when our eyes met in the hallway, something men just don't do unless they are posturing, which this rail-thin seventy-something fellow had no business doing. As I passed directly in front of him he raised his hand to his forehead in a sarcastic military salute, a gesture I perceived to be just shy of a middle finger.

It was then I noticed what I had to presume he wanted me to see: his thumb was missing, cleanly severed at the palm.

NOT knowing precisely how well the hallways and elevators were monitored—along the lines of the Pentagon, I presumed—I waited until I got back to my room to narrate a detailed report to Sherman about my morning. Not that people wandering the halls of Xanadu talking to themselves was all that odd an occurrence.

I stood by the window, looking out at the air-conditioning units, holding the Droid in my hand as if I was dictating a business letter. I needed to explain how it had been circumvented right out of the blocks, something that might happen again soon. And he needed to know about the Lou Mancuso connection, a name I was confident would ring a bell, and the fact that Lynn could link him to the murder of her daughter once they had her under their Federal thumb for conspiracy to murder her husband.

I tried to keep any trace of smugness out of my voice. But it was a challenge. Day One, and I was already on the scoreboard. All I had to do now was get it on tape.

THREE hours later I was back in the Xanadu gym. Not out of duty or some hope that I might run into Lynn Valentine. Fact was, I was bored silly. After dictating my report I decided to walk the strip. The day before I had discovered that Las Vegas during the day is a different experience than Las Vegas at night. Sin City turns into Fat City in the presence of sunlight. Mobs of tourists from Wisconsin wander the streets in curious shorts and funny hats, many clutching a cardboard cup full of nickels in one hand and a tourist map in the other. The Bellagio's water show—you saw it in *Ocean's Eleven*—lacks luster without the spotlights, and Treasure Island's lost ship—many fewer people saw that in *Miss Congeniality 2*—just sits there like a reject from Six Flags. No panhandlers, no hookers, not even all that many drunks to laugh at. Even the buffets are boring.

So, with my trusty Droid in my hand, I headed for a workout and another soothing hot tub, hopefully alone this time.

I wasn't by myself for long.

Two men were in the gym. One short and white, one very tall and black. They were doing free weights, and initially merited very little of my attention other than a fleeting curiosity regarding their Mutt and Jeff nature. I had settled onto a Lifecycle recumbent peddling machine with the latest Phil Margolin legal thriller, when I felt a tap on my shoulder. I turned to see the shorter of the two men standing next to me.

"Get a spot from you?"

My brain processed several transactions at once. It was odd that he would ask me to spot him on what I assumed would be a bench press, since he'd been working out with a buddy who could bench a small backhoe. My peripheral vision informed me that said partner had left the gym, at least for the moment, which also seemed odd. The other thing that struck me was this guy's hair. Perfect, in a 1970s Donald Trump sort of way. The color of street tar and thick as a horse's mane, greased back into Danny Zuko perfection, right down to the wayward strand that descended to just above one eyebrow. I hadn't set eyes on a real mullet since Randy Johnson cut his hair short, but I was staring at one now. The entire locked-down sculpture of it reflected the ceiling lights. I could almost smell the Paul Mitchell. I was looking at Rocky Balboa, ready for the weigh-in. He was stocky and moderately well built—too many carbs, this guy—with a tight wifebeater T-shirt more apropos to an audition for *West Side Story*. Finishing the ensemble was a quarter-inch braided gold chain attached to a crucifix bearing a realistic image of the

body of Christ, the size of a house key. That and the fact that
the shirt was tucked into snug nylon shorts, not to mention gym
socks stretched to the knees, told me all I needed to know about
this guy.

We all create the dark niche into which we crawl.

I had to bite my tongue to keep from grinning. But other
than looking like a *Saturday Night Live* skit he was sort of
handsome in a Joe-Pesci–on-steroids sort of way.

Gym etiquette had been breached. You just don't interrupt
someone's aerobics for a spot. For that matter you didn't darken
the doorway of a gym looking like a refugee from a Richard
Simmons video, either.

And that's when it hit me. When the gears clicked and the
memory of a photograph lying on my Portland coffee table
emerged from the fog of my present dilemma. I'd noticed the
mullet then, too.

My stomach did a full gainer that was almost audible.

This was Phillip Valentine. In the *Obsession for Men*–
scented flesh.

29

I followed him to the free-weight area, where a bench loaded with 315 pounds awaited. Three big plates on each side, enough to make the bar bend under the strain. This was not exactly Olympian if you were in a college gym full of sweaty off-season linemen, but in here it was positively Herculean.

I positioned myself behind the apparatus while Phillip Valentine smoothed a towel over the bench before assuming the prone position, his feet barely touching the floor.

"Lift off?" I asked, an obligatory query from spotters. Gym protocol dictated that this was all the conversation that was allowed at such moments, especially among strangers. No introductions, no *nice day for benching, don't you think?*

He declined with a quick shake of the head, adjusting his grip on the bar.

No liftoff for this guy. Then he whipped out ten smooth reps. I'd never seen *anyone* do a full, clean ten at that weight. In my experience a scarce few guys in any given gym could do *one*. A very few others could squeeze out three. NFL tackles, maybe five. On caffeine and steroids. This was freak-show stuff.

His form was perfect. Each rep lightly kissed the mounds of his pectorals, all without taking a breath or betraying even the slightest grimace.

I hated this guy.

By the time he'd reached five reps it dawned on me that he hadn't required a spotter at all. This was about something else. This was about me.

"Now you," he said, sitting upright as he used the towel to wipe down the bench and then his neck, both of which were perfectly dry. He wasn't smiling, either.

"Not my chest day," I said.

"Sure it is."

He didn't shift his eyes from mine, even though I sensed someone approach from behind. I turned to see his workout partner, who towered over my six foot three by a head. He wore dark-blue sweats and had a perfectly shaved head. He wore a Bluetooth headset—hadn't seen *that* in a gym lately—in case his parole officer called. He wasn't smiling, either, nor had he since he got cut by the Packers.

I just stared. The game, whatever it was, was on.

Valentine began pulling plates off the bar, as did his monolithic friend. They left one plate on each side: 135 pounds, the standard warm-up for lifters with any experience.

"Show us what you got, trainer boy."

It was a true Quentin Tarantino moment, sans guns. Everyone froze, eyes on eyes. There were no options. I searched for something witty to say, but the chamber was empty.

"Two plates," I said. "I'll go higher from there." First point to me.

The two men exchanged a glance, then snatched another plate from the nearby rack and slid them onto the bar, securing the plastic collar when they were done.

A little challenge between assholes. I positioned myself

under the bar and found my grip.

"Lift?" he asked with an infuriating smile.

Without answering I pushed the bar up off its seat, held it for a moment at lockout, then slowly lowered it to my chest. Upon contact I bounced it up and down a few inches, a standard though admittedly unwise move used by some lifters to warm up the pecs before getting started. Also a good way to tear a cold tendon. A little testosterone splashed right back at him.

As I began to press the bar upward, I felt the weight of the world crashing down on me. Literally. Both men were jamming another plate onto the ends of the bar. Suddenly there was 315 pounds of cold steel resting on my ribs.

And then, to my horror, they kept going. Two more plates, for a total of four on each side. That would be 405 pounds. I was pinned, barely able to breathe were it not for the full force of my arms trying to push some of the weight upwards. What relief that gave would only last a few seconds at best, until my shoulder tendons snapped.

Phillip Valentine came into my inverted view, standing behind me where a spotter should be, though the only one touching the bar was me. Jesus dangled from a chain above my eyes, but he had his own problems.

"A little download, you and me," he said. I was surprised at his voice, which I'd expected to have a certain obligatory Jersey lilt to it. It was understated, the cadence deliberate, a smooth and confident baritone.

"This is *my* house. You work here, you work for me."

I wanted to tell him that if this was his new employee orientation program, it sucked. But all I could do was grunt.

I think he grinned. Hard to tell through watering eyes.

"Allow me to clarify. You work for my wife, you work for me."

I nodded, hoping it wouldn't pop a vein.

"And . . . if you work *on* my wife, you take your chances. How's that for clarity?"

So much for clandestine water sports.

"You piss me off, maybe you lose a body part."

For a moment I forgot about the weight on my chest, the image replaced by a snapshot of the old man with an attitude and a missing thumb. Suddenly the bar was even heavier.

I wheezed, "Nine-one-one," which made him grin.

"I had you checked out." Then the smile vanished. "And you know what? It reads like the crap Lynn reads by the pool."

Sherlock and I would be having a little download of our own, should I live to tell the tale.

"One thing I know. Lynn doesn't hire douche bags. Only the best for my little facility manager. She had that fat cook—what's his name, Englebert . . . no, *Emeril*—flown in for a fucking charity luncheon. Ten grand and a suite. So I'm wondering, why you? I mean, a pretty face, that's nothin'. They're all over the place, dealing cards and bussing tables. So why, I wanna know, with a résumé like yours, does she hire *you*? They got better trainers at 24 Hour Fitness. You got any insight on that, Wolf? Feel free to speak up."

"Not a clue, Phil," I squeaked through a clenched jaw.

"Me neither. I fucking hate it when that happens."

He paused, patting the bar that was bending my rib cage in strange and unintended ways. I expected to hear muted snapping sounds at any moment.

"So here's what *you* need to know. I'm going to find out why you're here. And while you're playing footsie with my wife, know this: I'm watching you. Everything you do, everything you say, I'll know. Frankly, I don't give a shit what Lynn does or who she does it with. Knock yourself out, she's a lousy lay anyhow. But you cross any other lines, start to get close to the business, show the slightest interest in one thin dime of mine outside of your salary, that's a different game. Then we'll talk again."

I nodded, as best one can nod lying beneath a steel girder.

He glanced at his associate and stepped aside. The larger man took his place over me and lifted the bar from my chest as if it were a golf club. He hesitated for a moment, the clear implication being that he could drop it at any moment—in case he got a call, perhaps—thus ending further negotiations.

Note to self: do *not,* under any circumstances, piss this guy off.

Clearly, Phillip Valentine knew about my morning face-to-face with Lynn in the spa. One only had to look up at the little mirrored spheres in the ceiling of every room in the hotel, including the gym, to understand how. Based on the fact that I was still in possession of all my appendages, I had to assume the transcript of that meeting went unheard.

Or not. It occurred to me that Phillip might want the scheme to play out, see how far she'd take it. Maybe use the evidence of her intention to kill him as leverage in dividing the property in court. But if that were the case, why the intimidation job with the barbell, which was enough for anyone with a lick of common sense to clear out of dodge?

Maybe it was all just a sick, twisted game between people with too much money, and I was the puck. Renee—a.k.a. Nicole—probably told them that common sense wasn't my strong suit.

Maybe I should just take my chin and go home while it remained intact. Before they got warmed up.

*   *   *

IF there was one thing I learned from my previous outing as a federal snitch, it was the necessity to size up people and situations in less than an adrenaline-fueled heartbeat. More often than not survival in those moments was a matter of confidence, even if it was cloaked in bullshit. I'd been playing the game ever since in the safety of my living room—guys do all the time, especially short ones with issues—mostly with poseur tough-guy celebrities that popped up on *Entertainment Tonight* trying to look badass on a red carpet. With a glance I could tell with ninety-nine percent accuracy who I could take down and who I couldn't.

The point: I was in over my head here. Any way you cut it, Phillip Valentine and the bodyguard he didn't need were out of my league. I could press all the panic buttons Sherman could put at my disposal, but by the time he showed up, guns and badges blazing, I'd be toast.

After a moment of silence and the thin confidence that Valentine and Godzilla would not come back for a postscript, I hung my head, a move which pointed my mouth directly at the Droid phone resting on the floor beneath the bench. I covered my mouth and spoke softly to elude the digital ears that surely surrounded me.

"We have to talk," I barely whispered. "Tonight."

30

So how do you follow *that* act? You don't.

I hit the streets to walk it off. Down to the Luxor to check out the fake catacombs. Then it was up the street to the fake medieval splendor of the Excalibur, where I lost a hundred very genuine bucks on four straight hands of blackjack. Across the street to the fake skyline of Manhattan, where a woman with fake boobs gave me a fake smile while she served me an imitation kosher hot dog. I then took my stomachache across the street to laugh at the fake Eiffel Tower and the Japanese tourists madly taking pictures of it, then down the street to watch some very confused Midwest tourists take fake gondola rides on the fake canals of The Venetian—one couple, fresh from the McWedding parlor two doors down, wore a tuxedo and a bridal gown while toasting their union with bottles of Heineken—God help us all—before heading across the street for the cheesy fake pirate extravaganza at

Treasure Island. Then a drink at the newest crown jewel of Vegas, called Aria, which looked like a setting for a Ridley Scott movie.

I needed a shower. It, and much more, awaited me back at Xanadu.

I emerged from the shower butt-naked, frantically drying my hair with a towel as I blindly navigated toward the bed. As I bent to grope the bedspread for the television remote, an unexpected sound shot a bolt of ice through my flesh.

"Nice view." A woman's voice.

I dropped the towel to find Renee-Nicole sitting in the chair by the window, arms folded, her face consumed with a smug smile that once upon a time made my nipples hard. A smile that said *gotcha*.

"Very nice, indeed," she repeated as I scrambled to cover my gear with the towel. She was dressed for a night on the town, a slinky little black number cut tantalizingly low, killer heels at the conclusion of crossed legs, and lots of borrowed bling. Had to be, on an FBI paycheck.

"You on the clock?" I asked, "or on the make?"

"A girl needs her cover," she replied.

"Me too," I said, dropping the towel. I showed her my best side—that would be my ass—as I began rummaging through a bag for some shorts and a pair of jeans that didn't smell like Mickey Rourke's breath.

She studied me a moment, the smile fixed.

"Lynn was impressed. She particularly liked your abs. Personally, I like this better."

I looked up. "Aren't these rooms, like, bugged? I could have sworn you told me they were bugged."

It was hard not to glance at my Droid phone, which was resting on the dresser next to my wallet.

Her smile morphed into impatience.

"Think it through, Einstein. You work for Lynn Valentine, I

work for Lynn Valentine. You were assigned this room precisely *because* it's not bugged."

"So we can talk freely. Cuss, even."

"Actually we can have sex, if you're up for it. One of Chad Merrill's boys sees me going in and out of here, we need a story that floats."

"Does that explain your shoes?"

She glanced at her strappy little heels and giggled. "Hey, we're talking about it, aren't we?"

"Then tell me more about the part where she likes my abs."

"She told me to pay you."

"I concur."

"I need an account number."

I allowed a poignant moment to pass, my lips pursed thoughtfully. "A little problem there."

I hoped Sherlock was paying attention.

"My account has gone cryogenic. I open anything new off shore, you guys can grab it, too."

"That wasn't us."

"Sure it was. But it doesn't matter. There's no safe harbor for my funds. Which means we have a problem."

By now I had on a shirt and was running a brush through my hair, which was short enough not to need one. It was early, so I thought I'd sample the fabled Xanadu nightlife, see if anyone from the cast of *That '70s Show* was on the property. Rumor had it.

Without looking at her I said, "I'm thinking cash."

"You want a million dollars in cash?"

"Think it through. I have no other options."

"Not a chance, Wolf. Sorry."

I calmly tucked the Droid into the vest pocket of my sportcoat. I pictured Special Agent Sherlock huddled in a van with a sack of burgers and tepid coffee.

"It's not protocol," she added.

"There's protocol for this?"

"Or what? You'll walk?"

I stopped primping and looked at her squarely. "Oh, I'll walk. Straight to the case officer on my last gig. Name's Wissbaum. Who can forget a name like Wissbaum? Not me. Not you, either. What you forget is that I'm not on the payroll. I'm a contractor, and I have terms. Maybe even a union."

This one was spinning her wheels. Only time would tell if I'd just blown my cover or played a trump card. Either way, once Sherman Wissbaum and I huddled up, it was over. I wanted no part of Phillip Valentine and his man-child from the genetics lab.

Or the million dollars. I was yanking her chain at the moment, just for kicks.

"I'll make some calls," she said.

31

I assumed our meeting was over when she stood and headed toward the door, purse in hand.

"Was it good for you, too?" I asked.

Ignoring me, she opened the door and peered down the hall, carefully looking both ways, then closed it and returned to my side. She sat on the bed and patted the mattress invitingly.

"Guess you weren't kidding about the sex," I suggested.

"Sit." Her voice was different. Softer, no nonsense.

I complied. The volume of the ensuing exchange would be markedly lower, and I was grateful I'd stashed the Droid close to my heart.

She opened the purse and pulled out a vial of an injectable liquid the color of pale honey. Her eyes studied mine as I squinted, trying to make out the label.

"Lynn wants a game plan. You're looking at it."

"Do I get a playbook?"

"I'll tell her what you're planning to do, that you explained it to me tonight between orgasms. I don't know if she'll ask you about it. Maybe not. But she'll know, and she'll think it's perfect, because it is. You have to be ready with a story if she does."

She handed me the vial. I held it to the light, read the label: *Depo-Testosterone*. The listed patient was Phillip Valentine.

"That explains the bench press," I mumbled.

"Phillip's a psycho, a freaking health fanatic. Eats boiled chicken, edamame, blueberries, and, I swear to God, raw broccoli. Snacks on almonds and Meuslix. Pops fourteen nutritional supplements a day. And he's been injecting this shit into his ass every Sunday morning for the past six years."

"The freedom to worship as we see fit," I mumbled again.

"This guy worships two things. His mirror and his money. In that order. His daughter's not even on the map."

I handed the vial back. I'd known guys who used medical testosterone, and so far nobody was complaining. There were no real side effects, a visible improvement in body composition, new all-time bests in the weight room, and erections you could use to pry up a sidewalk. For my money, a diagnosis of diminished natural testosterone production and an ensuing prescription was nothing short of a medically endorsed fountain of youth.

"What's it to me?" I asked.

Her smile had shades of evil in it. That, too, used to turn me on. Before it was real.

"It makes you a genius."

"This genius wants cash," I reminded her.

She ignored the comment as she stared at the vial, keeping her eyes fixed as she spoke. Her voice was almost lyric.

"There's a substance in this particular vial. I know for a fact he has an unopened vial in the upper-right drawer of his vanity, next to the sink. Tomorrow night you'll replace that vial with this one. When he injects himself the next morning, he'll fall ill by early afternoon. Horrible, violent, unstoppable vomiting, with a fever. He'll think it's food poisoning, but he won't call the house doctor or anyone else. Phillip doesn't do doctors. Over the course of the week he'll feel better, and then on Sunday he'll give himself another injection. That will begin the worst week of his life. Doctors will run tests, but they won't find anything, they won't know what is happening to him. By the third Sunday he'll most likely be in a hospital, but because his vanity is stronger than any instinct to survive, he'll have his goon bring him the vial and he'll shoot himself again."

She looked at me with eyes I'd never seen on a woman. "He'll be dead by the end of that week. After a postmortem they'll decide on spinal meningitis, exacerbated by liver infection, which is how she'll get away with it."

The ambient silence between us was frightening. It was as if the sounds of the city had faded away, replaced by a thick fog of realization. Her eyes returned to the vial with appreciative eyes that lent the moment a cinematic quality, a witch holding an apple to the firelight, relishing the thought of the venom within.

"What's in it?" I asked, barely whispering.

She hissed the word, a Droid tearing through flesh. "Arsenic."

A moment passed, quickly filling with questions.

"Arsenic isn't invisible in the human body. They'll find it."

"Not this arsenic."

I swallowed hard, my throat suddenly dry. "Pardon me all to hell, but I thought we were just stinging this guy and his wife, not killing him."

She shrugged. As if my point was moot.

"I didn't sign up for this."

She put a hand on my shoulder, the heat of it penetrating my shirt. "Deep breath, Wolf. This is the version we tell Lynn about, if she asks. She may not. This is precisely what she wants, and precisely why you're here."

My eyes were hopeful as I said, "So it's not arsenic."

"Of course not."

"Where'd you get this shit?"

"You don't need to know that."

"What if she asks where *I* got it?"

"She won't."

It was a nice try, one I hoped Sherlock would appreciate.

"This stuff mimics the symptoms, then."

"He'll suffer. She'll get to see it, hold his hand, wipe the sweat from his brow, and say *there, there*. Watch him slowly dying, sipping it like a fine liqueur."

The visual shot a chill up my spine.

"What *is* in it?"

"A synthetic derivative. Harmless, if treated in a timely manner. Which will happen, once we move on Lynn Valentine."

"Which happens how?"

"We come in, probably when he's hospitalized, find the so-called arsenic, open a criminal file. With your testimony, we pin the intent to kill on Lynn, and she'll sing like a bird on Mancuso to get the deal we'll offer."

"The FBI just shows up? Yeah, that'll work."

"That's why I'm here."

"You've been in Phillip Valentine's bathroom."

"Many times."

Her eyes confessed the unspoken. I wondered if Lynn knew.

"Then why not just switch the vials yourself?"

"Because I'm not the one getting paid to do it, or to think it up in the first place. I can't just walk in with this idea. This is the work of a *pro*. There's video, Wolf, remember that. She needs to see you do it. She needs to believe this is real. Chad Merrill will show her the tape, and she'll pay him off to keep it quiet. That tape and Merrill's testimony both become part of the evidence she'll believe we plan to use against her in court."

"So Merrill's her guy."

"Totally. He'll get his own deal and throw her under the bus."

I thought a moment, my hands held prayer-like over my chin.

"I go in, plant the vial, get out. Without Valentine knowing. Tell me how *that* works."

"You'll have a card key. In and out in two minutes."

"He'll be somewhere else. As in, miles away."

She grinned again. "Phillip Valentine has a standing ten o'clock appointment at a very special loft downtown with an L.A. dominatrix. He flies her in for the sessions. He'll literally be tied up for two hours, sometimes they play all night."

I stood up and began pacing the room. Several minutes passed, Renee-Nicole quietly allowing me to process it all.

"What happens to me?"

"Lynn will never know you were a plant. We'll tell her you've been arrested and that you're singing like Kelly Clarkson. That's why you have to play this out, star in the music video, say your lines. When we have her you'll walk out of here with your money."

"And the sense of achievement that comes with serving one's country."

She paused, not sure how to take that one.

"It's easy, Wolf. We've *made* it easy."

I paced a moment more, then stopped and looked at her with narrowed eyes.

"Cash. By tomorrow. Maybe I'll make it worth your time and effort if you make it happen."

She thought a moment.

"You talking sex or a tip? I suggest five figures."

She got up and came to me, lacing her arms around my neck.

"And maybe I can show you that loft sometime."

She moved in for the kiss. I blocked it with my fingertips.

"I don't do dungeons."

I was lying, but she had no need to know about my past. Tracy had possessed a dark imagination. Part of her charm.

She laughed, that awkward moment when her pride surfaced to conquer the sting of rejection. She stepped back, then grabbed her purse to deposit the vial. A moment later she withdrew an envelope and plopped it onto the bed.

"Someone slid this under your door when you were in

the shower." When she reached the door, she added without looking back, "Have fun."

When she was gone I opened the envelope, which was sealed. I looked closely to see if the seal was wet, meaning she had opened it. Which would explain the "have fun" comment.

The envelope seemed pristine. It contained a ticket for the 10:30 showing of *Zumanity,* the Cirque du Soleil kink-fest showing across the street at New York-New York.

One ticket. Could be Renee playing games. More likely it was Sherlock responding to my call.

32

It didn't occur to me that the worst nosebleed seat in the house would also be the most secure. Top row, on the aisle. Nobody behind to listen in. Nobody to my left to listen in. Conveniently, the two seats in front of me would remain vacant. I had expected to find Sherlock occupying the seat to my right, and was prepared to play a game of innocent chitchat for any onlookers with binoculars and an agenda.

I was seated for a few minutes when a couple arrived, looking as if they just got off the bus from Sioux City. Dockers and wingtips for him, Laura Ashley and thongs for her. I had to hold my tongue when the woman took the seat next to me—surely this was a mistake. Sherman Wissbaum would arrive at any moment . . . I'd let him take care of it.

But Sherlock never showed.

The program began with a mistress of ceremonies dressed like Catwoman—a nice start, that—giving way to two Rudolf

Nureyev protégés in pink tights engaging in a full-contact ballet smackdown. When I glanced over to see how Mr. and Mrs. Middle America were holding up, I was surprised to see that the woman was looking at me with a curious smile.

She leaned closer.

"Sherman wants to know how you like the seats."

My expression announced confusion, so she pulled her hair back to reveal an earpiece. Then her eyes told me to glance down, where the palm of her hand cupped an open wallet with an FBI I.D. and a badge.

"Tell him I think he'd really enjoy this part."

"He can hear you," she said, glancing down at the Droid, which I was carrying in my hand. Then she put her hand to her ear. "And I can hear him."

"How do I know it's him?"

She listened to Sherlock's reply to my question.

"He says to ask you if you've had the chicken piccata at the Ceasar's Cheesecake Factory lately."

Renee would know about that. We'd eaten in that restaurant twice, albeit in other cities, and I'd order the piccata both times.

"Ask him the name of the lawyer from hell."

This was a reference to my previous FBI case involving a billionaire, three killer women—literally—and a jet I liked a lot. A euphemism Sherlock would know and Renee certainly would not, even if she'd studied the case file.

The woman smiled. "Lee Van Wyke. Leather pants, solid gold broomstick, kicked your ass on the tennis court."

That she had. And not just on the tennis court.

"So where is he, the Danny Gans show?"

"He's dead."

"Really? Maybe it's a trick."

"No, he's dead. He says details like that will get you killed."

Now she covered her mouth casually as she spoke.

"There's a good chance someone is watching you. Since you'll likely be meeting up with him later on, it would look suspicious if it happened twice. This is safer."

"Tell him I'm glad he's more paranoid than me."

She grinned. "He says that's not easy to do."

The two dancers were now prone on the floor, one gyrating on the other. A bona fide *Brokeback Ballet*.

The woman put her hand on her ear again, listening carefully, the grin having vanished. She said something to her male friend, for appearance's sake, then leaned back toward me.

"He says the husband sounds like a piece of work."

"You should see his friend. Tell him it's too dangerous."

She listened again, her face stoic.

"He says to tell you he found your money."

"How convenient."

"He wants to know what he should do with it."

"Tell him to put it back where it belongs."

She listened. "Won't work. They could just take it out again. And that it would alert them that they're busted."

"Tell him they won't know it's there so they won't look. I need to see it online. It's the only way I'll know it's back. Two words—good faith."

A pause. "He wants to know why you don't trust him."

"Because he wants me to do something illegal, which in all likelihood will get me killed. Besides, the guy'll say anything. He's done it before."

"He says you didn't die."

"Good point."

"You owe him this one."

"Tell him to sue me."

A longer pause. "He says that's a funny thing to say to the guy who has your money. And speaking of suing, you should know that the IRS wants you to call them when you get back to your room."

That hit below the belt. Which always gets my attention.

"Tell him he's a bastard."

"He says he knows."

Another pause. "He wants you to play it just the way your friend has teed it up. Says the plan she gave you will be the one they'll execute, except it will be his people and not hers when the wheels fall off."

Now I covered my mouth, just as she had done.

"So what happens if she's lying about the synthetic arsenic? What if it's real?"

She listened intently, her brow furrowed. She leaned closer, her hand even tighter to her lips as she spoke.

"Why, he wants you to consider, would FBI agents, even a rouge splinter group, want to kill the very person they're trying to incriminate? They can't arrest a dead perp. He wants you to think about the implications of that."

I nodded. I didn't know why.

Her eyes told me she was listening to him again.

"A contingency medical team will be on standby. If it's real, that just puts their ass in a tighter sling."

"Tell him Phillip Valentine thanks him for his concern."

Her eyes went to the Droid phone in my hand.

"You just did."

"I forgot. Under a lot of stress here."

"He says Phillip Valentine should be the least of your concerns."

The boys on the mat had worked up a good sweat and retired with a flourish to the dressing room, where salads surely awaited. The catsuit lady was again addressing the crowd, waving her riding crop for emphasis. Which meant that a certain percentage of the audience were dealing with erections.

The agent next to me tapped her male friend on the arm—perhaps on that very topic—whispering something that prompted him to produce a pen and a notepad. She jotted down a series of numbers, tore the sheet off and slipped it to me.

"Swissfirst Bank in Zurich. This is your account number and user I.D. Your money is there. He suggests you do the same with any incoming funds."

"Tell him I've got it handled."

She listened again. "He's got your back. There'll be a visual on you when you're not behind closed doors. Says there's new information about your handle, he'll brief you on that later. For now he needs you to be a good soldier."

Hand to ear, more intense listening.

"He says you need to get something on tape from the wife. No whirlpools this time. He needs it on the record."

"Tell him that the wife is smarter than both of us."

She listened without sharing Sherlock's response. Probably something to the effect that this is usually the case.

I watched the show for a few moments. A woman with a bright red wig dressed in what appeared to be a mesh of black belts was striking a cowering man with a whip that looked as real as it sounded.

Yes, those erections were coming along nicely.

"He wants to know if the two of you are cool."

I smiled, but not at her. "Tell him he's never been cool a day in his life."

33

As if in a Faustian time warp, Lynn Valentine was waiting for me in the gym the next morning, working on the same recumbent peddling machine, reading the same newspaper, again dressed in black tights, a throwback headband, and matching leggings to go with the obligatory *gee-I-didn't-know-you-were-here* attitude. At least her hair was pulled back into a tight ponytail, rather than the cheesy *Madonna-on-a-Starbucks-run* hat.

Only thing in a gym dorkier than a baseball hat on a woman is any kind of hat on a guy. My opinion.

As for me, I wore a long-sleeved Dry-FIT shirt, neon blue and snug enough to get her attention. No more cute little deltoid cuts for her estrogenic amusement. The Droid was on the floor at the base of the wall with my wallet, unobtrusive but easily noticed.

"Ready to work?" I asked, noticing that she didn't look up as she folded the newspaper.

"I've been working for half an hour," she muttered.

She did, however, glance at me with sudden alarm when I touched my finger to the back of her neck, checking for sweat. This, I assumed, was not something the typical Xanadu employee did unannounced. I glanced at the dry results and said, "Not hard enough, it seems."

She appeared more irritated than amused.

"Think you can make me sweat?"

"I guarantee it."

"Earn your money, Wolf."

The way her eyes burned as she said this led me to believe this was a deliberate and timely double entendre.

"Then," I said, "allow me to introduce you to my balls."

EVERYTHING we did that morning involved a rubber ball. Core work laying on a fitness ball the size of an ottoman. Dumbbell flies on a smaller version. Cables and curls kneeling on a BOSU ball. A game of underhanded catch with a weighted sphere. Some yoga stretches—this I made up as I went along—using a towel. Very little verbiage was exchanged, though not for any lack of trying on my part. Fact was, she was straining too hard to speak. My training style proved very hands-on—this, too, was improvised—as I used the gift of touch to adjust her posture and emphasize the burn in a particular muscle. This was accompanied by a smooth narrative of encouragement uttered at close range as I leaned in to share the moment. All of it was overtly flirtatious, and I hoped Chad Merrill and Phillip Valentine were taking notes down in spy central.

I also had an agenda.

As she was cooling down, her neck definitely moist and tender at this point, I put my hand on the small of her back and leaned close to her ear.

"We need to talk," I whispered, consummating the agenda.

"I suggest the spa," she said, louder than me.

"No."

She smiled. "I hear you met my husband."

"Little fucker? Big gold chain and a mullet?"

She grinned. "He liked you, too."

"I could tell."

The smile turned bitter. "He got to you. I wouldn't have guessed that."

"He said that? What, you saw the video?"

She shifted to another position, causing me to move with her to maintain a whispering proximity.

"No more whirlpools . . . what's a girl to think?"

I moved her arms into a slightly different position. Very firm and trainer-like. She resisted, preferring control.

"You want the truth?" I said softly.

Her look said *don't insult me.*

I put my lips against her ear. "You got to me."

She nodded again, only barely hiding a smile.

I pulled back a few inches. "I have a job to do."

"I heard."

"How much do you want to know?"

"Nothing at all."

"Smart girl."

"Smarter than you know."

"That's what I'm afraid of."

She was lying on the mat, me kneeling over her. Suddenly she rose to her knees, put her arms around my neck and buried her face under my chin. The cameras be damned, and not coincidentally, the microphones circumvented.

Her voice was air without tone.

"You'll never have to fear me, Wolf."

She pulled away so that our eyes could engage. Then she took my hand and brought my fingers to her lips, her voice now barely audible. More stealth than seduction.

"Unless you cross me. In which case I'll bury you. Just like I'm about to bury my husband."

Then she bit my hand. That part was seduction.

There it was. Just what Sherman needed, on the record.

"Do the work, Wolf."

She leaned in and kissed my forehead, her lips lingering, their heat penetrating my skull. She smelled like delicious, disgusting sweaty sex.

Lynn Valentine rose with the grace of a ballerina and walked out of the gym with the disquieting confidence of a woman who knows when men are watching.

The next time I saw her, Phillip Valentine would be well on the road to hell.

THE elevator smelled like smoke. Of course it did, this was Las Vegas. The churches smell like smoke in Las Vegas. I barely noticed a young girl already occupying the elevator upon my arrival. Until I heard her say, "Dude, nice shorts."

I glanced down; they looked just fine to me.

"You're Wolf," she said. It wasn't a question.

There was something vaguely familiar about her, but the comment was too jolting, her eagerness too arresting, to put it together. She wore a tennis outfit, at least that was my conclusion based on the fact she held a racquet and a can of Penns.

"You're that dude, my mom's new personal trainer."

Caitlin Valentine. The centerpiece of this rapidly deteriorating Greek tragedy. She was already a woman-in-waiting, destined for great beauty that would surpass her mother's, with dark hair worn in a pony-tail that defined the word *perky*. Dangling earrings were out of synch, the influence of her surroundings. Her body was thin and without features, a colt finding its legs, yet somehow graceful. This was in stark contrast to eyes, her father's, already alive with mischief and a startling confidence.

"If that's true, then you must be Caitlin."

I extended my hand. Then I had to stifle a smile when I experienced the contrived tightness of her grip.

"My dad was wrong," she said.

"First time since Elvis died, I bet."

She didn't get it or didn't care.

"He said you weren't as pretty as your picture."

I didn't recall submitting a picture to the Valentines. Renee, in her role as Nicole, had done her homework.

"Did you just play?" I asked, glancing at the racquet. The elevator was going up, and there were no courts on the roof.

"I take lessons at the MGM," she said.

"I used to play a little. Shouldn't you be in school?"

"It's Saturday. You want to hit sometime? I'm pretty good."

"I bet you are."

"I'm gonna play on the high-school team next year. I'm serious, you want to hit?"

"Love to. Maybe ask your dad if that'd be okay."

A sudden wave of guilt arrived, completely unexpected. The dad in question was the subject of a pending murder conspiracy, the machinations of which I would put into play that very night. Even monsters have fathers, and too often the innocent have fathers who are monsters.

I had to look away. Because suddenly the monster was me.

"Do you like Coldplay?" she asked.

The image of my felonious ex and this thing she used to do with ice cubes and Carmex flashed into my mind. Then I realized Caitlin was talking about the band of the same name.

"Sure," I lied. Coldplay was the worst rock band since Kiss. At least Kiss looked good.

"You should put them on your cell phone," she said, reaching out to tap the Droid phone in my hand. "That's what I do."

"I'll be sure and do that."

The elevator door opened. Her smile was brighter than the sunlight streaming in from across the hall. She held up a hand and offered a perky goodbye, calling me by name. I raised mine in return, unable to think of anything to say.

As the door closed I happened to notice someone standing there, as if intending to come in. But he didn't. He just stood there, arms folded eyes narrowed, shaking his head at me.

It was Chad Merrill, the guy who really ran this place. And

somehow he's managed to get from his spy seat in security central where he'd been listening in on my banter with Lynn Valentine's daughter, and arrive at those doors when they opened.

If there was a wild card in all of this, I had a feeling it might be him.

YOU meet some people in life and you want to take a shower. Had a lot of that lately. You meet others and you want to reassess your life. They make you want to play tennis and listen to Coldplay. Because in your heart you know you didn't merit the simple kindness to which you were just exposed.

That's why I hadn't stepped out of the elevator as intended. That, and the guy in the suit with the death glare.

I had encountered innocence moving among the creatures of the night that inhabited Xanadu. Caitlin Valentine had, in her way, reached out, casting for a possible friend in a world where friends are hard to come by.

There I stood, frozen by truth, unable to respond. Unable to be real.

In the midst of my fraud I stood naked, once again myself.

34

I was in the shower when the door to my hotel room opened and closed. I assumed, like last time, that it was the pseudonymous "Nicole" arriving with a sack of significant cash and a vial of trouble mislabeled as testosterone, so I decided not to hurry. I'd spent the afternoon walking off a severe case of nerves, the effect of which had turned my stomach into a gastric version of that high-tech vacuum cleaner advertised on television, the one with no moving parts and a centrifugal force equal to five hundred times the force of gravity. Enough to suck the serial numbers off a stack of fresh one hundred dollar bills and send me back to Portland with my covert tail between my legs.

But the game was on. A victory of economics over cowardice.

Just for kicks, I emerged from the bathroom butt-naked, my head swathed in a towel as I frantically dried my hair. I took my time with it, imagining the expression on her face when I dropped the towel, feigning that I had no idea she was there.

After a moment I executed the plan. The face I saw was that of a man leaning against the wall with a barely contained smirk. I'd seen the face before. His arms were crossed, revealing a hand that was not inconspicuously missing a thumb. Lynn Valentine sat on the bed, exquisitely nyloned legs crossed demurely— seams running up the back, gets me every time—her expression more embarrassed than amused.

The towel quickly found its way around my waist.

"I take it you were expecting someone else," she said, forcing the sarcasm.

Her lanky, thumbless friend was shaking his head, as if to tell me to watch my step. Or, perhaps, that I was an asshole.

"Would you believe room service?" I replied.

Her eyes narrowed slightly, darkening the moment. She was dressed for a night out, but then again this was Lynn Valentine's normal work attire at Xanadu, a cross between a gallery opening and a state funeral. She avoided eye contact, the fact of which I assigned immediate meaning. She was jealous. Which meant, at this particular instant, she was dangerous.

"Are you sleeping with her?" she asked.

"Sleeping with who?"

Her gaze held. "You were expecting my personal assistant and a million dollars of my money. I ask again, are you sleeping with her?"

She sounded every inch the disgruntled CEO. Or a lawyer on cross. I didn't buy it. This was a desperate *woman* talking from a bruised heart.

"Would it make a difference if I was?"

She shifted on the bed, the moment of silence painful for all of us in the room. Especially those of us wearing only a towel.

"Where is she?" I asked.

"I'm so sorry to disappoint you."

Suspicion confirmed. I vaguely remembered Renee saying she would tell Lynn that we were having sex when we weren't swapping ideas on how to kill her husband, so this all seemed a bit out of synch.

"I'm only disappointed if that bag doesn't contain my money."

My eyes flicked toward a black athletic bag resting at the man's feet. The Xanadu logo was emblazoned on the side in gaudy gold lettering, in keeping with the hotel's corporate colors and complete lack of subtlety. Black and gold, a nifty little metaphor for wickedness and cash.

She nodded once, in response to which the man picked up the bag and put it on the bed. As he unzipped it—not easy with no thumbs—I sensed that Lynn's eyes were on mine.

"Nicole will no longer be handling our affairs," she said.

It was full of bills. Bundles upon bundles of hundreds, though my glimpse was brief. Thumbless Joe had zipped the thing back up as quickly as he'd opened it.

"Is there a problem?" I asked.

"You tell me," she said. "Is there a problem, Wolf?"

Based on her tone, there certainly was.

I tried to be nonchalant as I cast a look at the console next to the television—another primetime rerun in midseason—where I'd left my wallet and the magic smartphone. Sherlock would be getting the whole thing loud and clear. A great opportunity, I realized, to give him his money's worth where Lynn Valentine was concerned.

"You think Nicole and I are running a number on you."

She pursed her lips, as if this was a fresh notion to consider. "She comes to me suddenly asking for a million in *cash*. What would you think?"

"I'd think I had trust issues."

"Precisely."

"The cash was my idea," I said.

Her eyes narrowed even more. Her voice was softer, which made it more ominous. Her eyes had a certain dare in them, a definite *he-who-blinks-first-dies* twinkle.

"Let me tell you what was my idea," she said back. "I have absolutely no knowledge of how the two of you know each other. She offered to tell me, but people I do trust told me that

I didn't want to know. As far as I was concerned she'd done her job. But then my husband comes to me, tells me that my new personal trainer's résumé stinks like last week's fish, that I should watch my back. Phillip's a bit paranoid and he's a jealous prick, so this is no big deal. Of course your résumé stinks, you're a covert freelance assassin, your résumé is bullshit. But then Nicole, who is linked to you in this unknown way, asks for cash at the eleventh hour, and it hits me that *she* suddenly smells like the same batch of bad cod."

I started to protest mightily, something witty about those trust issues and cod, but she stopped me with a raised palm tipped with the most elegant of French manicures. A quiet two-count punctuated its intention.

"The only person I know who can sense a rat quicker than I can is Phillip. So I asked Nicole to tell me where and how she found you. And that's when it happened. I'm in the business of spotting cheaters and liars, Wolf. There are a dozen tells, little pantomimes that give a liar away. Professionals can spot them, liars can't help them. That's why I know you're not lying to me now. And that's why I know Nicole was."

I stared her down for a moment, thankfully for little gifts I didn't know I had. Then I said, "She wasn't lying to you."

"Ah, but you see, you have no idea whether she was lying to you. Maybe she'd have shown up here with your money. Or maybe she'd have walked out the back door with it and gotten into a car, never to be seen again. That's the question I no longer had an answer to. And because I have trust issues, I had to intervene, you see. To get what I want while protecting my investment."

Something deep down in my plumbing eased, a sensation of relief washing into each of my limbs like a good hit of Percocet. Which made it harder to pretend to be shocked by the possibility that little Miss Nom de Plume was a felon.

"I don't even know her," I offered.

"I get that now."

"She found me through an intermediary, she gave me a nice

retainer. I liked the color of her money and the sound of her story. That's it. I wasn't fucking her."

Now it was Lynn who was conducting the stare-down.

"I believe you, Wolf."

"You want me to kill her? I can do that."

Her grin said she wasn't buying this bluff. Or that it was unnecessary.

"That's not who I want dead," she said slowly.

Time to set the hook. I chose my words carefully, delivered them slowly. "Let's be clear. For the record."

"Who's record?"

"Mine. I have an ass to cover."

"What isn't clear about this picture, Wolf?"

"You want to me to kill your husband. Slowly. That's the gig."

For a moment I thought I'd inserted my size thirteen where no footwear was intended to go. But then she shot her lackey a look. He reached into the inside vest pocket of his baggy suit coat, pulled something out, tossed it to me.

A vial of liquid the color of honey landed in my hands.

"Like Phillip," she said, "I'm clinically paranoid. The business does that to you. Unlike Phillip, I don't let it paralyze me. So I'm changing the terms of the arrangement you made with Nicole."

My intestinal vacuum cleaner suddenly kick-started once again. There was something I wanted to get on the record while it was still fresh, and this was pushing it.

"You have nothing on her. Just your little hunch."

"She's lying to me."

"Call it what you will, it's still a hunch."

"It gets you paid. You should be thanking me."

I paused for effect, as if I gave a shit, then said, "What have you done with her?"

Her brow creased, as if I just possibly *did* give a shit.

"What do you care, Wolf?"

I had to be careful here. Jousting with a jealous lady was like bobbing for bratwurst with a school of piranhas.

"I just want to know what happens to people who violate your trust."

That made her smile, in a scary sort of way.

"Nicole's on reassignment until we see what happens. You switch the vials, just the way she told you. Phillip is off with his little leather therapist, and the guard situation has been dealt with. When you're done you come back here, go to bed. I don't imagine this type of thing causes you any loss of sleep."

I conjured a scary smile of my own. "Not lately."

"There is one slight change of plan, however."

I raised a skeptical eyebrow, waiting for her to continue.

"There's a picture of Phillip on his bathroom counter. In the morning, when we meet in the gym to keep things looking normal, you tell me what logo is on the hat he's wearing in that picture. And then you get paid."

I whistled softly. "This trust thing is big for you."

"I've been burned by better liars than Nicole. Or you."

I pretended to carefully ponder it all for a moment. I had already decided this wasn't a deal breaker. Hell, for a million dollars I'd eat the damn picture.

"Humor me," she said. "Do the drop, look at the hat. I'm not asking you to risk anything you aren't already risking."

"Why not just switch the vials yourself?"

"Because I have a previous engagement this evening. Because tonight is the best time to do it, everything has been arranged. They call it an alibi, Wolf. I'm the one with the motive if things get ugly."

We locked eyes. I wondered what mine were telling her.

"Give me a reason I should trust *you?*"

A little gem of a smile came and went.

"We keep up the façade in the gym, my husband gets sick, then he dies. Of course I terminate the training because of my grief. You go home, I put another million into the offshore account of your choice."

It was not lost on me that I was sitting on my bed wearing only a wet towel, under the watchful eye of an over-the-hill palooka with no thumbs, all of which made negotiating from a position of power a bit on the ridiculous side.

She smiled. As if she'd been waiting to say the next line all night.

"Like the man used to say, Wolf . . . deal, or no deal?"

She didn't quite have Howie Mandel's style with the line.

I glanced over at the Droid, disguising it as a look of contemplation. Nothing really had changed, the same game was in play, the same stakes up for grabs. The only thing that had been compromised was me. Business as usual in the wild and wacky world of covert criminal intelligence, where the good guys get screwed and the bad guys get, well, screwed.

I pivoted on the bed, causing the towel to come undone.

"Look at my eyes, Lynn."

"Sort of hard when your johnson is winking up at me."

I grasped her chin. Thumbless Joe flinched, but I put my other hand up to stop him in his tracks, just as Lynn had done to me moments earlier. Then, because that's the kind of guy I am, I moved the towel back in place, keeping my eyes on hers.

"Hear this clearly. Be aware of the consequences of crossing *me*."

"I know who and what I'm dealing with."

I hoped to God that wasn't true.

"I told Nicole this, now I'm telling tell you. It doesn't end if I disappear. Or if I have an accident. I have peers, people who do what I do. People with retainers."

I imagined Sherlock gagging on his Starbucks at that one.

"And *that*," she said, "to answer your question, is why you should trust me. I'm not stupid."

She smiled. It was either the calling of my bluff or a simple disregard for my bluster. Her hand went quickly to the back of my neck and pulled me toward her, our lips meeting with a certain violence that was as thrilling as it was unexpected. The woman was, after all, wearing seams.

Pulling away only slightly, so that our lips still touched and the tips of our tongues still danced, she whispered, "Kill him for me, Wolf. Make him suffer."

Then she bit my lip, hard enough to leave a mark. She got up and quickly left the room, smiling, with Thumbless Joe holding the door.

"You might want to take a look at those trust issues," I called after her, but the door shut nonetheless.

I stared at it for a long moment, conscious of the pace of my heart. I drew a deep breath and flopped back onto the bed, realizing that the plan called for me to be in Phillip Valentine's room within the hour.

When I sat up, I saw that a room card key had been placed on the desk while Lynn and I were kissing.

And that the Droid was gone.

35

The telephone in my room rang fourteen minutes later. I had already packed my bag, anticipating the worst. I'd hoped that Sherman had heard enough to intervene, so the ringing was good news. And I was dying to hear what he'd heard *after* the Droid left my possession.

A male voice identified himself as the concierge. "There's a woman here, sir, claims you are expecting her."

"Is there a problem?" I said impatiently.

"No sir, certainly not. But we like to check before we allow, uh, these *ladies* to come up. We have to be careful."

"How's forty dollars sound?"

"Careful enough, thank you."

"What does she look like, if I may ask?"

"I think you'll be quite pleased, sir." I imagined him looking her up and down with a lascivious security-guard smirk as he spoke.

"Tell her to hurry," I said before hanging up.

*   *   *

HE was right about my not being disappointed. Not so much because of her looks, which were terrific—upscale *Girls Gone Wild,* thick blonde hair, obligatory Pamela Anderson autograph implants, strappy little sandals you could use to hunt deer—but because the door had hardly closed before she was digging in her purse for a Bluetooth headset, which she handed to me. She smelled like Juicy Fruit, which she was chewing frantically.

Sherman Wissbaum was already on the line.

"You get all that about Renee?" I asked as I slipped it over my ear, as if we were resuming a conversation abandoned prematurely. The girl, who had yet to smile, was sitting on the end of my bed watching television with an odd seriousness. I had no idea if she was a federal agent or a hooker making the easiest five hundred of her career. I guessed the latter.

"Is Agent Barry okay? Any hassles getting her up there?"

What do I know.

"Sort of hard to talk while she's sitting on my face like this, but yeah, it's all good. Talk to me, what the *fuck* is going on? Where's my phone?"

"That would be our phone, Wolf. Transponder has it somewhere in Lynn Valentine's suite. Dead quiet, too."

"So am I busted, or what?"

"I don't think so. I'd say Renee is busted. You, she still likes."

"She said that?"

"They're just being careful, Wolf."

"The deal's off. I'm outta here."

"It's not off and you're not going anywhere because your million bucks is still in play. In fact it's better this way. My guess is they took the phone to isolate you. The woman's scared and she's wicked smart. It was a good move."

"Meaning what?"

"Meaning you still go in. Status quo."

"Not without the Droid."

"I'll get another one to you tomorrow."

"Meanwhile I potentially put Phillip Valentine's life in danger? Be the fall guy in a frame job? I don't think so."

I glanced at the girl to see if that got her attention. It hadn't—she'd flipped to CMT and was watching Kenny Chesney pretend he and his tractor were sexy.

"Chill out, Wolf, and listen to me. Nobody's going to frame you for squat. Remember what this is about. It still works. Do the job. Get it on video, just like they want. If it's real, if the guy gets sick, we jump in and pull him out of it. All the better to nail the bitch. If the substance in the vial is bogus, then we get her for intent to commit. Remember, she *thinks* it's real, because that's what Renee told her. That's the key. She's ours either way, because once we have her in custody, she knows only what we tell her."

"What if she switched out the vials? If she didn't buy Renee's line and really *did* put poison into it?"

"All the better for us."

Sherlock had flunked the academy's sensitivity training.

"Just step into Renee's shoes, get the collar."

"Something like that. And you get the million dollars."

"Two million."

"I don't think Lynn Valentine will be inclined to pay you the back half once we have her under indictment. Just a hunch. Nice move on the cash, by the way."

I allowed that one to sink in for a moment.

"Nothing's changed," he said. "You bail now, the whole thing goes down in flames. We're counting on you."

"Really? Like I'm counting on you to put my money in that new account?"

"Every dime. You're golden. *We're* golden."

Sherlock had been watching too much WB.

"You meet your lady in the morning," he continued. "All you have to do is make her happy until we show up."

"How will you know without the phone?"

"I'll get you wired beforehand."

"What about Renee?"

"You let us worry about Renee. We'll extract her before Lynn decides to tie off any loose ends."

"You know where she is?"

"You could say that. Let me talk to Agent Barry. Good luck, Wolf. We've got your back."

I slipped off the Bluetooth and extended it to the lovely Agent Barry. She held it to her ear and mumbled something, then grabbed her bag and got up, heading for the door.

"How was it for you?" I asked.

"Your secret's safe with me," she said, grinning while holding her fingers about two inches apart. She winked before turning to walk down the hall, working it as she went along, as if her ass had eyes.

36

Lynn Valentine's words echoed in my ears, along with my footsteps, as I raced down the urine-scented stairwell. The place had the acoustics of a mausoleum.

"Do your job, just the way she told you."

Maybe Lynn Valentine was smarter than all of us. If she was, I was squatting squarely on the horns of a dilemma. I had only the time it took to reach Phillip Valentine's bathroom to decide what to do.

The walls of the stairwell were concrete and the steps corrugated metal, rendering the ambiance nothing short of *Shawshank*. A more suitable, upholstered stairwell served any of Xanadu's paying customers who grew tired of waiting for the elevators. This one had, according to Renee, been Phillip Valentine's preferred route for exiting the hotel unnoticed, as he had done earlier that evening on his way to an appointment with a woman dressed like Emma Peel. Which would keep him busy long enough for me to get in and out of his apartment with no one except the lovely Chad Merrill noticing.

That, I had to take on faith.

I climbed the stairs to the door to the nineteenth floor. I'd passed fourteen similar doors on my way up here, none of which were even locked, much less equipped with digital security. The scene of the crime was at hand. I paused to put on a pair of medical latex gloves—a lot of good that would do with a video labeled Exhibit A—before taking out the card key.

I stepped into the hall. Everything here was different: the temperature, the scent—it was the only place on the premises that didn't smell like an ashtray—the warm ambience of the lighting. The décor was markedly lighter than the neo-whorehouse motif of the rest of the hotel, more classic New England in muted green and beige. The designer had a thing for oversized potted plants, which I guessed would never survive in the oxygen-compromised atmosphere downstairs. There were three double doors, unmarked and waiting. An empty chair stood sentinel next to the elevator.

Lynn had been right about that much.

My hand shook as I slipped the card into a slot next to the nearest door. A small green light blinked twice, then went dark, which meant it liked me. I pressed the gold-plated handle, pushed it open, and slipped inside.

I had been in the hall less than six seconds. Thus far, I thought to myself, I was being grossly overpaid.

I paused a moment to take it all in. The lights were off, but walls of glass admitted the Las Vegas night, a galaxy of Hoover Dam–fueled bling. The design was starkly contemporary, everything in blacks and whites, lots of chrome trim, everything shaped in squares and rectangles. One wall appeared to be a huge mirror, but closer examination revealed it to be the largest high-definition television screen I had ever seen. The place felt sanitized, like a high-end furniture showroom, as if the master of the house hadn't been here in weeks.

My inspection was quick. I knew precisely where the prize

was kept, and how to get there. The trick would be to do it before rupturing an aorta.

I passed quickly through the bedroom in quest of the master bath. The pallet here was black on black, made all the darker due to the fact that the curtains had been drawn. Just for grins I touched the fluffy black bedspread, and I didn't need to remove my hemorrhoid-dressing glove to know its DNA: genuine suede. Phillip Valentine was a very bad boy, indeed.

The bathroom was nearly void of all illumination. Even stray reflections had been absorbed by the pit of the adjoining bedroom. I had brought a pen light for just this eventuality, purchased that afternoon from the gift shop at the Monte Carlo. As I opened the upper-right-hand drawer, I wondered if that clerk would testify at my trial.

The drawer was full of unwrapped syringes and a small rectangular box. I picked it up, read the label: Depo-Testosterone, for one Phillip Valentine. Twelve refills authorized. Instructions to inject two ML IM—that would be intramuscularly—every two weeks. Which, based on the vascularity of the guy's forearms and biceps, meant Phillip Valentine probably shot up at least once or twice a week.

I opened the box, shook out the small bottle. The small plastic cap was still in place, meaning it had yet to be opened. Then I reached into my other pocket to withdraw the replacement bottle given to me by Lynn Valentine about an hour ago.

I fumbled both vials in the palm of my hand. Then I slipped one of them back into the box, put it back where it was, and closed the drawer.

I closed my eyes, taking stock of what I had just done.

I was almost out of the bedroom when I remembered the most important detail of my visit. At least if I wanted to get paid. I turned back and scanned the countertop with the light. My heart skipped one of its staccato beats when I saw the picture, right where Lynn said it would be. Phillip Valentine was kneeling, either at a golf course or a ballpark, his arm around his two daughters. The girls were beautiful, identical dark-haired clones of their mother, about eight years of age. One of them had flirted with me in the elevator earlier that day. The other was dead.

Phillip was wearing a Chicago Cubs baseball cap.

As I made my way back to my room, tracing my steps down the forbidden stairway to the fifth floor, my mind was not on my heart rate or what I had just done, the fuse I had just ignited and the explosion that would ensue. Instead I was fixed on those three smiles in the picture, and the dark poetry of fate that would deal them the cruelest hand of all shortly after it was taken.

Most men wouldn't be able to bear looking at it. Hell, I'd only met Caitlin Valentine once, and even I got misty. But Phillip Valentine, a man who supposedly gave his dead daughter and her surviving sister no more thought than a Hallmark card, chose to face the truth every morning. I pictured him touching it as he left the room for the day to run his hotel, perhaps in the quietest of nights holding it to his chest, closing his eyes to remember the scent of his daughter's hair.

I had made the right decision. Sherlock would just have to find a way to compensate for the fact that I had not switched the vials. The poisoned bottle of testosterone was still in my pocket as I departed Phillip Valentine's suite, leaving it precisely as I had found it.

37

The night was an eternity of voices, each with their own tone of truth. Mine was the weakest in the choir.

Upon arriving in my room I flopped onto the bed, the chaos of doubt and hypothetical outcome running amok in my mind. In the context to the purpose of the mission, I had done my job. A video—assuming Sherlock could get his hands on it—would show me entering Phillip's suite at Lynn Valentine's behest. This would be enough to convince her that they had her dead to rights, and that she should begin singing in their studio. Mission accomplished. By not leaving the poison behind, I had eliminated any chance of a screwup that might cost Phillip his life. These were the Feds, after all. And besides, I still had the poisoned vial Lynn had given me, which was evidence enough. Especially if it were, as I feared, the real thing.

The ace in the hole was me. By telling Lynn Valentine that I would testify at her trial, that I was, in fact, acting as an undercover agent the whole time, she would realize she had no options. She'd jump at whatever deal they offered, perhaps eagerly if it involved the downfall of the husband she so loathed.

Sherlock may not have agreed, but none of this required Phillip Valentine going through the agony of arsenic poisoning, real or not. Not on my watch.

Three o'clock came and went as I juggled the outcomes. Lynn had been wrong—sleep wasn't in the cards. I thought about raiding the minibar, then I remembered I don't really drink, and adding dry heaves to my problems didn't seem like the best remedy. Casually, more out of habit than hope, I dug my old mobile phone out of my bag, on the chance the Droid had been turned off, or that the battery had bled dry.

My money was on the latter. I had one message waiting.

As voices in the night go, this one would change everything. The call was from my friend Blaine, with whom I'd left the wine glass bearing the fingerprints of the two supposed FBI agents who had extorted me into this mess.

"DUDE, listen up, okay? Whatever you're into, man, get the fuck out of it, okay? That wine glass, man . . . holy shit. There were two prints besides yours, one likely male, one likely female. Male came up dry. Which is problematic because you said he was FBI, right? All agents have prints on file, so he's bogus, man. Ran FBI, the NFF, even the NSA. Nada. But the female, holy shit. Name is Charleen Spence, d.o.b. nineteen seventy-five. Two indictments for conspiracy to extort, one charge dropped, the other a copped plea in Miami, did six months. But here's the red flag, and pay attention. She's FBI all right . . . she's on an FBI organized-crime watch list. As in, she's the girlfriend of the son of one of the grand fucking puh-bahs of the fucking mafia, man, I shit you not. Guy's into racketeering, murder, extortion, offshore money laundering, the whole Tony Soprano enchilada. Take care of yourself, dude. Hope this helps. It never happened, by the way. Peace out, bro. And you're welcome."*

*   *   *

MY nightmare had become a can of chubby, garlic-breathed worms. Why had Sherlock told me the FBI agents I'd met in Portland were a rogue faction looking to take down a big fish? Either he didn't know and he was marking time with a tasty little lie, or he was simply lying outright. Where was my Cayman money, and who had hijacked it? And how, then, did he get it back? Why had Lynn Valentine suddenly lost faith in the very woman she'd trusted to hire her husband's killer, and then sent me into the same shitpile of that woman's creation? And for the love of God, why was Phillip Valentine still wearing his hair like 1990 Billy Ray Cyrus?

These were questions of sudden and urgent importance. But with my Droid gone there was no one to talk to. I could wait and ask Lynn Valentine about it all in a few hours, but that wasn't the ticket. The weight of the moment demanded counsel, and I was alone.

By first light I realized I had no other options. I had to leave Xanadu. Before the shit arrived at the proximity of the fan.

SOMEONE knocked on the door to my room at the precisely moment I was zipping up my suitcase. It had taken me less than two minutes to pack, if you didn't count the five-minute meditation in the middle of the process, which I'd needed to talk myself through it again. The only change to my plan to flee was that I'd leave the hotel for anonymous ground, but return in the morning for my meeting with Lynn Valentine to collect my money. There was, I reminded myself, the issue of my mother's nursing home and the million dollars they would ask me to produce on closing day.

Another victory of economics over fear.

The effect of the loud knocking on my physiology was akin to someone starting a spinal tap with pruning shears.

I looked through the viewer in the door. Four men stood in

the hallway, two of them wearing police uniforms. Thank God, Sherlock had sent the cavalry to rescue me.

I opened the door. A short guy with a suit and no hair gave me a look that would melt the mascara off the face of an evangelist's wife. He flashed a badge: Las Vegas PD, detective division. Very shiny. The other suit stood there, expressionless, a large house with nobody home. The cop who gets shot first in a Samuel L. Jackson movie.

"Wolfgang Schmitt?" said the one with a brain.

I nodded. So did he, but at the two officers. This was their prompt to enter the room and pull my hands behind my back, one of them efficiently slapping on handcuffs.

The detective eyed the suitcase on the bed. "Checking out, Mr. Schmitt?"

"What is this?"

They were already ushering me out of the room.

"You're under arrest for the murder of Phillip Valentine."

PART
THREE

38

The small jet executed a tight turn onto its final approach toward
runway 19-Right at McCarren Field, roughly paralleling the
fabled Las Vegas strip as it descended silently, flaps flared, gear
down. The sun was barely above the horizon, casting a surreal
glow over the city. Renee, deep into her guise as Nicole, sat on
the right side of the tiny cabin, her forehead pressed against the
glass. She had slept little; in fact, she had used her room in Reno
for nothing more than a place to change. But she was wide
awake now, unsure of what awaited her.

She saw nothing, thinking instead back to the evening before. It had all been such pure and utter bullshit.

Lynn Valentine had summoned Nicole to her suite just
after dinner. She wanted to go over the plan again, in minute

detail this time. Nicole had made her request—Wolf's request, actually—for the million in cash that afternoon, and Lynn had responded with anger. For a few minutes the entire operation was dead. But in a few more minutes, however, Lynn remembered that she would be much happier if it were her husband who was dead instead.

Nicole went over it all, even taking out the vial of spiked testosterone and putting it on the table in front of them. Lynn's personal valet—that thumbless hand made Nicole shiver whenever she saw it—remained in the room, the first and only sign that something unusual was about to unfold. Thus far their dark discussions about Phillip's future had been private, very carefully concealed.

And then Lynn pulled the plug. It was for Nicole's sake, she claimed, providing her with an alibi should one be required. Enthusiastic protests fell on deaf ears. Lynn would deliver the money herself. Being close to it, she claimed, made it more satisfying, and her satisfaction was the point. Everything had been arranged to divert the nineteenth-floor guard, a contrived meeting while both of the Valentines were away from the hotel.

That's when the thumbless valet stepped forward and snatched the vial from the table.

Moments later Nicole was being whisked off to the airport by one of Lynn's bodyguards. They'd gone into her room and packed an overnight bag and a sexy outfit for the evening. The so-called assignment, as contrived as it was useless, was what Lynn called "a mystery shop," wherein Nicole would take Lynn's personal jet up to Reno for the night, check into one of the larger hotels, and immerse herself in the available nightlife and amenities. Which included a former Broadway dancer hung like Secretariat, if that was her pleasure. Ten grand in cash was in her bag, she was told, enough to sample the casino from a VIP perspective. Lynn claimed she was thinking of buying the place, something that had never come up before and was therefore suspicious. It was a job she could entrust only to someone she trusted, someone of Nicole's abilities.

* * *

As the jet taxied to its berth, Nicole looked out to see the Xanadu limo, a white stretch Mercedes with an obnoxious logo on the doors. As she emerged into the sun she saw that a ramp worker had already removed her bag and was carrying it toward the limo, the trunk of which was open and waiting.

The back door of the car, too, swung open as soon as her feet hit the tarmac. The only surprise in the entire sequence was when she saw Chad Merrill waiting in the back seat.

"How was Reno?" he asked, patting the seat as she slid in.

"Fucking cold."

"You don't look like a particularly happy camper."

The car began moving toward the gate, the monolithic expanse of the MGM Grand filling up the horizon.

"Why are you here?" she asked.

Merrill shifted in his seat. Then he hit a button to raise the barrier between them and the driver.

"There's been a development." He paused for effect. "Phillip is dead."

Nicole could sense that he was watching her closely, studying every nuance of her reaction as only a professional could. She didn't have to act. Her jaw fell open, but she remained speechless as she inhaled sharply. She froze as the words sank in, eyes wide, the sudden release of adrenaline coursing through her skin.

"Not what you expected to hear, is it."

She shook her head in rapid little demonstrations of denial. "What happened, for God's sake?"

Merrill leaned forward and hit a button on the VCR—it was a ten-year-old company-owned limo—which was right below a small television that normally showed a Xanadu promotional video for VIPs on their way in from the airport.

"What is this?"

"Please watch."

The opening visual was a static shot of the lobby on the

nineteenth floor. Black and white, a little fuzzy, shot from a ceiling mounted camera.

"I've edited this from camera to camera. Got a pretty realistic timeline, if I do say so myself."

A man appeared from off-camera to the left. He walked forward with hesitance, then stopped in front of the first set of double doors. After looking both ways, he inserted a key card and went inside.

Wolf.

Nicole tried not to look away.

The image switched to a ceiling POV shot of Phillip's living room, which connected to the entry foyer. The man stopped for a moment, more out of fascination than fear, even going to the wall to touch the huge television screen. Then he turned and walked into the dark at the back of the room.

Cut to Phillip's bedroom. He passed through it quickly, eyes forward.

Then the bathroom. He produced a pen light, though the camera image was clear because of the low-light technology of Merrill's system. He opened a drawer, withdrew a small box, shined the light on it, and studied the label. Then he replaced the box and started to leave. But he stopped and turned back, picking up a framed photograph on the counter next to the sink.

Merrill leaned forward and pressed the stop button.

Despite her sudden nerves, she had to play this straight until Merrill tipped his hand. This could end up being any number of scenarios.

"Tell me what that was."

"I was thinking you might tell me."

She studied him with the same intensity he had directed toward her. The unspoken was screaming in their ears.

"Phillip's suite."

"Of course. You've been there many times, haven't you."

This was a dare she knew she shouldn't take. Somehow the bastard knew she'd been sleeping with Phillip.

"Who was that?"

"Cut the shit, please."

An uncomfortable silence ensued, lasting several blocks. Which in Las Vegas can take several minutes.

"Tell me what you think you know," she finally said. Jousting with this guy was like going one-on-one with Kobe Bryant. Turn the wrong way and you just might take it up the ass.

A strange, bewildered look came across Merrill's face.

Then he smiled and said, "I've never liked you."

Nicole's eyes narrowed. "How about you cut the shit."

This made him laugh. Whatever anxiety he had shown earlier had calmed to the point of arrogance. This was now his show.

"Your background was puzzling at first. Nothing I could put down. But I have a sense about these things, about you. A sense of smell, actually."

"Just say it."

"The entire hotel is wired. I see everything. Who you tell off, who you blow in the elevator."

He paused. That, too, had happened.

"I see into your room. I see into Lynn's room. I see into Phillip's room."

"It's called a God complex, you sick little fuck."

"That's occurred to me, yes."

"Lynn thinks her room is secure."

"Lynn says what she believes is true. She believes it's true because that's what I told her. You know another room I see into? I see into the trainer's room."

Another pause for effect. "You've been there, too."

He let that one float between them for a moment. Nicole remained still, staring out the window, again seeing nothing. The car turned North onto Las Vegas Boulevard, missing the turn that would return them to Xanadu. Morning tourists with white skin and pastel shorts wandered the streets.

"Are we going to the police?"

"No. We're going to talk. Wolf told the police he didn't switch the vials. Which means the injection Phillip gave himself when he got home was from a vial that was already there."

"If you believe Wolf."

"I do, actually."

"That's unfortunate."

"The truth often is. I believe you and Lynn conspired to make this happen. That you hired Wolf to be your front man. That you or perhaps even Lynn planted the poison in the drawer beforehand, and gave Wolf another poison vial just in case he bailed on you. Lynn likes to cover all the bases."

"That's complete horseshit."

He snorted a contemptuous little laugh. "Is it? The point was to get it on tape, because Lynn is well aware that I monitor Phillip's suite, at her request. That tape nails the trainer for the killing, because either way it goes down the police find another vial of the stuff in his room. Something I'm sure you anticipated. He'll tell a story about being in bed with you and Lynn, but you'll both hide behind your lawyers and claim this couldn't be further from the truth. Then Lynn will admit to an affair with the guy—his looks being a big part of your recruitment criteria, after all—which establishes motive and seals his fate."

Nicole was shaking her head, with a complicated little grin designed to throw Merrill off his game.

It didn't.

"Last night the police get an anonymous call that something is wrong in Phillip Valentine's suite. The same caller fingered your boy."

"I was in Reno on business. You can check that."

"Easy enough to arrange."

Her smile vanished, replaced by the same staccato shaking of her head, an urgent plea of denial.

"I can't believe this is happening."

"The police have asked me if I have any video from the stairwell or the hall."

"What did you tell them?"

"I told them I'd review the footage and let them know."

Merrill again allowed the silence to set the stage for what was to come. The way he had phrased his answer was a deliberate opening of a door to her possible salvation. He leaned back and watched his prey squirm in her seat, as comfortable in the moment as a seasoned prosecutor setting up a witness for the kill.

"What does that mean?" asked Nicole without looking up.

"That's up to you. Because I do, indeed, have it all on tape. Not just Wolf in the suite, either. I have you negotiating the deal in his room, I have you and Lynn planning it all in hers. I even have you in Phillips bathroom night before last, though one can't quite make out what you're doing when you open that drawer."

Merrill could now see the strain on her face. The ice queen was cracking, and he had more ice picks in his bag.

"It may very well be that we are on the same page."

She inhaled deeply. "That would be fortunate for all involved."

He slid the inside of his lips over his front teeth nervously, squinting. She could tell a bomb was forthcoming.

"I know who you are. Your name is Charleen Spence."

A bomb, indeed. She closed her eyes, as if it were suddenly over.

"I ran your prints. You're not officially an employee of the hotel, and because Lynn pays you personally it didn't come up. At first at least. But when Lynn asked me not to run you, curiosity got the better of me. I know you work for the Germano family out of Miami. You're a very bad little girl."

Nicole, now Charleen, said nothing.

"You're here to move Mancuso out. Does Lynn know?"

"Yes."

"And she approves? Trading one devil for another?"

"If the new devil puts her husband in the ground, yes."

"Which is precisely what you did, isn't it."

Again she remained motionless.

"Is Wolf a hitter?"

"No. Wolf's a mark."

"Not healthy to set up a real hitter, is it."

"I needed a face. None of the real guys look that good. And you're right, that'd be bad business. I'm not stupid."

Merrill shifted in his seat, audibly inhaling. A subtle shift that Nicole—once Carolyn, then Renee, then Nicole, now openly Charleen—easily perceived.

"Lou Mancuso has been sucking the blood out of this business for the past three years," said Merrill. "That's after he took the life of an innocent little girl and corrupted the souls of the two people who loved her most. He's a cancer, consuming more and more of the host flesh until it dies."

He paused, emotion gripping his throat. He waited for it to pass, then said, "I can't let that happen."

She squinted at him, as if he had morphed into something she didn't understand. Then she smiled, something evil having come alive inside her.

"You're in love with her."

He drew a deep breath, his eyes falling away.

"So what are you saying?" she went on.

"I'm saying I want what you want. I want Mancuso out. And if that means replacing one devil with another, so be it. Without that video, Wolf will eventually lead the bloodhounds to Lynn, and then to you. I'm offering to stop that."

"And how will you do that? Your tapes prove our complicity."

"I'll do it by selling these videos to you. All of them. With them, you can pressure Lynn to sign on with team Germano. Other than Wolf's word, the videos are all that ties her to Phillip's death. Then you and Lynn can set up shop with whoever you want."

"You said *sell* the videos."

"I need to finance an early retirement."

The woman formerly known as Nicole whistled softly, in and out, her brain processing rapidly.

"How much?"

"I think the cash you were intending to pay Wolf will suffice."

"He already has it."

"What am I, stupid? Lynn withheld it. Remember when he paused to look at the picture on counter? That was one of Lynn's little tests. She wasn't going to pay him until he told her what was on Phillip's hat in that picture. Her way of insuring he did, in fact, go into the suite."

Charleen chuckled softly and shook her head. The laugh dissolved into further contemplation as the car neared the end of the strip, turning off toward the Las Vegas Hilton. She remained in that position long after the limo turned around and again turned onto Las Vegas Boulevard, heading south, back toward Xanadu.

"I'll have to check with her. It's her dime."

"Of course."

"She won't like it that you're betraying her."

"I'm saving her life. Tell her that, too."

She considered that a moment, her eyes distant.

"Provided she approves, I'll accept your offer, with one contingency. Something I want you to handle discreetly."

"I'm listening."

"Wolf is problematic. As long as he's insisting that he's been set up, there'll be someone considering the possibility that it's true. If you position it as a crime of passion, that he was trying to eliminate his lover's husband, then you open all sorts of avenues that could resolve this issue."

"Go on."

"Is he in custody?"

"He was released this morning."

She turned toward him, putting her hand on his leg. "What if the betrayed lover can't handle the heat? What if the poor man commits suicide in a fit of drug-fueled self-pity? He's nailed dead to rights on the frame, and Lynn is turning her back on him to save herself. That's plenty of motivation."

"For what?"

She paused for effect. "For him to commit suicide."

Merrill had trouble holding her gaze. Evil this pure burns the eyes when you stare at it too long. Even to a grizzled veteran of the Las Vegas strip wars who had seen everything and done more. Everything, that is, except murder.

She leaned closer. "A swan dive off the roof of Xanadu. A perfect solution to everything that's in our way."

She extended her hand, a businesslike sealing of the deal. He stared at it, forcing his face to remain stoic.

"I have something I want from him first. I'll let you know when."

"After I get paid."

That smile again, chilling his flesh.

"Of course," she said, as if the proposition was sexual.

Merrill nodded, happy to have the time to arrange what needed to be done. He took her hand and shook firmly, his own deal with the devil now sealed.

He was not surprised to find her touch to be cold.

39

I was marched unceremoniously through the casino and then the lobby, hands cuffed behind me, out the front door, and into an unmarked LVPD sedan commanded by the two suits. The black-and-white followed as we drove to police headquarters and what would be an interesting session of Q&A. They had read me my rights in the elevator on the way down, and had been nothing short of by-the-book on the way to the car.

That's when, as Sherman had put it, the wheels came off.

The larger suit with the blank expression suddenly turned into Matt Lauer. He pivoted in his seat, the seams of his suit jacket stretched taut, his expression smug. Sweat beaded on his upper lip, making it easy to look away.

"So, what do we call you, eh? Wolfman? Pretty boy?"

"Three words," I said. "Low fat diet."

The big guy shot the little guy, who was driving, a commiserating look. But the little guy didn't crack a smile.

"Mouth like that, I'm surprised you made it this far."

"Don't I get to call a lawyer or something? I think I heard that."

"Sure you do. I was thinkin' maybe you'd like to sing us a song now, make things easier on everyone."

"Do I *look* stupid to you?"

"Well, you don't look scared. *That's* interesting."

"You want I should puke here in your car? I can do that."

"I'd rather you just told us what happened. Let us help."

"Right. Guess I *do* look stupid to you."

Another exchange of glances, the big man seeking the little man's approval. It came in the form of silence.

"Mr. Valentine comes home after midnight. Relaxes, opens a V8, gives himself his weekly injection. Ten minutes later he's calling 9-1-1. Medics arrive, the guy's stone dead. M.E. comes in, and based on the evidence suspects arsenic poisoning, probably a massive injection."

I smiled, just to piss him off. "What evidence?"

"For starters, the place smelled like garlic. Blood-red piss in the guy's pants. Actual cause of death was him choking on his own vomit. M.E.'d seen it before, he says arsenic."

"I'm dying to hear how this relates to me."

"Funny choice of words, there."

"Hey, I'm here all week."

Big Man's eyes narrowed, tired of me one-upping him.

"Anonymous caller says you and the vic weren't exactly having sleepovers."

Chad Merrill. No surprise there.

He reached down, then held up a plastic sandwich bag, inside of which was a vial I'd seen before. The plop of acid in my stomach was almost audible.

"Did we mention we had a warrant to search your room?"

He put on a pair of frameless glasses and squinted.

"Depo-Testosterone, prescribed for Phillip Valentine."

He folded the glasses back up and pocketed them, returning his attention to me.

"So we're wondering two things at this point. One, how did it come to be in your suitcase? And two, why were you checking out of the hotel at five in the morning?"

"An anonymous caller told me to get out of dodge."

I could feel the heat assaulting my cheeks, wondering what shade of red I had turned.

"I don't think so. Any other wisecracks, Mr. Wolfman?"

"You know that South Beach Diet? You should try it, make you feel like a new man."

He turned to his partner. "He don't seem too worried."

"Shut it, Vince," said the partner.

"I'm just sayin', an innocent man, he's scared shitless. He's not making cracks that might get him a broken rib."

My interrogator turned back to face me.

"You fucking the man's wife, Wolf?"

"Shut it, Vince," I echoed.

"I mean, Jesus, who wouldn't want some of that, you know?"

We locked eyes. It was easy to stare him down with a smile, because his gambit was obvious. They had nothing. They had an anonymous call that was not so anonymous as far as I was concerned, and they had the vial of Phillip Valentine's testosterone. I had some explaining to do, but it wasn't enough to hold me. Especially when one of Sherman's lawyers arrived to bail my ass out of this mess.

I watched the sweaty man's arrogance bleed away like air seeping from a child's balloon. Apparently he decided there was nothing more to be gained by our little give-and-take, so with a snort and a shaking head he turned back to face forward, leaving me to contemplate my next move.

Unfortunately, I didn't have a clue what that might be.

40

I sat in a concrete box the color of green olives until seven o'clock, the hour at which I was supposed to be taking possession of one million of Lynn Valentine's dollars. The scent of bacon wafted through the station, the thought of which made me nauseous. I imagined the guards chowing down on omelets and toast while the prisoners slurped runny oatmeal and coffee the consistency of crankcase oil. It wouldn't have surprised me if they had a Keno girl on the premises.

I had given the admitting officer Sherman Wissbaum's name and private telephone number, without mentioning that he was a Special Agent for the FBI. No one else had tried to interrogate me, nor had anyone arrived with a platter of that special institutional oatmeal. Which meant I had ample time to process it all, which was the true source of my gastric distress.

I was in the deepest shit of my life, and I had swum in some pretty smelly waters in my time.

My dark reverie was interrupted by the hollow sound of footsteps on the linoleum floor. I heard a key sliding into the lock—there were no bars, just a solid metal door that matched the gastrointestinal shade of the walls—and looked up to see a small entourage standing at the threshold. A man emerged from their midst, wearing a crisp suit and sleeves sporting cuff links. Prettier than me—I love it when that happens—cockier than the cops who brought me here. I was never so happy to see someone I would normally make fun of.

He approached, and with a hand on my upper arm guided me to my feet. With the others behind him it was easy to mask his words. He spoke softly, but with deliberate clarity, almost a whisper.

"I'm your lawyer."

And that was it. Not another word was exchanged as we navigated what seemed like a labyrinthine series of hallways and locked doors, finally emerging into a parking lot flooded with sunshine.

Across the lot was a black Lincoln Town Car. The back door was open, and I knew it was for me.

TWO men waited in the front seat, the first clue that my rescuer had never seen the inside of a law school. My supposed lawyer—he looked a little too much like one of the Baldwin brothers for my comfort level—held the door and closed it after I got in, then went around and got into the backseat next to me. The scent of cologne quickly overwhelmed the interior.

I almost made a crack about Sherman being too busy to come, but stopped myself. The FBI didn't spring for rides like this, and no agent in the history of criminology had worn gold cuff links the size of walnuts.

"Do you know who I am?" he asked.

While he did look vaguely familiar, I was more certain about the guy in the passenger seat up front. I'd seen him around the hotel with a small coiled wire coming out of his ear, standing watch in front of rooms not open to the general public. Which, given the circumstances, was not necessarily a good thing.

I shook my head. Any tendency to spice things up with a few edgy bon mots was diluted by the context at hand: I had been rescued by the wrong team.

The pretty guy bit at his lower lip thoughtfully, as if trying to make up his mind about something.

"I'm not your lawyer," he finally said.

"Had a hunch."

"It's in your best interest to behave as though I was. Which means, you tell me everything you know, even what you don't know, so that I can work on your behalf."

This could mean anything. He could be one of Lynn's foot soldiers, sent to whisk me away to safety before her name came up downtown. In that same capacity he might have been instructed to dispatch me in some unpleasant way. The woman, after all, had a thing about her men writhing in pain. Or, he might be one of Renee's goons, a junior rogue agent already dressing the part of a player, bailing me out of the shitter as part of his oath to serve God and country and the ghost of J. Edgar Hoover.

Not a chance. This guy smelled like the president of the Frank Sinatra fan club.

"My name is Bradley Pascarella."

That was supposed to ring a bell, and it did. He was the muscle backing Phillip Valentine's title, the Chief Operating Goombah, the first lieutenant in the kingdom. The guy who made things happen at Xanadu, some of which never found their way to the balance sheet. I had been warned about him by no less than three people, only one of whom I actually trusted.

"Can we stop for breakfast?" I asked.

"Absolutely. Right after we have a little dialogue."

"Had that feeling, too."

Bradley Pascarella suddenly whipped a backhand across my face. It felt as if he'd pushed my nose to the back of my skull, the burn radiating outward in waves that made me want to bite off my tongue. I cupped my face in my hands, and when I looked up I saw that they were covered with blood. It would be the third time my nose had been broken.

He was adjusting a cuff link, as if the motion of the blow had disturbed the symmetry of his fashion. The guy in front had produced a very large handgun, which was pointed directly at my head in case I wanted to engage in the aforementioned dialogue right here. Were it not for the gun, that would have *been* fine, too. Just like Bruce Willis, I knew I could take this clown.

"A little warm-up," he said. He offered his handkerchief, embroidered with his initials, the ironed creases of which were still crisp. Smelled like a department store Polo counter. We were heading east, away from the Strip, toward the brown hills bordering the desert beyond.

Not a good thing for the Wolfman.

If ever there was a time a guy needed a federally reengineered Droid phone with a range of up to twelve feet, it was now.

41

Not long after it was certain we'd officially driven out of the city, the Lincoln turned onto a dirt road that wound toward some minor hills. About a quarter mile ahead I saw a collection of old buildings which could have been trailers, what appeared to be a barn, and the remains of hundreds of eviscerated cars. A salvage yard, something from a John Carpenter movie, where bad things happen.

A guy appeared out of nowhere and slid open a huge set of double doors leading into the barn. A huge pile of tires was visible on either side of the building, which wasn't a barn at all. It was the place where cars met their maker in the jaws of a crushing device that could compress a Buick to the size of a toilet in about three seconds.

Speaking of Buicks, an '85 Electra station wagon was parked in front of the machine that would swallow it whole. Its tires were gone, the condemned having been looted of all remaining value.

The two front seat thugs quickly got out of the Town Car. This had been carefully choreographed, no conversation required. One of them opened my door and the other grabbed my arm and pulled me out. When we began moving toward the Buick I tried to shake loose—let it not be said that Wolfgang Schmitt goes down without a fight—but within seconds I was on the ground with a Florsheim planted on the back of my head. Which was a convenient position for someone to strap my wrists together with a set of plastic cuffs, the kind you have to cut off after the torture has lost its edge. The floor was concrete creased with faults, but had not been swept since the Eisenhower years and was therefore more akin to a sawdust pit. The place smelled like a typical garage, heavy on the burned rubber.

I was then hauled back to my feet and unceremoniously dragged toward the open door of the Electra, where I was inserted behind the wheel, my head smacking the top of the door frame along the way.

Bradley Pascarella put his hands where the window used to be and leaned down.

"Sorry about all the drama," he said.

"Not half as sorry as me," I replied.

"Guy like you, someone with balls, ya gotta be creative, know what I'm sayin'?"

"I do," I said back, my voice sounding like someone with a bad cold thanks to the fracture in my nose. "But this has holes all over it."

He cocked his head, smiling slightly. "How so?"

"You show up at the station, posing as my lawyer. I go missing, they know who took me. Guy like you, someone with balls, you're easy to find in a town like this. My guess is you're a bona fide personality already."

He nodded, casting a quick glance to his compadres to share the moment. Then back to me.

This one made him really smile.

"See that guy over there?"

I turned my head to see who he was talking about. It

was the guy who had driven the Town Car, the one who had dragged me out of it moments earlier. He returned my gaze with slitted eyes.

"He's a lawyer. For real. Ain't that the shit?"

"Well I'll be."

"From out of town, too. So you see, Wolf, there aren't any holes. Anything else I should know about? I'm all ears."

The smug bastard.

"I'm hoping," I said, "that sooner or later, and sooner would be good, you'll ask me a question or something."

He stepped back, nodding to someone off stage. An ear-splitting sound engaged, and the car began moving forward on its rims, up a slight ramp, then onto a platform. It sounded like railroad cars being pulled over a grate. Gears shifted, the ambiance dropped, and the platform began to lower, stopping so that what had been the floor was now at my eye level.

I looked up to see Pascarella, gazing down at me.

"You ready for your question now, Wolf?"

"Fire away, Bradley."

"Who you workin' for?"

"Lynn Valentine."

"She hired you to kill Mister Valentine?"

"She hired me to help her with her abs."

Pascarella once again nodded to the unseen bit player with his hand on a switch. The sides of the box in which I was sitting began to compress, clamping onto the side panels of the Buick. Very hard on the paint. They kept on compressing until they crushed the door panels like candy wrappers. The first thing to crack in half on the inside of the car was the dashboard, right before my eyes. One of the radio knobs shot off, barely missing my face. Then the windshield exploded, showering the interior with a million tumbling diamonds.

My eyes were closed, so I didn't see him nod to stop the presses.

"You killed Phillip Valentine," he said.

"No fucking way," I said back.

"The good folks with the shiny badges think you did."

"No. Slow down so we can talk. You got this wrong."

Another nod, another jolt of sound and motion. The car began to cave in on itself, forcing me to the middle of the seat, which was buckling beneath me. After a moment the roof snapped downward, striking my shoulder so that I was forced to lean to one side. The steering column suddenly shifted, the wheel slamming into my rib cage on the left, as the passenger door cracked at its hinges and swung inward until it touched my right shoulder.

Then it stopped. One more note and the dance was over.

I was breathing rapidly, as fear tends to do to someone who has never ridden a Buick into a car-compressing machine before. The expression on my face, the purest form of pain and terror, was the real thing. I almost forgot that the guy had broken my nose. That was the least of my problems now.

"Stop it, I'll talk!" I screamed, intensely enough to score the skin on the inside of my throat.

Pascarella bent down to a catcher's stance. His voice was infuriatingly calm. "Who's paying you?"

All bets were off. It was every rogue agent for themselves. All I was risking was a million-dollar payday.

"I was hired by Nicole."

"Who's she working for?"

"I was assuming Lynn Valentine. That's how it played."

"On behalf of whom?"

"I don't understand the question."

"But you do understand what will happen to you if I tell him to hit that button one more time."

I nodded. I was fresh out of Denis Leary bluster.

"Who's backing Lynn Valentine?"

I took a few badly needed breaths. "Nobody. At least as far as I know. The woman is obsessed with the death of her daughter, and she thinks it's her husband's fault. That's it. If you've ever crossed a woman you'd know how that works."

He nodded slightly in a moment of commiseration.

"That's all I know."

"I think there's more."

"Then ask Nicole. If you're right, it's her thing. I'm just here to give Mrs. Valentine what she wanted."

"So you're a killer, right, Wolf?" He was grinning widely.

"Looks like I am now."

He thought a moment, weighing it all. "What if I told you Nicole was in the trunk of this car?"

"Then I'd say she better speak up fast."

"You're saying you did kill Mister Valentine, at Mrs. Valentine's behest. You're admitting that."

Strange, hearing this palooka use the word behest.

Another deep breath. It was hard work balancing terror and anger at the same time. Nonetheless, it occurred to me that he looked more like the fat Baldwin brother than either of the pretty ones.

"Listen to me. I didn't switch the vials. I was supposed to, but I didn't do it. I wanted the money and I wanted out. I'm guilty of conning her, nothing else. She thinks I planted the vial, I get the money, I'm gone. Someone else poisoned the guy. I was the patsy all along. I knew it, so I went for the money. That's it."

I choked on the next words.

"I swear on my mother."

Pascarella nodded, a bit sadly this time. He stared at me for many seconds, igniting the slimmest of hopes that he was buying my version of things. Which was mostly the truth.

"Funny you should say that," he said.

A cold wave of panic washed over my already extended nervous system as Pascarella reached inside his coat pocket. He produced a photograph, staring at it for a moment before leaning down and holding it to the shell of the window where I could see it.

It was my mother, sitting at a card table with some other women at the nursing home where I had left her in Portland. She looked confused. And very alone.

"Your cover stinks like day-old gefilte fish, but your story is too chicken-shit to be anything but true. I don't know who you are or why you're here, other than you're a bottom-feeder looking to make a quick buck. *That* much, I buy."

"That about sums it up, yeah."

"Just a guy with a hard-on for a lady with an agenda."

"Right again, Brad."

He smiled. Thought a moment.

"I'm gonna offer you a shot. Consider your employment status transferred to me."

I had a feeling Sherlock would like that just fine.

He nodded again. The same sound effects, only in reverse this time. The car raised back up, stopping when the two floor surfaces were level. One of the thugs reached through the crushed door, turning me slightly to extend an arm behind me and slice off the restraints. I guess all of them carried knives.

"You ever seen a nursing-home fire, Wolf? Swear to God, it's the ugliest freakin' mess. It's terrible."

"Point made," I said, suddenly in no mood for snarky humor.

"You go back to Xanadu. You're gonna want to run, find a real lawyer, do this by the book. But remember who has a snapshot of your mother. See this through, it all goes away, including the murder rap they're trying to pin on you. You tell Lynn Valentine and your friend Nicole that the police just wanted to question you, then they let you go. That's actually the truth, isn't it. Tell them you're scared shitless, which is also true. Tell them it's your ass on the line now—true again—and you want in on their deal or you'll go back and answer some more questions. Convince them you're still their boy. Get them to talk to you."

All I could do was nod. I was still in the car, and the only way out was through what used to be a window.

"Find out who's backing them. That's all. Easy game. Just find that out. You keep whatever money they've paid you, and you get to go home to your mother."

They began walking away.

"I told you, Lynn was in this for blood. What makes you so sure there's more?"

Pascarella just raised a hand. One of the thugs opened the back door for him, and he folded himself neatly inside without another look in my direction.

"Hey, a little help?" I called.

The Town Car fired up and backed out, leaving me to—literally—crawl through cut glass. Once I was out I went to the trunk, which had compressed and folded inward, opening a portal to the interior.

No Nicole. I was almost relieved.

42

It took awhile, but I finally realized the late-model Honda Civic parked near the crumbling building was intended for my use. It didn't make sense that Pascarella would send me off on assignment by leaving me stranded fifteen miles from town, and it was this sudden realization that made the car pop out from the depressing environment of the wrecking yard. The keys were on the seat, the tank was half full, the smell was month-old gym socks with just the slightest hint of urine. Probably stolen, but that was someone else's problem today.

Other than the contents of my suitcase being strewn over the bed, my room at Xanadu was just as I'd left it. In spite of an overwhelming desire to take a shower, I had an even stronger need to hear the sweet voice of Special Agent Sherman Wissbaum. I'd half expected him to be waiting in my room upon my return, or at least to find a spanking-new magic Droid under my pillow. All that was there was a pair of my briefs.

My first call was to his office at the regional FBI center in Seattle. It was Sunday, a day of rest for all federal employees, so no one with a pulse answered at the switchboard. I knew his extension so I left a message, the tone of which was something short of cordial. At this point the need for candor superseded the covert state of my assignment, so I used my laptop to e-mail Sherlock with the following: *"Call me, call me now, the bottom has fallen out, mayday, S.O.S., 9-1-1, could use a little help here, NOW! Have a nice day."*

My head was spinning. The shower didn't help, but it was something to do and absolutely necessary if I was to venture forth into the real world in search of a few answers. Which I absolutely intended to do. Lynn had some serious explaining to do, regardless of the fresh state of her widowhood. The bitch formerly known as Renee had even more questions to answer, provided I could keep my cool while I choked them out of her. As long as I didn't run into Phillip's six-foot-nine bodyguard from the weight room, I liked my chances of getting through the day without someone dying, either way.

There was one more base I had to cover before I went on the attack. I called the nursing home in Portland where my mother was playing cruise director. A dull-witted weekend receptionist put me on hold for two minutes—she sounded more like one of the patients, actually—then returned to inform me that my mother was asleep, and to call back the next day if I had any questions about her condition.

It was less than five seconds after I hung up when the telephone rang, sending a jolt through my cardiovascular system that in calmer times would have caused me to find a quick chair. Today it just pissed me off.

It was Renee, her voice unusually warm, as if nothing had happened. She even asked how I was doing, to which I simply responded with a chipper lyric, "Other than a broken nose, I'm fine . . . you?" She asked if I could meet her for coffee in the Denny's up the strip next to the Venetian in thirty minutes. I told her to make it fifteen and bolted out the door.

* * *

I was in a back booth when she arrived wearing jeans tucked into black boots and a fluffy white blouse, her hair tied back. She looked like a junior league wife meeting one of the girls for a quick bite before meeting with her divorce attorney. Only with a switchblade in her bag.

I had no idea what I would say. If I would tell her I knew about her street life as Charleen Spence, or if I would play dumb and see what transpired. The former would be satisfying if for nothing more than the expression on her face, but there was no turning back from it. The dumb route was the ticket, a ruse she would easily believe from me.

She slid into the booth, smiling innocently, her eyes on my red, bulbous nose.

"That's gotta hurt," she said.

I didn't smile back. "My condolences on the death of your boss's husband."

The shift-weary waitress arrived with two water glasses, offering coffee. My date took her up on it, I ordered the Grand Slam, extra syrup.

"We have a lot to discuss," I said as we watched the waitress depart.

"You have no idea," she said, her expression dark. "My guess is you don't know which end is up, who to trust, who fucked who. Am I close?"

"Couldn't be more wrong. I know exactly who not to trust. And as to who got fucked, that would be me."

The coffee arrived. The waitress came and went.

As she took a sip she said over the rim of the cup, "You think it was me who screwed you."

"Wouldn't you think it was you?"

"I spoke with Chad Merrill this morning. You'll be interested in hearing what he has to say. He says he has video of the whole thing."

I couldn't help choking on the sip of water I was taking.

"There's a shocker. How'd I look?"

"He has a video on file of Lynn in Phillip's suite yesterday afternoon, switching out his medicine. Wearing gloves. About four hours before you were there."

It was safe to say I didn't believe this for a second.

"And she'd do that because . . ."

"Because she doesn't trust you. She doesn't trust anybody. So if you switch teams, decide to not swap out his bottle with the one I gave you, he still injects the poison. And you're still on video, nailed to the wall."

It was a setup all along.

"Good to know," I said softly. "Of course she'll deny it when I ask for my million dollars, which gets me exactly nowhere. I prefer to have more options."

"I don't think she was planning on paying you today. I think she assumed you'd be sharing a cell with someone who thinks you're even prettier than she does. Someone made an anonymous call to the police, you know, fingering you."

"My money's on Thumbless Joe. Guy's good with his fingers. What's his story, by the way?"

"Just a rumor, but supposedly he used to deal pai gow and got caught with the thumb he used to have in the cookie jar. Same rumor says Phillip beat him unconscious and then cut off his thumbs with a steak knife. Lynn hired him back for big money to prevent him from going to the authorities."

"A paradox, our Mrs. Valentine."

"You know what this means, Wolf." She took another sip, speaking over the rim of her cup. "It means mission accomplished. Congratulations, my people are pleased."

Holy shit. She still believed I was buying her role as a federal mole. Which, in turn, means she knew I might not swap the vial, in which case she's the one advising Lynn to create that little contingency plan. God, I wished I had a bugged Droid phone right about then.

"Thanks. Will your people still pay me the million?"

A bluff for a bluff. She doesn't know I know who she's

really working for, she thinks I think she's a Fed, which makes my inquiry legit.

"You get your Cayman money back. That should count for something. Maybe we can come up with something else."

Yeah, like a long vacation in the Mojave desert, about six feet south of the sand.

The waitress swung by with a refill. We paused as we watched her work her magic, patiently awaiting her departure.

"So I get to go home now."

She sipped again, thoughtfully this time. "Not quite yet."

That was the sound of the other shoe dropping.

"Lynn will sing once we get that video from Merrill, which he'll happily fork over. He was Phillip's man first and foremost, and he's pretty upset. Which is half the battle here. We have a shot at the big fish, and we'd like you to land him for us."

"You mean be the bait is more like it."

"Whatever. You do the bait thing very well."

Bait *and* switch, actually, but that's another story.

She set the cup down delicately and leaned over the table. This would be the good part, on final approach.

"Lou Mancuso will be very concerned about Phillip's death. They had an arrangement, one that Lynn never signed off on. There's history there, and it's dark. He'll want to make changes. That's where you come in."

I pretended to think about that for a moment.

"As the guy in first place in the *who-killed-Phillip-Valentine* sweepstakes, I don't think he'll send a car for me."

"That's exactly what he'll do. Your job will be to talk fast before he pries off your toenails with a lobster fork."

Not quite, but she had the idea. Lobster fork, car crusher . . . it was all the same to me at this point.

"I'd rather just go home. You can keep your money."

She took a sip of coffee, smiling through it.

"You'll have a copy of the video showing Lynn doing the switch. That will get his attention. That video will make her popular down at the D.A.'s office, and you'll tell Mancuso that you're there to offer her to him, on a platter, in return for the million she stiffed you for."

"What's to prevent him from feeding me to his Rottweiler and just take the tape? That sounds cheaper."

"The promise of your testimony. Think about it, he can't just come forward with the tape and get what he wants. He needs you to run point."

"Why isn't Chad Merrill the starting point guard here?"

"Mr. Merrill has already made a deal and is looking at early retirement."

"Deal with who?"

"With us. It's how we're going to get the tape."

"And where's Lynn while all this is going down?"

"In our custody. It'll look like she's taken flight. All of which gives Mancuso precisely what he wants."

"Which is?"

"An open door for Brad Pascarella to take over the operation. He's running it anyway, this just puts the lid on any future stockholder dissent. Pascarella comes forward with a buyout offer, which given Lynn's predicament will look very attractive to the other stockholders."

"Wait . . . stockholders? I thought the Valentines owned it free and clear."

"No. They were a front to keep the gaming regulators happy. The majority of the shares are owned by investment entities controlled by Lou Mancuso."

The Grand Slam breakfast arrived in all its coagulated glory. Two thousand calories of pure carbohydrate heaven, seasoned with over a hundred grams of animal fat. With extra syrup.

I stuffed the first half of a sausage link into my mouth and said, "So how does this set him up for you? I'm not wearing a wire to Mancuso's, if that's what you're suggesting."

"No. They'll check for that. You'll set up a meeting to deliver the video file on a thumb drive. Which will be coded to reveal an IP address once they play it. They won't check for that."

I chewed. On the sausage and on her plan. If either weren't so coated with slime, they would both be brilliant.

"Quick question."

Her smile was positively affectionate. She thought she had me right where she wanted me, which was dead center beneath the heel of her boot.

"You're entitled."

"How does that get me off the hook with the police? When they said don't leave town, I took that to mean they'd be back when they had my balls in a sling."

She shook her head, snorting a little laugh.

"Wolf, think it through. You're undercover for the federal government. One phone call from us, you're off the radar. You'll have to testify, of course, if it ever gets to that point. And if that doesn't make you feel better, there's footage of you in the suite, clearly showing that you didn't make the switch."

She paused for a cocky swagger with her head.

"Anything else?"

A bite of hash browns this time. "No, I'm good."

And I was. The game was back on, with higher stakes than ever. Nothing smothers the smell of manure better than the smell of the barn burning down.

And all of it played right into Bradley Pascarella's greasy little hands. When he heard I had the videos he would literally kill for, with the added benefit of my assistance in bringing down the lady of the house, he'd drive me to Lou Mancuso personally.

Never mind I'd be tied up in the trunk at the time.

My only challenge now was getting Sherlock back in the Loop, and soon. There were enough loose ends flopping around in the air to shut down. Until then I was flying solo, without a parachute. Hell, without an airplane, was more like it.

43

The tall man with the long eyelashes left the restaurant first. Three minutes later, after finishing her coffee and picking at the remnants of the man's unfinished breakfast, the flashy ash blonde with the tight jeans also left, a cell phone already affixed to her ear.

A nondescript middle-aged woman sat at a booth near the door, with a clear line of sight toward the table where the two beautiful people had just shared breakfast and what was obviously a very meaningful conversation. More important than the line of sight, however, was the line of access for a directional microphone hidden in her bag, which rested on the tabletop pointed directly at them.

When they were gone, the woman, selected for her keen ability to blend invisibly into a crowd, pivoted the purse toward her, then leaned down looking at her watch as she spoke with a very soft voice.

"Nine-zero-four hours. Subjects departed. Observation terminated. Hope you got it."

She then put the purse on the floor between her feet, turning her attention to the morning paper in front of her, which until now had been nothing more than a prop.

ROUGHLY a mile away, Chad Merrill sat in the Xanadu security ops center located directly above the casino floor. He was in his private suite, the door locked, headphones over his ears. He'd just listened to Charleen Spence's dialogue with Wolf, watching the levels to be sure the digital recorders were capturing it all.

He had intercepted the telephone call to Wolf's suite that had started it all. Charleen would have known he'd hear the call, but she had no choice if she wanted to contact Wolf before he left his room for who knows where, and she'd selected what she believed to be a secure location for their meeting.

That part made him smile. But what he heard had made him laugh. It had been so much more rewarding than what he'd expected. Bullshit had never sounded so compelling.

He punched a key that terminated the recording. Then he removed the headphones, picked up the telephone, and punched in a number from memory. Moments later he spoke quietly.

"It's all going down. You're good to go."

He hung up, a smile of satisfaction on his face as he leaned back and closed his eyes.

It was a good day to get rich at Xanadu. And it would get nothing but better.

CHARLEEN Spence went directly from her coffee with Wolf at Denny's to a FedEx Office store on Hughes Center Drive, catching a cab for the two-mile hop. There she grabbed one of the rental PCs for the twenty-cents-per-minute Internet access, punching in a Yahoo mail account that was so anonymous and deeply buried among tens of millions of other largely anonymous users that it was considered secure. Only two people on the planet knew the account existed, one in Nevada and one in Florida, and unless the Feds employed someone to read all one hundred million Yahoo e-mails sent out daily, there was no problem. Nonetheless, the tendency to be cryptic was in their DNA.

HEY babe—thought you'd like to know things are working out well here. First phase complete, the wicked witch dead. Better outcome than we hoped because of an unexpected avenue of opportunity where phase two is concerned. Timeline is urgent, as in, tomorrow. Need your best cleanup hitter out here ASAP. Throwing a party for your special friend, need the piñata shattered on-site. There's a vendor involved, same guy who catered phase one, who needs a serious pink slip as well, same time same place. Please advise, it's moving fast. Lovies.

44

One would think the chances of Lynn Valentine seeing me unannounced would be lower than a John Edwards nomination for, well, anything. It wasn't exactly like I was family—that very morning I'd been taken in for questioning regarding her husband's sudden death. Which she was rather hoping would not be so sudden, which I'm sure had her completely confused.

I'd know soon enough.

A steroid-infused doorman allowed me in without a word. This was, I realized, where all the undrafted linemen of the past two decades came to work.

Lynn was sitting in front of the 18-foot floor-to-ceiling glass wall that overlooked the Kingdom of Sin, enveloped in a chair with her legs crossed, a glass of red wine in her hand. She wore a smart black pants suit, her hair tied back with a shimmering silver scarf that matched her belt and shoes. She wore huge sunglasses to mask her grief from the staff.

Or to hide the fact that she was nervous.

She didn't look at me as I entered her field of vision. I took a seat across from her, remaining respectfully silent. We were quite alone, other than the absolute certainty that Chad Merrill was listening in. I was tempted to wave, but I had no idea where the cameras were hidden. Perhaps it was good that Lynn didn't know, either.

"What did the police say to you?" she asked, still not meeting my eyes.

"They strongly suggested that I not leave town," I replied.

"Have *you* spoken to Nicole?"

I swallowed hard. Lynn was fond of little pop quizzes.

"No."

I was keeping my options open here. If I ratted Nicole out to Lynn, that would sabotage her agenda to gain control of the hotel as Lynn's ally. Which didn't serve my goals, because I needed that agenda to proceed unhindered in order to give Sherlock something to work with.

Lynn took a slow sip, holding the rim of the glass against her lower lip as she shifted her gaze to me.

"I don't know quite what to say to you. Let's start with why you're here."

"Let's start with my million dollars."

Her laugh was shallow. "You didn't do what I hired you to do."

"I think we need to clear the air here," I said. "You think I crossed you. I didn't. Why would I?"

She shifted in her seat. "Really? I was under the impression it was you who put the vial of poison in his drawer. That this was precisely what you came here for, and why I was paying you, only with a different outcome."

"The vial was given to me by *you*. Through your proxy, which legally is still you. Which means you're accountable for its contents."

"You could have switched it out."

"Right. And jeopardized my money. Because . . . ?" I added a pair of upturned palms and shrugged shoulders to make my point. "You're the second person today who thinks I look stupid."

A smug grin emerged. "Because a third party is paying you more than I am."

"That's ridiculous."

"Is it? Tell me."

"You're suggesting that someone else wanted your husband dead, and that they paid me to kill him quickly instead of the slow painful demise you'd paid for. And that there was some upside in that for someone. I'd say that's pretty out there, far enough to qualify as ridiculous."

She just stared at me.

"Sounds to me like I'm the one getting set up here. That's the only non-ridiculous motive available."

She took a sip, set the glass down gently.

"What are you saying?" she finally said.

"I'm saying whoever gave you the vial is responsible for Phillip's death. That someone is protecting you in this thing."

She paused. "Nicole."

"I was thinking Chad Merrill."

She waved that one off.

"Have you spoken to Nicole?"

"We're meeting this afternoon. What possible reason would she have for shortcutting my intentions, other than protecting you? Dead is dead."

I took a deep breath, to show that I was about to break open a new can of worms.

"Maybe she's working for someone else," I suggested. "Someone who wants you alive and well enough to sell the hotel you now own free and clear. Just a thought."

Her eyes drifted. I waited for a response, but it wasn't coming.

"It wasn't me," I continued. "I came here to tell you that. And that I want my money. Then I'll get out of your hair. Disappear. You can tell the story any way you want from there."

I was treading a fine line. It was indeed me who placed a

deadly vial of poison in her husband's nightstand, especially from her point of view. And the man was dead, which was also the expectation. So in saying it wasn't me, I was opening a can of worms that posed more questions than I had the ability to answer. I wondered if it was me in a corner here, or her.

I needed Sherlock back in this, like, now. But he wasn't taking my calls.

She took off her sunglasses and narrowed her eyes, fixing me with a look that reminded me of my mother on Jack Daniels.

"The terms of the arrangement were violated. There's no money, Wolf. Not for you."

I knew precisely what she meant. I leaned forward, lowered my voice. "You're vulnerable right now."

"Not from you, I'm not. You're as good as dead."

"Scary, but I'm not nervous."

"You should be. Alive or dead, I control what happens to you."

I summoned my best cocky smile, allowed it to evolve into a look of genuine concern.

"Let me help you get out of this," I said. "I know about the video of you coming in the room earlier yesterday. Switching the vials. I don't know why, to be honest, but I can make assumptions, and they all have to do with me taking the hit. There's video of the whole thing going down."

I paused before repeating, "So let me help you."

She cocked her head, face twisted. "Why on God's green earth would you want to do that?"

My smile was ironic. "To get paid."

She got to her feet and went to the window.

"I want you out of my hotel."

"Of course. But think about what you're saying. When they try to pin this on me, I'll have no choice but to testify. You hired me to kill your husband. I have more documentation than you know that proves it. You gave me the poison to do it. I'll cut whatever deal they want, in exchange for that video."

"You don't have a video."

"But I know who does."

I found it interesting that she didn't seem to want to know who, in fact, did have the video. This particular silence was telling.

She turned, took a step toward me. Then she threw the content of the wine in my face. A dry pinot noir, very nice. I realized this wasn't just about her husband. It was about us, something unrequited, a hope cast to the ground.

"Never bullshit a bullshitter, Wolf."

I smiled, wiping red from my eyes as I turned to leave. The stain was going to play hell with the carpet, which was the color of wedding cake.

It wasn't my problem anymore.

THE elevator stopped on the tenth floor on my way down to my room to change shirts and retrieve my things. I would dump the entire clusterfuck into Sherlock's lap and go back to Portland. Deal with the significant fallout later. There were certain benefits in working for the Federal government, and I was sure Sherlock would advocate for me when it all came down.

Three men got into the elevator with me. Two had shoulders the width of Freightliners. The other was Chad Merrill.

There was no eye contact. Without a word he put a key into the elevator control panel and opened a small door above it. He pushed a four-digit code into a numeric keypad and closed the door. I noticed the light on the control panel button for the fifth floor, my destination, had gone dim.

I was being hijacked.

At that moment one of the cyborgs grabbed my upper arm with enough force to facilitate a field amputation.

Merrill turned and smiled.

"It's time you and I sat down together," he said. "You don't mind, do you?"

"Hey, as long as you give Quasimodo here a Tic Tac, I'm good."

Merrill shook his head, genuinely amused, as we rode the

elevator down to the second floor, access to which was not among the available options on the panel.

The other guy, however, wasn't amused.

45

We ended up in a small office that had every electronic toy you won't find at Radio Shack. I counted three computers, six flat-screen monitors, a scanner, a bank of digital recorders, and a switching panel that reminded me of the cockpit of an Airbus. Two impossibly comfortable leather chairs swiveled before the bank of images, and a plush matching couch flanked the wall behind, so new the place smelled like a retail coat store. The room was dark, illuminated only by the glow of the screens. I was invited to sit on the couch with a small shove to my spine, while Chad Merrill took one of the chairs. He was smiling casually, as if he did this sort of thing all the time. We were alone, the troops camped just outside the door, no doubt sharing a protein bar.

"Get you anything? Water? Coffee?"

His teeth were yellow, his face weathered, his suit impeccable. The three rudiments of Vegas street cred.

"Got any arsenic?"

He chuckled, not a trace of posturing in evidence.

"Someone recently told me I have a God complex," he said. "I think maybe she was right."

"Really?" I replied dryly. "Because I could use a little divine intervention right about now."

The chuckle became a soft smile. There was a connection between us, indefinable, perhaps dangerous if I misread it.

"You have no idea what's going on here, do you."

"Apparently not. I mean, I thought you were just gonna *whack* me. That the right term these days? Or is that not cool, too Hollywood?"

As he studied me I recalled the primetime casino drama starring James Caan. This was him.

"I was with Lynn last night," he said, "at a charity thing. I would have stopped you if I could have."

From the look on his face, I had the feeling he was considering a quick jab to my jaw. The rope he was giving me had just about played out.

"Lynn pays me to take care of her and her daughter. I do that work happily. All she cares about is getting out of here, and staying in one piece until she can."

I glanced at my watch. "What's your point here, Chad? I've got an appointment with the D.A. Drinks and artichoke dip at Ghostbar. Happy hour."

Merrill sat back, crossing his hands.

"Your friend Nicole believes she and I have congruent interests where the Valentines are concerned. She told you all about that this morning at Denny's. You had the Grand Slam, extra syrup."

I whistled silently, then mouthed the word "Wow." There was something to that comment about a God complex.

His eyes drifted for a brief moment, a crack into his heart. Then he snapped his gaze back, the fissure sealed. His tone was different, urgent now, but softer.

"I care very deeply for Lynn and her daughter. She's in

trouble with this Phillip thing. And you might just be in more trouble than you know."

"Oh, I think I've got my arms around it, thanks."

I was suddenly angry, and had no reason to hold back.

"Listen," I continued, "talk to Lynn or Nicole about how the poison got there. Me, I'm just the dumb ass they're trying to pin it on. You have no idea how . . . *complicated* my role in this is."

"Try me."

"As Lynn's guy, my assumption is you're all over it on her behalf. My guess is you already know precisely who I really am."

He sat back, almost amused at my energy. "You have no idea what I know."

I suddenly realized he was right. So far this conversation had no destination, though I knew one was coming.

"Framing you for Phillip's death doesn't get Mancuso and Pascarella out of Lynn's life. *That's* what I want, Wolf. Even if Nicole brings her people in and take it over, that just trades one hell for another. These guys are all the same breed of asshole."

I pursed my lips, then nodded.

"You're right about that," I said. "Which is why I'll take my chances downtown."

"Not with this, you won't."

He reached behind, hit a button on the console, bringing one of the monitors immediately to life. There I was, entering the foyer in front of Phillip's room, wandering through his suite, then standing before his bathroom sink and digging around in a drawer. When it was over he hit another button, returning the room to an ominous silence.

The air was suddenly much too warm. It was the hot seat upon which I suddenly found myself.

"It's a clusterfuck, Chad, I promise you that."

"That it is, Wolf."

Sherman surely had my back. As soon as I got out of here, I planned on calling in the Director of the FBI to help find him if I had to. I preferred to believe that he would find me first.

"So let's end this little dance," he said. "I have something you need, and you have something I want."

"I have resources of my own. Better than yours."

This made him smirk. "That, my handsome friend, is either a bluff or a matter of opinion."

"So call me."

We stared at each other for what must have been a minute, an eternity when there are chips on the table between you and the guy you're trying to bullshit.

"What did Nicole mean this morning when she inferred that the two of you were working undercover for the FBI?"

My mouth fell open, almost as wide as my eyes.

He smiled. "You said your role was complex, don't look so surprised."

"I'm just wondering if now it's you who is bluffing.

The smile widened. "In Nicole's case, I know that's not true. I know precisely who she's working for. But you, I'm not so sure of."

I was as still as a Madame Tussaud statue.

His voice was suddenly calmer and lower. He leaned forward.

"Divine intervention, Wolf. I can give you what you want, no matter who you work for—Lou Mancuso and his people, maybe Nicole's people in Miami, too. And, you get to walk out of here when it's over."

The unspoken flashed between us. A faint humming tone from the electronics filled the room.

"I'm not sure what, if anything, I should say to any of this."

"I'm asking for two things. First, you continue to play your role. Do as Nicole asks, meet with Pascarella, be the go-between. Maybe make a few dollars for yourself along the way, that's fine. Only now you report back to me. When the time is right, we pull the plug, take them down. This video keeps you in the game until that happens."

"Whatever that means."

He was nodding as he shifted, his own defining moment having just arrived.

"Two, the Attorney General will offer Lynn full immunity for her cooperation in landing two of the most significant organized-crime figures active today. Also, a manslaughter plea for any complicity in the death of her husband, and for any improprieties they dig up relative to the operation of Xanadu since her daughter's death. She'll walk."

I swallowed, my eyes still huge.

"This is what you came here for, Wolf."

"You assume a lot about my ability to cut deals. Trust me, that's *way* above my pay grade."

The room was receding into a tunnel before me. I no longer heard the faint drone of the electronics in the background.

"You have twenty-four hours," he said.

My eyes flitted around the room, a nervous tick I'd first noticed when an outgoing girlfriend confronted me about the incoming squeeze of the month.

"What if I'm just a schmuck out to make an easy buck? What if I'm exactly who and what Nicole sold me as to Mrs. Valentine?"

"Doesn't matter. Same outcome for us." A pause. "There's nothing easy about what I'll be asking of you. I know that."

A long pause, the ambient humming louder now, competing with the rushing of the blood in my ears.

"Talk to me, Wolf."

I looked up at Chad Merrill. And then I told him everything that I knew to be the truth.

46

Clusterfuck, indeed.

There was Nicole, a.k.a. Charleen Spence among a long list of other recent a.k.a.'s, and her offer to facilitate a way for me to earn one million dollars to deliver a video to Bradley Pascarella that would incriminate Lynn Valentine. She believed I would buy it because she thought I was still invested in her FBI cover— I'd liquidated that investment the previous day—and the plan was a way to bring down the bad guys, which was our original mission together. But why this plan, really? To arrange, perhaps, a meeting at which both Lou Mancuso and Bradley Pascarella would be in attendance, during which, I assumed, everyone in the room would be annihilated, Francis Ford Coppola style. That would enable Nicole's Miami people to come in unhindered, and Lynn would happily hand over the reigns to Xanadu for a better deal and the sweet peace of mind that comes from knowing your husband died a horrible death by arsenic poisoning.

My fate in this scenario, I had to further assume, was a bullet in the back of the head.

Then there was Bradley Pascarella, resident hands-on king of all things Xanadu, he of the gold chain and the oppressive eau de toilette. He would offer me yet another million to find out who Nicole was working for—million dollar bills were flying around Vegas like free buffet tickets—hinting at the strong likelihood that he had anticipated her takeover agenda. Which would eventually get her killed. With a few more answers from Chad Merrill I would have the information he sought, and I would, once again, receive a bullet in the back of the head for my efforts.

Enter Chad Merrill. He of the God complex and the forty-million-dollar covert observation system. His allegiance and some unexpressed sexual tension was devoted to Lynn Valentine, and to save her from Nicole and separate her from further dealings with the Mancuso folks, he had enlisted me as his eyes and ears. The purpose of my involvement, I had to assume, was to intercept the news of a bloody meeting between all interested parties, and either make sure the FBI had an invitation, or perhaps facilitate all the right people ending up in a box when the dust settled.

I couldn't help but suspect that one of those boxes was reserved for me, and I would occupy it with . . . wait for it . . . a bullet in the back of my head.

That left Special Agent Sherman Wissbaum, he of the FBI and the Martin Sheen hair, my official employer for this little field trip. Sherman would approve of each and every attempt to hire me in the last twelve hours, and he would implore me to juggle each nametag the best I could, with a spanking-new clandestine wire stashed securely on my person that would allow him to indict anyone who came within earshot. In his spare time he was promising to return my missing Cayman Island money, and was dangling the possibility of even more tax-free funds for my time and trouble and the ridiculously high risk that I would lose a body part in the process.

But Sherlock was missing a good game. And until he punched back on the clock, I was on my own, without a program.

I nibbled on this buffet of the sublimely absurd yet insanely dangerous on my journey back to my room. Chad Merrill had suggested with some urgency that I remain there until one of the players threw me the ball, promising the services of the entirety of the protective resources at his disposal, which rivaled that of a small armed-tank division.

We've already agreed that the shitstorms do indeed come in threes. It's just that nowhere in the manual does it say they will descend upon your head within the space of three minutes.

When the specially wired Droid phone given to me by Sherlock was confiscated by Thumbless Joe yesterday in my room, I'd resurrected the services of my trusty old Verizon flip phone, which I'd stashed in a pocket in my suitcase. This was the number I'd given the nursing home and, more politically relevant, to Blaine up in Portland.

There was one message.

"MR. *Schmitt, this is Riley Parsons, from the nursing home. I was just calling to tell you that your mother left most of her things when she checked out this morning. And, that you have a balance due, which you should have remitted when you were here. Our Sunday morning crew doesn't normally process checkouts, so it slipped through. If you could give me a call at your convenience, actually as soon as you can, I'd appreciate it.*"

ALL kinds of things run through your mind when you realize your mother has been kidnapped. Especially when you know who did it, and why.

And that if you didn't jump through their hoops, she was dead. And because you have no idea what those hoops are, this is the supreme ultimate in crazy-making, the kind that makes your guts feel like a spool of barbed wire.

I sprinted the rest of the way to my room, causing the two housekeepers in the hall much alarm. The effort had no effect on my pulse, which was already red-zoned from the call.

This was when shitstorms number two and three fell from the sky, a tandem jump.

The telephone in my room was ringing.

"Wolf," said Chad Merrill. "Thank God."

Strange. We hadn't been *that* close.

"Listen," I said, no humor evident, "I just got news . . . I have to leave. I'm sorry."

"I don't think so, Wolf. Listen to me."

The bomb that exploded in my stomach had to have rung a few bells at the nearest seismic lab. My first thought was that Merrill was behind my mother's abduction. He hadn't sounded surprised and certainly not remotely concerned. But then I remembered that Pascarella had already foreshadowed the possibility. Perhaps they were ass-buddies after all. Nonetheless, I knew in my heart that whatever Merrill was about to say would relate to my mother's whereabouts in some dark way.

"Better explain that," I said, "and fast."

"I didn't tell you everything when you were here. But now something's happened, something bad, and you need to know. It affects everything we discussed."

Never unpack at Xanadu. I'd heard that.

"Someone kidnapped my mother, Chad. You know anything about *that?*"

I heard him exhale, then murmur an expletive that evoked the name of a certain savior with the middle initial "H."

"No. But it fits. Pascarella's leaning on you. Just like they leaned on Lynn. He plays rough."

"What happened?"

"Caitlin is gone. Taken from a safe house this morning. When Phillip was found dead we decided to get her out of here."

"How would he know?"

His laugh was a snort of irony.

"Jesus. It was his people who took her, Wolf. Everyone on the property works for Pascarella, whether they know it or not."

"You've heard from him?"

"No. And we won't for a while. He's got the ball. All we can do is wait. He wants us to sweat it."

"Does Lynn know?"

There was silence on his end. A long silence.

His voice was barely audible. "Yes. And no."

"Shit, Chad, what the hell does *that* mean?"

More silence. This was bad.

"Lynn found out an hour ago. We talked, I told her not to discuss it with anyone until we knew more."

This explained her attitude when I met with her in her suite. That of a woman who had just lost everything she loved, and somehow it was my fault. I'd assumed it was because of Phillip, some twisted guilt transference thing.

"We have to talk, Wolf. Now."

"I'll be right down."

"No. Go to the Bellagio, ask for a bellman named Clyde. Be there in ten. And be careful. If you're followed, don't come."

His voice had no life, not a trace of anger or urgency, in spite of the John Le Carré context.

"Chad, talk to me. What the hell is going on here?"

"It's Lynn."

I paused, already grabbing the wall.

"She's dead, Wolf. She shot herself in the heart less than ten minutes ago."

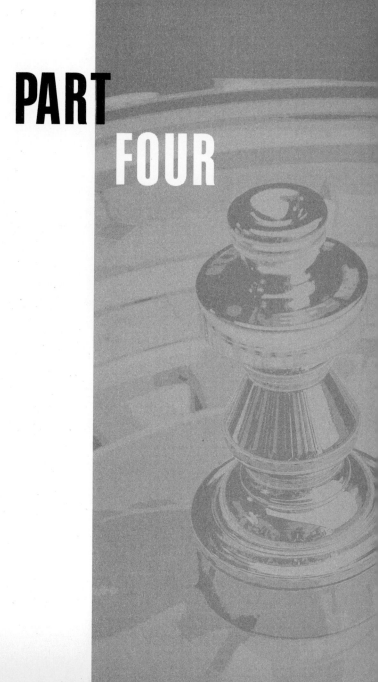

PART
FOUR

47

This would be an excellent time to exit the hotel. When news of Lynn Valentine's death hit the street, I would suddenly be the most popular person of interest in the precinct. I used the same back stairwell that had facilitated my wayward assault on Phillip Valentine's suite the night before, happy to step out into the sunlight next to some trash bins and a bevy of carcinogen-ingesting blackjack dealers who barely gave me a look.

The Bellagio was a twelve-minute walk at my pace. The whole time I couldn't get little Caitlin's face out of my head, the supreme confidence, the unbridled joy at meeting a new friend of her mother's, the way she opened the door to a relationship by asking me to play tennis with her.

I walked faster. My mother probably really *did* think it was me who checked her out of that nursing home. Caitlin had lost both parents in the space of twelve hours, and she was in the company of men who smelled like analgesic balm.

I prayed Chad Merrill's God complex was still up to speed.

THERE was the usual crowd at the overwrought entrance to the Bellagio, with enough bellmen to put together a drill team. A rock band was checking in, roadies piling off a bus airbrushed with black clouds and faces of females wearing cat masks. I asked one of the uniforms where I could find Clyde, and the guy he pointed to was already watching me, as if I had been aptly described. He nodded as I approached, code for *I know who you are,* and I nodded back in kind, code for *I'll tip your ass next time, pal.*

He raised his hand in the opposite direction of the taxi line. A white stretch limo pulled away from the curb down the access road, did a loop around to the entrance cue, then stopped fifty yards short of the competition. The Xanadu logo was unmistakable on the door panel. A huge yellow scar.

The limo door opened. Clyde nodded again, and I was off.

Chad Merrill was on a mobile phone when I got in. As soon as I closed the door we sped off, traveling much too fast for a parking lot, even here. Merrill's eyes met mine, though there was no other acknowledgment. He was listening intently, nodding occasionally to himself.

Shortly after we turned onto Las Vegas Boulevard, I heard him mumble "Jesus H. Christ" and close his eyes.

Then he hung up. He stared, his head shaking slightly, almost tremorlike.

"Just when you think the shit couldn't get any deeper."

"What happened now?"

His eyes narrowed to slits, remaining fixed on me.

"You, my friend, are in a very deep hole."

Two metaphors in fifteen seconds. Not bad.

My head began to shake a bit, too. I raised both arms to a half salute of exasperation.

"That was a contact at the newspaper. Lynn's death has already leaked and he wants a blurb. Said he had something I might like, so we traded."

"And?"

"Last night they found a body out at an abandoned warehouse east of Henderson. Poor bastard was inside what used to be a Buick, a block of scrap about yea high."

He was holding a hand at waist level. My stomach felt like it was being stretched to the same dimensions.

"Police won't confirm or deny, but rumor has it there was Federal I.D. on the body. FBI."

"Holy hell," I breathed, barely.

Sherlock. That explained the silence of late. I had feared the worst, but in my mind the worst was a bureaucratic fuck-up improvised by someone wearing a suit.

Suddenly Chad Merrill was looking like my only friend.

"You think it's your guy?" he asked. Not thirty minutes earlier I had been telling him about Sherman Wissbaum and the fact that he had ceased to exist.

"Could be a ruse. Could be something completely unrelated."

"It's not a ruse that my handle has disappeared from the radar. No way that happens without . . . something like *this*."

Emotion was the last thing I thought I'd feel, but a tug of something like it was gripping my throat. Sherlock, with his thick-chinned lame comebacks that made me laugh. Sherlock, with his willingness to bend the system to get an outcome, which made me respect him. Sherlock, with his wife and two kids at home, proud of the man they called Special Agent Daddy. Somehow, if I got out of this with a pulse, perhaps sitting in an institution of federal discipline awaiting my appeal, I would figure out a way to make this all my fault.

I breathed deeply, allowing the sensation to pass. Merrill respected the moment.

Then he tossed me a large manila envelope.

"Read this," he said, sort of disgusted by the necessity.

I tore it open and slid out a thin sheath of what were obviously legal documents. Dense font the size of spilled pepper. Awareness dawned with the recognition of two sets of words. The first was *Power of Attorney*. The second was my name.

"Lynn's lawyers are none too happy about this," said Merrill.

"Neither am I." I looked up. "What the hell?"

Merrill was nodding sadly. "It was her idea. When Lynn found out about Caitlin she went off. What you'd expect. We had to give her two clicks of Valium to shut her up. When she calmed down, it was clear what she needed to do, and I agreed with it."

I wondered what he meant by *needed* to do. The woman was, after all, dead.

"You agreed to give me control over Xanadu? That's freaking absurd. That's . . . it's beyond any and all reason."

"Absurd, absolutely. But easily explained. We've been down this road before with Mancuso. He knows it, that's why he took the girl. A slam-dunk move, because there was already equity in the threat. He doesn't get Xanadu, Caitlin *dies*.

That simple. We had no choice and he knew it."

"No choice for *what*? Needed to do *what*?"

"Sell him the hotel. At his price. One of his corporate shells will come forward and make an offer for Xanadu. It's a privately held company, completely unconnected to him on paper. The bidder will be clean, the seller will be within their rights, and the Commission won't be able to touch the deal."

I paused, long enough to take a drink of water from one of the available bottles in the console.

"What the hell does any of that have to do with me?"

"At a glance, that's a reasonable question. People will ask, and there'll be no good answer to give them, other than the fact that the two of you were lovers. Lovers do crazy things. This was one of them."

"We weren't lovers."

"As of now, you were."

"She hired me to kill her husband! Are you fucking nuts?"

Another ironic, sad little laugh.

"Perhaps. Selling the hotel to Mancuso to get Caitlin back was Lynn's idea. Giving you power of attorney over the deal was mine."

I stared at the man. *He* was fucking nuts.

"Think about it. It keeps all the balls in play. It allows you to negotiate your mother's return. It allows Nicole to believe her interests are being taken care of by someone she controls, giving us time to tee her up. Pascarella will deal with you because you'll give him what he wants from you. This is what you and I discussed, putting you in the middle of it all, the efficient, under-the-radar puppet master."

We locked gazes, both of us processing it all.

"We can make this turn out any way we want," he added.

We drove awhile, in no particular direction. By now we were near UNLV, the basketball stadium and track off to one side. I could use a good run, right about now. Straight off a very steep cliff.

"I think," he said, his eyes distant, "when I told her how it would work, it gave her some peace. She knew she couldn't handle it. And she knew Caitlin would be taken care of."

It hit me a moment later, awareness triggered by the look on his face.

"You and Caitlin?"

"I'm thinking Texas, somewhere with horses. Maybe Oklahoma."

I looked down at the paperwork in my lap, not able to make out any of it except my name clearly printed in bold type. A long minute passed in silence, the most peaceful of the day.

"When do we meet the man?" I finally asked.

Chad Merrill smiled slightly, nodding once. Approval.

That strange connection affirmed.

"Tonight."

"Will Lynn's attorney be there?"

"Just try and stop him. He won't like you either."

"Can't say I blame him."

The smile remained in place.

"You'll need to peel Pascarella away, have a one-on-one before you sign anything. Tell him what he wants to hear about Nicole. Find out what he wants done about it, then offer to give it to him. Tell him you have your own score to settle. He'll like that. Then, you're done. It'll be over."

I had trouble visualizing that reality.

"How do we get this into the hands of the Feds?"

He shook his head. "That, my friend, is your problem. You know my terms, and they extend to Lynn's memory. And, as Caitlin's guardian, to me. Are we clear on that?"

I wanted to say *crystal,* but that was so last year.

"Absolutely."

"Right now you're doing this for Caitlin. And for your mother. That should be enough."

I watched as another limo shot by. The windows were down, a bunch of college girls getting an early start on a bachelorette party. Probably heading to the spa for face-lifts and champagne. My life used to be simple that way, the next party, marrying off friends one by one. One day I was the only one left in the limo.

If you want to *matter,* be prepared to pay.

"It is enough," I said quietly, noting the sense of calm that was suddenly filling me, just hours from the most dangerous, foolish thing I'd ever done in my life.

It was over an hour later when I realized I hadn't asked about, or even thought about, getting paid.

48

Based on the décor of his office, Bradley Pascarella had also been watching James Caan *Las Vegas* reruns. When I saw a huge poster from *The Godfather* featuring Caan in his heyday, and that it had been signed—*"To my friend Brad, remind me never to piss you off, Jimmy C."*—it occurred to me that perhaps it was the show that had been based on Xanadu. The poster was one of many composing the primary interior-design motif, positioned in vertical pairs covering each wall, each signed.

Sharon Stone had written, *"To Brad, nice ass—SS."*

The office had a fireplace surrounded by deep burgundy leather sectionals. Above the fireplace was an oil of Xanadu's founder, Lynn's grandfather. The man looked plenty pissed off.

The office smelled of stale cigars. So did the seven or eight men there, all wearing exceptionally nice suits.

Except one. He wore a shimmering blue warm-up emblazoned with the logo of the New York Knicks, and thick black-rimmed glasses. No one spoke with him, leaving him by himself on one of the leather chairs.

When I arrived, alone—Chad assured me he would not be welcome here, and the lawyer who'd insisted on coming had been told to wait by the elevator—I saw that I was sorely outnumbered. An aide escorted me in, and as the double doors closed behind me, Pascarella disengaged from a conversation and approached, hand extended. I found it all very bizarre, this meeting among extortionists and child killers, that the tone would be that of a country club happy hour.

But that's as far as the cordials went. No one else bothered to introduce themselves, and if hostile looks had weight I'd be one black and blue power of attorney designate.

"I have what you want," I said, nervous about what would happen next. Chad Merrill had equipped me with answers that would keep me alive for the next ten minutes. What took place after that was up to me.

Pascarella grinned, an awkward state for the guy.

"Nicole."

I handed him a single sheet of paper, which had emerged from the printer earlier. On it was printed one word:

GERMANO

I watched his face. It was made of stone and every bit as cold. Only a slight twitching of the muscles where his jaw hinged indicated that he was chewing on what he saw. Without looking up he asked, "You'd bet your life on this?"

"I'd bet hers. Fingerprints don't lie."

Now he looked up.

"We didn't run her prints. She was Lynn's employee."

"I took the liberty of running them."

"Ran them where?"

"I have my sources. Her real name is Charleen Spence. Two indictments, six months served. What the record doesn't show is that she sleeps with Germano's only son, and is at the center of everything they do."

"How'd you learn that?"

"Like I said."

His eyes went back to the sheet. He mumbled, "Charleen Fucking Spence," to himself, as if he's heard the name.

Then he looked up, ready to move on. Just like that.

"Chad Merrill says you have something to tell me. I'm listening."

"Actually, I have something to show you."

I'd worn my best—make that my only—sportcoat for the occasion. From the breast pocket I withdrew a thumbdrive.

"What is it?"

"My admission ticket."

He stared at the drive as if it would explain what that meant.

"You know I went into Phillip's suite last night. You know Lynn and I were plotting to undo Phillip. I had no idea what it involved. I was told the medicine would make him sick, not kill him. Take him out for a few weeks while Lynn mounted an assault for control of the business. You know that already. What you may not know is why."

"I'm all ears."

I gave this one the appropriate low tone. "Lynn and I were lovers."

Those cold eyes never flinched as they bore into me.

"What's on this?" He held up the DVD in its case.

"Proof."

"That you were lovers? I'll pass."

"Proof that I didn't kill him."

He tapped the case against the palm of his hand. Knowing we were being observed, he motioned with his hand for someone without looking over. The fellow who came was the six-foot-nine defensive tackle I'd met in the weight room that day with Phillip.

"Take him outside and sit."

"I'll stand, thanks. Been sitting all day."

The big fellow took my arm, as if I wouldn't know where outside was. Using my free remaining arm, I went back to the breast pocket and extracted yet another folded piece of paper. This one would rock his world.

"Read this," I said as I held it out.

He took it from me, then flicked his head toward Jolly Green to get me out of there. To sit.

It was the Power of Attorney document, authorizing me to represent Lynn in the sale of Xanadu.

THE "sitting" took thirty minutes.

At some point during that time I knew they'd watch the digital video, which showed Charleen Spence entering Phillip Valentine's suite approximately six hours before I got there—a time-code was visible in the bottom right corner—entering his bathroom and replacing the bottle of testosterone with an identical one she'd brought with her. This switch was much clearer than the video showing me doing the same thing.

The slippery Miss Nicole had told me Chad Merrill possessed a video showing Lynn doing the switch. Neither Merrill nor I had a clue why she'd said that. Lynn's death changed everything, including Nicole's need for a video incriminating her, since it would no longer be of any benefit to Pascarella, Mancuso's front man at Xanadu. This unexpected twist explained her absence from my life for the past few hours, giving her time to confer with the rocket scientists in Miami about a new way to squeeze my balls.

The second part of the video showed Lynn and me in the spa on the first day of my tenure as her personal trainer. Lynn had said the spa was a camera-free zone, yet one more underestimation of Chad Merrill's desire to know about and control everything in his world. While not conclusive in its outcome—semi-nude mashing, lots of tongue, a few misplaced hands—it was certainly enough to corroborate my recent claim that I had been her lover, which in turn made it credible, if not particularly likely, that I would be given her power of attorney as we attempted to take over the world.

At least that's how we hoped he'd interpret it all. If he didn't, I wouldn't live to see what they were serving at the breakfast buffet the next morning.

As I waited, my thoughts focused on Sherlock. The news of his supposed compression was not something that I had taken lightly. In fact, it had made my physically ill all day, the nausea tempered only by regular infusions of fat-free yogurt. There are only so many options available to an undercover mole left high and dry and abandoned on the beach. I'd called the Seattle office again, leaving as much of the story as I could on voicemail, which I assumed was being listened to in real-time. Apparently those with emergencies knew the secret number required to actually reach someone. They'd arrive the next morning to some very distressing news, and if Sherman were alive it would get to him before his morning coffee had cooled. If the rumor of Sherlock's demise were true, however, then my fate depended solely on the likelihood that he had made our relationship official, as in *on paper,* or at least had told someone who counted about this case file.

Or, perhaps, that they'd at least want to talk to someone who claimed to be working for him on the side. Just a guess.

If I were a betting man, which I was, I didn't like the odds of any of these cards paying off. Chad Merrill had been right— this was now about getting Caitlin and my mother back. Those odds depended entirely on my ability to dance through whatever came my way as Lynn's power of attorney guy, and on Chad Merrill's integrity as my new best friend.

Deep shit, indeed.

49

Jolly Green remained behind when I was summoned back to the room. The office had been cleared of all but two people: Pascarella and a cartoon character of an aging man in a blue warm-up and Groucho glasses without the plastic nose. They occupied the two leather chairs flanking the couch, facing the fireplace. Pascarella motioned with his eyes that I should sit between them.

"Do you know who I am?" asked the older guy.

I was sorely tempted by many responses. None would, I sensed, be in my best interests, so I simply shook my head.

"That's good. Names don't mean shit. What does mean shit is that you and me come to an understanding."

Now I nodded. A little chill of realization ran up my spine. This was Lou Mancuso.

Pascarella leaned forward. "This power of attorney thing is horseshit. But until we find out otherwise, we'll move this along. Our legal people will get involved, and once you accept our offer, so will yours."

It was here that I held up my hand, thus risking my life.

"Question," I said.

The two men exchanged glances, as if I were some sort of foreign species. I looked at Pascarella, and he nodded back.

"Where's my mother?"

He smiled. In happier times I would have launched from the couch and inserted my arm down his throat to the elbow.

"You didn't seem too, how shall I put it, *moved* when we met earlier today. I like a sure thing."

"Really? I thought that little machine of yours was, how shall I put it, pretty fucking terrifying. Where's my mother?"

"Kid's got balls," muttered the man I assumed to be Lou Mancuso. Pascarella, however, was not impressed.

"You'll learn that I don't take chances," said Bradley. "Took you, what . . ." he glanced at his Rolex, "twelve hours for you to get back to me with an answer? Guess the thing with your mother worked."

Now he smiled again.

"The car crusher would have sufficed."

"Whatever."

"So we're good. Tell me where she is and we can move on."

"She's safe, is where she is."

"That wasn't our deal."

Pascarella nodded slightly, his eyelids at half-mast.

"You negotiating, Wolf?"

"Didn't think I had to. I assumed you were a man of your word."

Mancuso chuckled out loud. When Pascarella looked at him, irritated, the older man held up both hands and said, "I told you guys, I'm talkin' balls."

Pascarella took a deep breath, obviously repressing his own desire to insert something deep into my esophagus.

"You'll get her back. I need you to do one more little task for me first. That's the new deal. We cool, Wolfie?"

"You want the hotel, you'll give her back."

Now the old piss and vinegar was boiling in his eyes.

"You want to die old and with all your parts, you shut the fuck up and listen to me."

Time to jack it up.

"Second question: where's Caitlin?"

You'd think I'd just told him the IRS was in the lobby.

"You took her, too," I said. "You bring her back, you return my mother, then you get your hotel. For a fair price, I might add. And skip the *make-him-an-offer-he-can't-refuse* bullshit. Brando is dead. We cool, Brad?"

"He prefers *Bradley*," chimed in Mancuso. "Last guy who called him Brad ate chopped food through a straw for a year."

"Good to know," I countered.

Pascarella got to his feet, an action that caused every cell in my body to indulge in small spasms. He went to his desk and picked up the phone, turning his back as he spoke, then as he listened.

Mancuso stared at me, a tiny grin twisting on his face.

"Balls," he said admiringly.

"How about them Rebels?" I replied, in reference to the local college basketball team, a perennial contender. What was I going to say, *beat up any hookers lately*?

"They suck," he replied, clearly knowing more about it than me. Thankfully Pascarella was returning to his seat to change the subject.

He put his hands over this face, as if praying, staring at me. Pondering my fate, I presumed.

"It wasn't us."

"Rumor has it one of your people took her out of the hotel, on Merrill's orders."

"Maybe you should ask Merrill about that."

"He says I should ask you," I fired back.

A deep breath. "We don't have her."

"Think about it," growled Mancuso. "Why take the girl and then deny it? Hell, that's probably what we *should* have done. But he's telling you, it wasn't us. And I'm telling you, don't go down that road. Not with him."

Now the deep breath was mine. "Then who? And why?"

"Clearly," said Pascarella, "somebody wanted something from Lynn. And as you say, if not us, then who?" He added an infuriating grin. "Take a guess."

"Charleen Spence."

He winked, made a funny noise with his mouth, and pointed a gun-finger at me. My old man used to do that after a few beers.

I said, "Help me get her back."

He shrugged. "Not our problem."

God, how I wanted a piece of this guy. I glanced nervously at the old man, who appreciated my balls.

"If you want your hotel deal, you'll help me get Caitlin back. Whatever it is you want from me, tell me and I'll do it if I can. Those are the new terms. It's win-win."

Pascarella flopped back on the chair, his hands again in front of his face in the steeple game of what was probably not his childhood.

"Okay," he finally said. "This might work. What we want is a meet with Nicole—sorry, Charleen Spence—and her people. I want old man Germano and his kid there. I want his lawyer and all his seconds there."

"So you can kill them."

"So I can make them understand."

"By killing them."

He looked at Mancuso and shrugged, mildly amused. "Hmmm. Think they'd understand then?"

"You want *me* to make the meeting happen."

"Those are *my* new terms."

"And she'll do it because . . ." I let the statement hang, which was the point. Or so I thought.

"Because you have a hotel she wants. You tell her you have Lynn's power of attorney, that you control the estate, and that you're ready to deal, she'll drop to her knees for you. You were Lynn's lover, so of course you don't want us stinking up the property any longer. This is what Lynn wanted. Tell her you want to set up a meeting, who you want there. Tell her you'll bring your people, you'll have cocktails, then you'll sign papers. Remind her there's a Nevada gaming commission who will be very interested in the deal, so she better show up with a clean buyer."

"I think they'd know that."

"Just sayin'. She can even pick the location. Their comfort level. Then you tell me when and where. That's it."

Both of my hosts looked smug.

"How does that get Caitlin back?"

The two men quickly swapped glances. Mancuso nodded.

"Let's just say I'm confident Charleen Spence will tell me what I want to know. Leave it at that."

"When?"

"Tomorrow. I want an answer by noon."

"I don't know where she is."

"I have a feeling she'll find you."

I thought a moment. Pascarella didn't get where he was, much less live this long in the company of sociopaths, by being as dumb as the people who watched his back.

"This could work," I offered.

"I just said that," said Pascarella.

I patted my knees. "Okay then. You boys have a nice evening. Drink some beers, go catch a movie."

I got to my feet.

"Your mother's a sweet lady, Wolf. Don't fuck this up."

"She's not, actually. She's just insane. Oh, by the way . . ."

There was one more item in my pocket, an envelope this time. I took it out and plopped it onto the coffee table between them.

"What's that?"

"The asking price for Xanadu. Have *your* response ready by noon tomorrow. And don't push your luck. There are other buyers out there."

Then I turned and headed for the door, wishing I had eyes in the back of my suddenly very light head.

"You got some fucking balls, kid," I heard Mancuso say as I opened the door. Again I fought off a thick catalog of responses and just walked away, past the hormonally enhanced bodyguard who looked as if he'd like to bounce me down the stairwell for exercise.

As I passed him I said, "Is it true all those 'roids make your testicles shrink up like little raisins? I heard that's what happens."

I didn't break stride to see what he thought of *my* balls, which had so recently been praised by his employer.

Never mind I threw up in the elevator on the way down.

50

Sleep was, of course, an impossibility. I had turned it over so many times, spun it and kicked it and tossed it up in the air, that I was beginning to doubt the details. Making up stories about what might have been and what might happen next. During such nights one loses any differentiation between panic and sleep, they blend into a horrific emotional stew that leaves you praying for the dawn.

I was in such a state of existential angst when I sensed I was not alone in the room. With the curtains drawn to shut out the stark illumination of the strip, the room was as dark as a crypt. So imagine my alarm when, in the midst of this silent and sudden awareness, I saw a flame ignite from the vicinity of the chair in front of the dresser mirror.

Spielberg would have appreciated the visual. In the yellow aura I saw two faces, the fire only inches from both as a beautiful woman lit a cigarette, the glow on her eyes and cheekbones positively satanic. One of the images was from the mirror. The other was Charleen Spence, come to claim my soul.

I fumbled for the bedside lamp, found the switch.

"I'm sorry, this is a no-smoking room."

She blew a slow and elegant stream of smoke toward the ceiling. Then she smiled.

"Maybe you should call the manager. Oh, that's right, the managers are both dead."

"I see you got my message."

"I've been a little busy. From what I hear, so have you."

Another slow drag, our eyes locked. It's always strange to see someone you've known as a nonsmoker suddenly playing for the other team. It's just a pinch of tobacco rolled into a paper cylinder, no different, in many ways, than chewing a piece of gum, but unlike a stick of Dentyne the impact is that of someone suddenly speaking in tongues, the effect being the uncomfortable conclusion that this is not the person you thought you knew.

Then again, I'd come to that conclusion long ago where this particular bitch was concerned.

I said, "You're the star of a fairly active rumor mill around here."

Her eyebrows raised. "Really."

"One of those rumors concerns an FBI agent found stuffed into a compacted car. Know anything about that?"

Surprise arrived on her face, taking a back seat to a sincere desire to remain stoic.

"I don't."

I stared. It made her uncomfortable, speaking volumes.

"You don't seem too upset about that."

Another slow inhale, as if she was auditioning for *Basic Instinct 3*. "I'm devastated."

"I mean, being an FBI agent and all, I'd think you'd be all fired up about that one. Maybe you knew the guy, know what I'm saying?"

Her smile reinforced the satanic first impression.

"I know precisely what you're saying."

We engaged in one of those unspoken bridges of time in which both parties are afraid to speak that which both parties already know, because it will change everything.

"Chad Merrill says your name is Charleen Spence. Just a rumor, though."

A last drag before she stubbed out the butt on the top of the desk, no ashtray.

"Well," she said, taking time to blow the last of it out. "That certainly changes things between us, doesn't it."

"Just what I was thinking."

"You believe everything Chad Merrill tells you? What if I told you he was playing you? That I own the guy."

"So . . . would that make you a puppet *mistress*? Sounds kinky."

"What else did he tell you?"

"If he *was* your boy, you'd know what he told me. Which means you're fishing."

Her eyes burned with an anger barely suppressed. "Maybe you should be asking what he told *me*. Now *that's* interesting."

This dance was certainly picking up its tempo. She was tangoing with the wrong partner, too.

"Why don't you just tell me."

"He told me that Lynn Valentine gave you power of attorney over the sale of Xanadu. Imagine that."

"Hey, Schmitt happens." I'd spent a lifetime getting teed up for that line.

"Cute. I mean, all those lawyers, all those loyal employees . . . and she names *you*? What's up with that, Wolf?"

"She thought I had an honest face. And a nice ass."

"Be a shame if anything happened to either of them."

I shook a finger at her. She smiled back, as if her words were more jest than threat.

"Nonetheless, looks like I'm the guy. Let me guess . . . you and your consortium are interested in making an offer. Just another rumor."

Any trace of humor or self-righteous confidence melted away, replaced with a sudden fierceness.

"Want to hear another one?" I said. "This is a whopper. People say it's you who kidnapped Caitlin, to use as leverage to get the deal."

She was already shaking her head. "No," was all she said.

"No what?"

"We don't have her. That sounds like Pascarella's style."

"Funny, that's just what he said about you."

"I don't know anything about it. A shame, too."

"My money's on one of you."

"Which makes no sense, you dumb fucking bonehead. If one of us took the girl, don't you think we'd send you a snapshot with our offer for the hotel? Maybe a finger? What's the point if it's not leveraged?"

"Sorry, I'm sort of new at the extortion game."

"You'll catch on. It's fun once you get the hang of it."

I felt the heat assault my cheeks, drawing a few deep breaths to keep it at bay. The banter was fine until it connected to Caitlin. At this point I wasn't above landing a firm left jab should the opportunity present itself.

She gave me that smile again. "You'd like to rip my throat out, wouldn't you?"

I nodded.

"Ah, but you see, I just *might* have the girl, and if you fuck this up she's dead. Which means I own *you*, too."

Amazing how the wrong kind of smile incites violence. Married folks know the feeling well, but it was new to me.

"You want the hotel, make an offer."

"I intend to. How's this for starters—you get to walk out of here without bleeding, and with that two million dollars Lynn was never intending to pay you. How's that sound?"

"Return the girl and we'll talk."

She nodded, perhaps appreciating my cool. Or, perhaps, visualizing me hanging by my feet off the Grand Coulee Dam.

"Tell me what you want," she said, her tone impatient.

"A meeting. Bring your people, I want to meet them."

She chuckled. "Not gonna happen, Wolf."

"You want the business bad enough, it'll happen. I know all the names, don't leave anyone out. You pick the place, within the next twenty-four hours. If I like what I see, including the numbers and the assurance of the safety of all parties involved, we can talk further. If not, Lou Mancuso has a few ideas of his own for the future of Xanadu. Now that Lynn's gone it's all the same to me."

I took a deep breath, dedicated to Caitlin.

"Interesting, how quickly you've forgotten the girl in all this. What's it been, thirty seconds? You're cold."

"Au contraire. Here's the bottom line. The team that brings her back first, happy and healthy, gets Xanadu. That clear enough for you? If you have her, then you win. If you don't, I suggest you find her."

It was a strange conversation to be having in the nude in the middle of the night, with a woman with at least four names that I knew of. A woman who *smoked*, for shit's sake.

"Let me get back to you," she said.

She stood up, smoothing the leather of the pants she wore.

"Soon would be good," I said.

She marched out the room without another word, leaving behind the stink of her true self, literal *and* contextual.

Bradley Pascarella would be a happy guy come morning. I wished the same were true of me, but it wasn't.

Unable to fall back to sleep, I opened the curtains hoping to observe the dawn of what I prayed would not be my last day. I was naked in the window, looking out over six tons of air conditioning toward the adjacent seven-level parking lot, which was strangely dark. The hour before dawn was when stillness reigned. When, as the saying goes, it is always darkest.

I spoke softly, but out loud.

"Sherlock, if you're out there, buddy, I could sure use an assist." I paused, an unexpected wave of emotion embracing me. "You were a good man, my friend."

And then the strangest thing happened. From somewhere in the depth of the parking lot, hidden within the sandwiched layers of cold gray concrete, a set of headlights flashed on and off, twice.

A chill ran up my spine, sending me diving back under the covers, refusing to entertain anything beyond coincidence.

I was tired beyond my ability to see straight. Which was my only explanation outside of coincidence, something I had long ago given up as an easy crutch. And when you give up on coincidence, what remains is *meaning*. If it's not coincidence, then, by definition, it has *relevance*. Utterly unavoidable. No matter what one's state of denial.

I fell asleep wondering how, in the end, I might be touched by it all. Thus far, it felt like a stiff kick to the head.

51

The answer came in the form of a note slipped under my tray when room service brought me the omelet I didn't order. The meeting would be that evening at nine, at the Palms hotel, which was definitely neutral territory. Worse than neutral—it was common knowledge that the Maloofs and the Valentines came from different planets, and that the doormen at the Palms had orders to evict anyone that was known to be associated with Xanadu. On the other hand, the doormen at Xanadu had orders to shoot anyone from the Palms on sight.

I knew the note was from Charleen Spence. It was written on a cocktail napkin from the bar in Portland where she and Duncan Stevens first approached me about this job, such as it was. Impossible for anyone else to know. Except Sherlock.

I immediately called Pascarella's office with the news.

Okay, not quite immediately, since a warm omelet is much tastier than a room-temperature omelet. He wasn't in, so I left a message with his assistant, a woman who sounded a little too much like Goldie Hawn in her *Laugh-In* days.

Pascarella called me back within sixty seconds.

"The Palms?" he began. "You sure?"

"Sort of hard to fuck that one up, Bradley."

I could hear him chuckle. "Smart."

I wasn't sure if he meant her or me, having just called him by his preferred surname.

"And then some."

"She's bringing the family?"

"I told her that I wanted to meet them, that the deal depended on it. Which brings up an issue."

"I'm listening."

"I'm not going."

"You're going, Wolf."

"I don't think so. Given what I know about the outcome, I don't think I want to be there when they cut the cake."

"Your mother says you're going."

The guy was good. I was on a roll, and he just threw a sack of nails on the road I was heading down.

"If you were me," I said, "would you go?"

"I wouldn't want to be you."

"See what I mean?"

"Come to the fucking meeting, Wolf. Nothing bad will happen there. You have my word. Make friends, have a few drinks. Make them trust you. Tell them what bastards we are over here."

"Easier than lying, I guess."

"You oughta watch that mouth of yours."

"I get that a lot."

"What possible good would it do us to fuck with you? Or to hurt your mother? Just do the work, you'll get your mother back, and if you don't push it too far you get to leave town with a big grin and a shitpile of cash. That's a good deal, Wolf. Don't kiss a gift horse on the mouth."

"It's *kick*, Brad, but I hear you."

"Bradley. Just be there. Or your mother pays the price on your behalf."

"How about my offer?"

"We'll talk later."

"I gave you until noon."

"Fuck noon."

He hung up. They really were bastards over here at Xanadu. And, as the Valentine estate's power of attorney, I was now officially one of them.

52

I'd had quite a day. I'd spent hours walking the street with my trusty old flip phone, calling every regional office of the FBI for which 4-1-1 would provide a number, a total of eight. Six had actually connected me to someone who pretended to care, saying little as I went through my story dropping Sherman Wissbaum's name, informing them I was on undercover assignment and had been inexplicably left unattended, and that I was in dire need of a lifeline. Or least some marching orders. I was flying solo and I barely had my learner's permit.

It sounded preposterous, even to me.

The other two just took my name and said someone would be in touch. All eight thought I was crackers, I was certain.

It was like a confirmed bachelor's long dreaded wedding day, wandering the mean streets lamenting the last time I'd ever do this, my final glimpse of that, my last meal from a fast-food joint, all the privileges of the unattached. Or in my case, the *breathing*. There was a pit of anxiety in my gut that wouldn't go away, the need to try something, to make a difference while there was a chance.

Chad Merrill was doing what he could to help. When I arrived back at the room there was a remote hard drive containing the last sixteen quarters of financial data filed with the Commission. Any buyer would want to see it, and offering it to the Germanos would further substantiate the legitimacy of the meeting I'd called. Otherwise, it smelled a lot like a load of bullshit.

Time had run out. Whatever happened was out of my control now, even if I failed to show. If I didn't make an appearance with the Germanos, the fate of Lynn Valentine's daughter and Wolfgang Schmitt's mother was up for grabs.

I couldn't live with that. Even if it meant I had only a few hours more to keep trying.

THE Verizon rang in the taxi on the way to the Palms. It was Chad Merrill, his voice agitated.

"I got something."

"Is it contagious?"

"One of the employees in maintenance is missing. Turns out he was seen going in and out of Charleen Spence's room in the past week."

"She doesn't do blue collar."

"For the record, she does *anybody*. I checked his employment record, and it coincides with her arrival. He was her guy. My guess is he took the girl. They're lying if they say they don't have her. They do."

I could sense the rate of my pulse accelerating.

"What do I do with it?"

"Don't back down. They want the hotel. Get the girl back. Give them whatever they want."

I hung up and told the driver to turn around. I asked him to take me to the nearest Fed Ex, and to wait. I wouldn't be long.

*   *   *

IT was a whole new ballgame at the Palms. From the bellmen to the wait staff to the dealers, these people were young and, compared to others hanging around the local labor union hall, basically fit. The staff at Xanadu was mostly just out of reform school when Nixon resigned, with enough mileage on their collective faces to start their own frequent flyer club, "flying" in this case meaning something other than air travel. The Palms was bright and colorful, full of pretty people and movie theaters and restaurants and things to do besides donate your money to chance. Xanadu had more cigarette machines than toilet stalls, and the only movies on the premises cost fifteen bucks a pop in the rooms, a selection of pornography to rival anything Caligula could have imagined.

And of course, there were all those stars. The hotel was owned by quintessential silver-spoon brothers who were more than willing to kiss a lot of celebrity ass between trips to Sacramento to watch their basketball team in the arena they would have to replace to keep the team in town. And to top it off, they were good looking as hell, the pricks.

But I would see no stars tonight, unless I happened to piss off Charleen Spence's boyfriend and he hit me over the head with his rap sheet. As I approached the front entrance with not a clue as to what to do from there, a young man intercepted me—he said he'd been told to look for a guy with Owen Wilson's nose and Denis Leary's scowl, and based on that I was easy to spot—and took me to a side entrance and a nondescript metal door. Just inside was an elevator accessible only by key, as were the floor buttons inside.

He sent me alone up to the fifty-fifth floor, to a private room down the hall from the famed Ghostbar, where Britney and Justin and Ashton and Paris all held court, as long as there were photographers around to chronicle it all. Where else would the most notorious family in all of crime hold a little soirée in my honor?

53

Team Germano was actually quite cordial, in an *I'd-rather-be-having-hernia-surgery* sort of way. There were six of them, in addition to Charleen—the father, the son and fabled betrothed, another obviously older and dumber son who had a thing for the shrimp they'd brought in—they both looked like diminished versions of the old man, a cross between a character actor and the maître'd' at an old-school steakhouse—plus a grizzled veteran of the mob wars who stared at me as if he'd like to rip out my throat, and two slick Ivy League geeks I guessed were attorneys, based on the fact they looked as if they couldn't fight their way out of a Mary Kay convention. I never met *them*, actually, but they were on call if needed. There were also four bodyguards, and the fact that they didn't quite look like the second team defensive line at Miami U. told me they would prove to be exceptionally dangerous in a tight spot.

There was enough tension in the air to fuel a joint session

of the Super Committee. I just hoped these guys had more sense than those elected officials.

Charleen introduced me to them one by one while the others stood around nursing drinks and checking out the view. It was clear this was a pain in their Sicilian asses, that they were perhaps impatient to hit the strip. Drinks were served by three hostesses straight out of Hefner's mansion, blonde clones with sculpted lips that were impossible to look away from. They occupied the strays with intellectual repartee while Charleen took the players through an obligatory schmooze with me.

It was all posturing and impatience, ridiculous really, since no one in the room wanted to be there. Most especially me. It was like a cancer charity reception full of tobacco executives. An exercise in the art of façade.

It took about ten minutes of this charade to get down to it. I'd finished with the older brother—he wanted to know if I'd seen any movie stars since I'd been in town—and the crusty long-time lieutenant, who said absolutely nothing to me at all.

We were down to Charleen's boyfriend and his father. Truly the opposite of love at first sight, and it was mutual.

I hadn't looked too closely at the boyfriend, not wanting to get caught staring. But now, as she brought him to me, I took a closer look. And recognized him immediately.

Charleen Spence's boyfriend was none other than Duncan Stevens. He shook my hand as she introduced him as *Craig*, his face full of amused victory.

"I liked Duncan better," I said.

"I bet you do."

Now he could add impersonating an FBI agent to his résumé. If you didn't know his job was interfacing with Colombian drug lords regarding the importation of ten thousand pounds of cocaine each month, you'd think he managed the nearest Barnes & Noble. Provided, that is, that he could read.

"So Wolf," he said, "What's up with this? Cost me nine grand in jet fuel to get out here on short notice. If the old man didn't want to play golf with fucking Wayne Newton someday, we'd be in Miami."

I smiled with as much plastic as I could muster.

"It's about you, Craig, or whatever your real name is. Think of it as an audition."

He didn't like that. The door to the patio and a fifty-five story drop was twelve feet away, and I saw him eye it for a quick second.

"You know what, Wolf?"

Charleen put her hand on his arm, her eyes telling mine I was making a terrible mistake. He drew a deep breath, closed his eyes. He was smiling again when he reopened them several seconds later.

"Charleen said you were a comedian."

"Hey, I'm here all week."

For the second time in that week, my listener didn't get it.

"So what gives? We gonna deal, or what?"

"I have two buyers. I'm just testing the water."

"How's it feel?"

"Chilly."

He got *that* one. Actually thought it was sort of cute.

"Way I hear it, you have one offer and one buyer. We are the latter, and the former don't count. Which means, you give us the nod, the suits arrange a signing with a nice neat little cover band, we file all the red tape bullshit with the gaming commission, and we're good."

"Looks like someone's been reading their Chamber of Commerce brochure."

His face went white as he said, "You got a big fucking mouth on you."

Charleen again grabbed his arm and quickly pulled him away. That's when old man Germano wandered over, his face alive with amusement. He'd been handsome once, to a degree that never quite yields to age. And I couldn't help but notice that he bore a frightening resemblance to Mancuso himself. They could be brothers.

It was then that it occurred to me that they *might* be brothers.

"My son don't like you."

"Really? I thought I felt chemistry."

"You got the power of attorney on you?"

I nodded. He held out a hand for it. *This* guy, Charleen had told me, you did not try to entertain with wit. I took out the paper, then reached into another pocket for the drive.

"What's this?"

"Financials. For your due diligence."

"Very thoughtful of you."

"Just tryin' to help. I didn't want you to fly out here just for cocktails and chitchat. This stuff is too sensitive to trust to an intermediary."

"An exchange of data between top dogs," he said.

"Something like that," I replied, smiling like I had an Old Boys Club membership card.

He stepped away for a moment, leaving me alone in a room full of people who could muster up a collective nine hundred years in sentences if indictments came with a group rate. I saw him hand it to one of the attorneys, who immediately put on a pair of reading glasses and began to earn his paycheck.

The other attorney handed the old man an envelope, which he brought back to me.

I stared at it for a moment, then took it from him.

"Don't read it here," he said. "It's straight up. The price is fair, but as you can imagine, a good value from our end. Our final offer, by the way."

"You haven't seen the financials," I said.

"That don't matter."

It didn't. After paying a token amount to send Caitlin safely off into the sunset, little of the money would ever change addresses.

The intensity of his glare drove the point home. The offer would be high enough to look credible to the prying eyes of the State auditors, but ridiculously low in terms of what the numbers would otherwise warrant. In every sense of the word, the Germanos were stealing Xanadu.

Then he said, "The little girl will have a very nice life."

My already taxed ticker skipped a beat.

"I'd like to talk to you about that," I said.

He nodded, aware of what I was going say. He looked at me with a cold intensity I hadn't seen since Charles Bronson stared down Henry Fonda in *Once Upon a Time in the West*. Shortly after that look happened, someone in the credits ended up dead.

"That isn't us," he said. "We don't work that way."

"I have information that says otherwise."

His face constricted. "That's bullshit. We don't have her. You're either bluffing or calling me a liar."

"Not a bluff. And I'm not that stupid. Either way, though, nobody buys the hotel until Caitlin comes home."

The old man was barely holding it together. I wondered how many men had squared off with him like this, and how many had lived to tell the tale.

"Listen to me. *You* gotta understand something. I've said it once, and I won't say it again. We didn't take the girl. Which means there's nothing to negotiate."

I returned his gaze as respectfully as I could. As much as I wanted to look away, that would be a sign of weakness, which would be as fatal as telling him his teeth looked like he'd been chewing chainsaw parts dipped in mustard sauce.

"Then I could use some help on that. Because what I said stands. No girl, no hotel."

"You asking a favor? That, we can negotiate."

This, I realized, was truly a deal with the devil. You can check out, but you can never leave.

But he was dealing with a devil of another kind—me. I was giving him an out. By asking for his help in getting the girl back, he'd never have to cop to taking her. He could make himself a hero by "finding" her and facilitating her return. We'd be buds for life. In appealing to his ego, I doubted he would see through the manipulative nature of it all.

Charleen was right. This was sort of fun.

"I'm just saying," I continued. "A man of your influence and reach, you might be able to help."

He worked his jaw in tiny circles, the way old men do who no longer give a shit what people think. "I'll see what I can do. Meanwhile, in return, you work with Charleen to get this deal done. We good on that, Wolf?"

"Good to go, sir."

I never did catch his first name.

We shook hands. I'd cleaned a halibut once with more warmth to it.

"We're outta here tonight. I got a tee time in the morning with a couple of guys from Venezuela. Ever been there?"

I shook my head. I guess Wayne Newton was tied up.

"Fucking hot," he said, then turned away to join his sons, who were making nice with Bambi and Thumper at the patio door.

That was my cue.

I was out of the room in less time than it took for Craig Germano to hawk up half his lung, which was my cover as I departed. I didn't want to be anywhere in the vicinity when the attorney-accountant guy opened up that hard drive.

I had been instructed not to call Pascarella upon my departure, unless there was something I thought he needed to know about their logistics. There was. He had less than an hour to do whatever it was he needed to do.

54

The hour following Wolf's departure from the fifty-fifth floor of the Palms was a confluence of intentions.

In a suite located on the forty-ninth floor, the Germano attorney opened up his laptop and connected the remote hard drive with a USB cable. After it booted and displayed a title page—the logo looked like someone had an accident on a place mat—he audibly gasped.

The page was white, except for a line of small type in the middle of the page. It read:

NO GIRL, NO DEAL.

The rest of the disk was empty.

He quickly grabbed the phone and called back up to the reception room on fifty-five. Mr. Germano wasn't going to like this a bit. And when that happened, everybody suffered.

*   *   *

THE executive terminal at McCarren Field resides in a corner of the property, in the shadow of the MGM Grand and The Excalibur kitty-corner from it. A sleek Gulfstream V jet had arrived just after six, deplaning ten men wearing golf clothes and strange shoes with no socks. All but one, the oldest, carried overnight bags or suit bags. One of the young guys carried one of each. It wouldn't be a long visit. Sometimes these private jets came and went within hours. Sometimes no one got off and a limo full of young ladies filed on without the engines shutting down.

One time a plane pulled up, the hatched lowered, and a body was dumped onto the tarmac. The plane was back in the air before anyone even saw the deceased on the pavement.

This contingent got into three rented SUVs and sped off. The pilots remained behind to fill out paperwork, a piece of which authorized a cleaning of the cabin and a restocking of the bar, which had been significantly depleted on the flight in from Miami. Then they got into a rented Taurus and headed to dinner.

One fellow, the largest of the bunch, stayed on board the Gulfstream with a stack of magazines and an iPod. He ordered a pizza from Dominos and settled in for the evening.

Shortly after ten o'clock a middle-aged woman wearing a jumpsuit adorned with the proper badges emerged from a van that had parked a hundred yards down the tarmac. She carried a large metal case, which she happily opened for the guy who was guarding the jet. It was full of candy bars and liquor.

He showed her the bar area, even opening the door to the refrigerator. He went back to his seat and took up where he'd left off, the latest issue of *Us Weekly*, with a feature on how Tom Cruise's daughter was already taking flying lessons, in little high heels, no less.

The woman took one of the candy bars from the case and affixed it with an adhesive strip. She then pressed it to the underside of the small sink, behind the drain pipe to hide it from view. Two small wires emerged from one end.

With a glance at the goon to make sure she was still being ignored, she withdrew a small device that looked like a digital watch without a wristband. Bending down, she inserted the tips of the two wires from the candy bar into portals on either side of the device, then pressed a small button. It, too, had been fitted with an adhesive strip, which she pressed onto the pipe just below the candy bar.

She was in the airplane for six minutes, making sure to keep a steady cadence of clanging wine bottles as she unloaded her wares and did her dark business.

As she left she smiled and issued a little wave at the guard. He nodded, barely looking up from his reading.

A pity. He was a nice-looking kid. She hoped there wasn't a wife and kid back in Miami waiting for his return.

BRADLEY Pascarella received a call, also just before ten o'clock. He saw from the caller I.D. that it was Wolf.

"We're good," said Wolf, his voice slightly breathless.

"Did they cop to the girl?"

"No. I told him I needed help with that. Made it easy to save face."

"Smart boy."

"What happens now?"

"Get your ass back here and wait. We sign tomorrow."

"I mean about Caitlin."

"Leave that to us. We'll do what we can. But Wolf?"

"Yeah?"

"In the end, Caitlin's not our problem. We sign either way. Then you get your mother."

A pause followed. Pascarella had no way of knowing that the mention of his mother had caused Wolf's throat to seize.

Then Pascarella hung up before giving the guy a chance to respond. He was tired of his mouth, and there was nothing left to discuss.

If Charleen Spence knew where the girl was, she'd tell him. That much was certain.

CHARLEEN Spence bid her garlic-scented companions goodbye from the doorway of her suite at the Palms, spending an extra moment with her fiancé, who wanted to tell her his plans for her their upcoming weekend in Cancun, which involved a set of identical contortionist twins recently fired from a casino in Atlantic City for engaging in prostitution with the customers.

Now there's a party, she thought to herself.

The old man was the last to leave. He took her aside, telling his youngest son to get his bag and meet him downstairs.

"This thing with the girl," he said.

"Where's he getting that shit?"

"It don't matter. In the morning you call him, tell him we found her. Tell him it was Mancuso's thing, that we had to waste a couple of his boys to get it done. Which makes for bad blood going forward. Tell him you need a signed contract, and that you'll wire a significant deposit to the account of his choice. His lawyers will need to see it all, of course, but tell him you need him to sign the intention document, which is binding. When he does that, say you'll tell him where the girl can be found. Seal it with a kiss, if you get my drift."

Charleen was nodding. She'd come up with this scenario herself, relayed it to Craig, who in turn had told the old man. Always good to make sure the old fart feels smarter than everyone else.

"Then what?"

"You get his signature, you take him to dinner, then you drive him into the hills and put a bullet in his head."

She smiled slightly. "I can do that."

"I know." He kissed her on the cheek. "You're a good girl, Char. You be safe."

He turned and waddled down the hall, as harmless as a retired caddy hanging around the clubhouse, which was precisely how he was dressed.

AT just after midnight, Charleen received a call from Bradley Pascarella. He wanted to meet, to see if there was a way out of what seemed like an inevitable declaration of war. She claimed it was not her place to have such a conversation, but he insisted they should at least view the playing field. Too much noise coming from a casino was a bad thing in this business, and Xanadu was already under scrutiny on a variety of fronts. Neither one of them could afford the mess of a war.

He had an offer, he actually said out loud, that she could not refuse.

He wanted to change teams. He would help her move Mancuso out of the picture, even set up a hit that would cripple that organization. He knew all the power players, he would help her take them out all at once, and, as most mob cleanups go, it'd never even hit the radar.

He wanted to stay at Xanadu, he said. He wanted an employer who appreciated his talents. Mancuso was a jackass.

As incentive, he told her he would give her the location of the girl, whom he'd taken as his ace in the hole. He assumed Wolf was holding the deal hostage for Caitlin's return. He'd planned on creating the illusion of an eleventh-hour rescue, blaming the Germanos for the abduction, thus positioning himself as the front-runner for the buy and further burying the Germano interests.

But all that had changed.

Caitlin was safely hidden nearby. He'd hand her over in return for a guarantee of a peaceful resolution and a place in the new kingdom, enabling her to use the leverage toward her own ends. And he'd do it, he confessed, for the chance to get to know her better.

He would send a car over in fifteen minutes. Long enough to put on something tight and negotiable.

After she hung up, she called her fiancé on the jet to share the news. But there was no answer.

Nor would there be.

55

I was waiting in the lobby of the Palms when Charleen Spence emerged from the elevator. She had changed into something more comfortably hedonistic since our previous social hour, a lot of black leather with a definite sparkle of bling. When I stepped in front of her just inside the door, she looked like she'd seen the ghost of John Gotti.

"Wolf. I was going to call you."

Her eyes went to the glass wall, and beyond to the curb. A black Chrysler 300C was waiting, passenger door open, a uniformed driver leaning against a nearby column sucking on a Marlboro. I recognized the guy from Xanadu, me being one who has trouble remembering names but never forgets a face.

"Let me guess," I said, looking her up and down. "Pascarella called. You're meeting for coffee."

"Dessert, actually."

"Don't go."

She smiled and touched my face with the tips of her fingernails. "Wolf, how sweet."

"He wants a meeting, am I right? Someplace discreet."

"More than a meeting, I think."

"You have no idea."

We both looked out at the driver, who was checking his watch. I placed the guy now, and he wasn't a driver at all. He was one of the muscleheads in Pascarella's office from that morning.

"Trust me, this isn't what it seems."

Her smile was of the mean variety. "Now *you* have no idea."

"Let me show you something."

I had brought my iPad with me. I'd been killing time in my room after I'd left here earlier, and when I saw what I was about to show her, I knew I had to find her before Pascarella did, and this was my best shot. Not that I didn't sympathize with Pascarella's agenda, at the heart of which was the return of Caitlin.

It's just that I had a better idea on how to get it done. And that I knew he hadn't taken Caitlin at all.

She tried to brush past me, but again I blocked her way.

"I don't lie. You know that about me."

"Unless someone's paying you. Then you lie like a pro. What are you up to?"

"Give me two minutes. Your life depends on it."

That made her laugh. But when she saw that I wasn't backing down, the humor disintegrated into confusion.

We moved off to the side, where I placed the iPad on a granite bell-station counter. The flow of humanity in and out of the lobby was astounding, like Christmas Eve at a mall, only half the people were carrying cocktails.

I opened the iPad, powered it up. The home page was *msn. com*, which was the page I wanted her to see.

She fidgeted, her eyes returning to the car and driver.

I put the cursor on a headline that read, "*Small Jet Explodes Over New Mexico.*"

"Read that," I said softly, touching my finger to the screen.

Her hand shot to her mouth, eyes suddenly wide. I said nothing as I hit the link, which opened to a page with the story. The headline there read, "*No Radio Contact Before Disappearance.*"

I watched her eyes as she scanned the copy. A small jet had taken off from McCarren Field shortly before eleven that night. According to the FAA, the plane had been progressing routinely along its filed flight plan when it disappeared from radar without any radio communications regarding a technical problem. The plane was headed for Miami, and believed to have been carrying several prominent South Florida businessmen, though no names had been released.

You could see the color bleed from her face.

"Mancuso did this," I said. "And now they want you."

I let this one sink in. It didn't take long.

"You're all liars and manipulators. What I do know is that you're dead if you go."

She looked out at the car again. The driver was pacing now, a cell phone held to his ear.

"Why? After everything I've put you through?"

"Because this is my fault. I told Pascarella the same thing I told your people—no girl, no hotel. If you're dead, the deal is over. I have no leverage. He'd do anything to keep Xanadu. This qualifies."

Our eyes locked. I added, "And . . . it's you."

Her breathing was rapid now, as if she'd arrived via the stairwell. She was staring at the driver, perhaps considering taking out his eyes with those lovely French-manicured claws.

"I don't know what to say," she said.

I spun her around to face me, keeping my hands on her shoulders. Those cruel eyes were suddenly red and wet.

"Leave now, use a back entrance. Lay low for the night. Meet me tomorrow morning at ten at Xanadu."

"You want me to march right into his backyard?"

"No. The Coleridge Room. Ten o'clock. Come alone."

It was a conference space named after the poet Samuel Taylor Coleridge, who invented the concept of Xanadu in a poem from the 1700s called "Kubla Khan." Naming a room after the guy was the extent of Xanadu's relevance to anything remotely academic, the other rooms being named, I would guess, something like Seagrams, Benson & Hedges, and the Valium Lounge. It had been empty and unlocked since I'd arrived—I like to jiggle doors when I'm wandering around a hotel—and I was betting the farm on the probability it would be empty come morning.

Her mouth gaped open for a moment as she weighed the offer.

"What are you up to, Wolf?"

"Saving people," I said. "One of them being you." I paused, adding sincerely, "Just be there if you want to get out of this in one beautiful piece."

Though she might have guessed, I hadn't told her everything. There was more at stake here than my mother and Caitlin, which were certainly the prime objectives. But there was me, too. What I did now, what measures I took, would define the rest of my life.

Charleen Spence wasn't even in the same league where my motivations were concerned. I just needed her to play an unwitting role if this was going to stand a chance of working.

I gave it about a one in five shot. But with no leverage, no gun, and no federal safety net, it was all I had.

56

If Lou Mancuso liked my balls before, he hadn't seen anything yet. I was about to blow the entire Xanadu drama to a Will Smith blockbuster fireball.

My day began at the UNLV gym. The jocks would be getting in their workouts before class, and I was hoping to find the biggest, scariest dude on campus. Hopefully a grad student, someone with a little life experience on their face.

The perfect specimen was doing squats when I approached. A weight room is not the kind of place where strangers approach, so the look he gave me was about as cordial as a father greeting the guy who got his daughter pregnant over spring break. My new friend was upwards of six-eight, weighed in at about three hundred pounds of pure protein, with what I guessed to be a thirty-eight-inch waist. His hair was barely there, an homage to the current Jason Statham vogue. There were five full plates on each side of the bar, meaning he was squatting 495 pounds. Easily. Probably a warm-up.

"You gonna put some *real* weight on that?" I asked as I approached. I was wearing khakis and a golf shirt. He was wearing a sleeveless shirt displaying arms that were bigger and substantially more defined than my legs. The tank top had been invented with this fellow in mind.

"The driving range is down the street," he said.

I extended my hand. "Wolf," I said.

"Coyote," he replied.

"No, my name is Wolf. I'm a talent scout. Sort of."

"NFL?"

"More like *American Idol*. Listen, you want to make five hundred bucks before lunch?"

"Legally?"

"Technically, yes."

"Is this, like, a reality show? Any babes involved?"

"No, but I may ask you to throw someone out the window."

"Cool."

"You own a suit?"

"I got a sportcoat."

"That'll do."

I gave him the *when-and-where* and left the gym feeling only a bit relieved. I had been serious about the window-tossing thing. When I got back to the taxi I'd asked to wait for me, I realized I hadn't asked for the guy's name.

AT a few minutes before ten that morning I was standing in the small foyer in front of Xanadu's several meeting rooms, which they laughably called a "conference center." The only thing people "conferenced" about here at Xanadu was how much they lost and who nailed who. I had been amused at how high the room-service crew jumped when I told them I was Lynn Valentine's personal associate, and that I wanted coffee service for twenty set up in the Coleridge Room for a press conference. And now here they were, a long table draped with white linen and two staffers in matching white jackets happily standing by.

They'd also set up a few rows of folding chairs and had taken the liberty of placing a podium with the Xanadu logo at the front of the room. A nice touch, that.

My massive new employee, whose name was Karl—with a "K," he assured me—stood next to me. That was in keeping with the sum total of the instructions I'd rendered upon his arrival: remain at my side no matter what, and look pissed off at all times. If anyone seemed like they were about to grab me, step between me and that person and fold your arms like Mr. Clean. Maybe growl. If they actually *do* touch me, anything other than a handshake, grab them by the neck and throw them to the ground. If someone produces a firearm, run like hell.

When I asked if that was all crystal clear, he grinned and replied, "fuckin-A."

It's amazing what you can get done in two hours.

I'd made fourteen calls since my visit to the weight room. So far nine people had arrived, standing in twos and threes with their coffee, their expressions politely confused. Some knew each other, some didn't.

None of that mattered. Because it would get more confusing as the morning wore on.

I remained out of sight, discreetly tucked into the recessed doorway of the neighboring conference room, which was empty today. Xanadu was not exactly the kind of place where people brought their sales teams for a President's Club retreat. More like where *Hooters* might send the winners of their annual wet T-shirt contest.

The first guest of honor to arrive was Chad Merrill. Upon seeing the set up he immediately began pacing in front of the meeting room, his walkie-talkie pressed to his mouth as he frantically sought an explanation. I thought about coming out from the shadows to greet him, but he wouldn't like what I had to say, and he had the clout to shut it down with a wave of his hand. Provided, of course, I didn't get to him first.

Bradley Pascarella and his own statistically improbable bodyguard were the next to show—he and Karl could have an interesting exchange of thoughts if things got dicey—arriving within two minutes of Merrill. When they saw each other they both stopped in their tracks, before exchanging mutual shrugs with the familiarity of two guys who shared a cubicle back at the office.

It was game time. To say I was nervous would be like suggesting that Paul Allen is socially awkward. Some things are obvious.

My entrance was upstaged, however, by the arrival of Charleen Spence. Both Merrill and Pascarella froze in their tracks at the sight of her—she was wearing the same scalding black outfit from the previous night, making me wonder how'd she'd passed the time—allowing Karl and me to approach unobtrusively from the rear. We arrived at the moment Merrill, Pascarella, and Charleen were all face-to-face, utterly speechless.

"Know what this reminds me of?" I said loudly.

All faces snapped toward me. It would have been a great time to have a camera.

"That Tarantino movie, where everyone's pointing a gun at everyone else because nobody knows who's gonna shoot who first."

"*Reservoir Dogs*," offered Pascarella.

Merrill had his eyes closed, his head shaking sadly. Again he reminded me of my departed father, who had been similarly disappointed with nearly every word that ever emerged from my adolescent mouth.

Pascarella leaned close, not wanting the new arrivals that were passing nearby to hear.

"What the *fuck* are you doing?"

And then, as if I'd ordered it up, a camera crew whisked past, two guys with equipment sporting the KVVU Fox logo— they never met a lead they didn't like—and a gorgeous talking-head field reporter. For a moment, my guests forgot I was there.

"Just a little news conference," I said.

Pascarella and the others watched the camera crew go into

the room, in as much awe as if it had been Britney Spears.

"Who's the meatball?" asked Pascarella, only now noticing Karl just over my shoulder.

"My insurance agent. One or two of your punk-ass goons, I could handle. But knowing you, I had to consider the possibility you'd bring the whole front line. *Them*, he can handle."

Karl tried not to smile. He was having the time of his life.

"This is a mistake, Wolf," said Merrill quietly.

My eyes caught Charleen's. She was barely containing a grin, having just comprehended my play.

Before I could answer, Pascarella grabbed my arm and turned me away from the others. Karl started to make a move, but I put up a hand to stop him, as if we'd rehearsed it. Pascarella's man had moved in, too. We were moments away from a sideshow.

He spoke through lips that barely moved, proving there is a thin line between ventriloquism and suppressed rage.

"You double-crossing little fuck," he began. "Your mother's sitting in a bus station in downtown Portland, waiting for someone to pick her up. We had a deal."

"That we did. You can go now. No, wait."

I pulled out my mobile phone and began to punch in a number. This, too, had been one of my calls.

"She's at the bus station," I said to Blaine Borgia, who had been sitting by the phone up in Portland, having been one of my fourteen calls. I listened to his response, then snapped the phone closed.

"Who was that?" asked Pascarella, not used to being on what is known on the street as the shit-end of the stick.

"My Portland associate will be at the bus station in five minutes. Then we'll see. I suggest you stick around until I get that confirmation. Anybody gets in his way, if I don't hear back in six minutes, I walk over to that podium and drop a few bombs."

Merrill and Charleen had been listening. All of their eyes went to the podium, awareness beginning to emerge like a nuclear dawn. My little cat was fully out of the bag now.

"See that guy there, in the brown coat?"

I pointed to a shoddily dressed guy badly in need of a haircut, awkwardly separated from his peers. I had no idea who he was. Definitely media, though, so I took a shot.

"Beat reporter for the *Sun,* their industry guy."

"That's not Ryan Dean," said Merrill, who apparently knew the industry beat reporter for the *Las Vegas Sun.* I should have anticipated that one. My stomach did a pirouette as the blood drained from my head.

"Dean's over there." He pointed to an older guy who looked as if he'd spent two decades spinning a roulette wheel. The blood flowed back where it belonged.

"Whatever. The crew is from Fox. There's people coming from KVBC and KTNV, too. My guess is one of those guys is from the Nevada Gaming Commission, probably that geeky guy, who actually thanked me for the invitation over the phone. And then there's the FBI and the local police, who I really hope will get along with each other."

As I said this, I recognized the detective who had taken me into custody the day before. I'd spoken to him personally, making a deal that if he'd let me play this out, I'd go downtown with him afterwards if that made him happy.

"Hail, hail, the gang's all here," I said, deadpanning.

Merrill ushered the five of us to the side.

"Hey," I said when we were safely tucked in a corner, "I told them ten o'clock, I gotta get up there, do my thing."

Now Merrill grabbed my arm, hard. Karl quickly removed it and pushed the smaller man back against the wall, keeping his hand on his chest to pin him there.

"He's just a pup," I said.

Merrill slapped the hand away. I inserted myself between them before the testosterone got out of hand.

"What, precisely, have you told those people?" asked Pascarella, his eyes back on the crowd instead of me.

"Oh, that's easy, Brad," interjected Charleen, definitely in the spirit of things. "He's going to tell them how your people blew my boyfriend and his family out of the sky last night."

"It's Bradley," he snarled.

His eyes snapped back to me.

"She's good," I offered, shrugging. "And that's just for starters. I told them I had an announcement regarding the death of Lynn Valentine, and the disposition of the hotel. You want the script, or do you want to know why you're here?"

The collective expressions on their face would have kept Norman Rockwell busy for the rest of the century. This is what George Dub-ya must have looked like when someone told him the CIA had gotten their wires crossed.

"I told you," said Pascarella, his lips thin and his jaw muscles tight, "I do *not* have that girl!"

"Gee," said Charleen, "I swore I heard you say that you *did*. No, wait, that was before you sent your guy to take me out. I get so confused . . ."

She turned to me. "Help us out here, Wolf."

"Happy to. I'm sick of your shit. All of you. You're pathetic. All I want is the girl. Then you can kill each other fighting over ownership of this toilet."

Merrill was shaking his head urgently. "Don't do this."

"No? Hell, Chad, it might be *you* who took her. Bradley's not that good a liar."

"You have no idea what's happening."

"Exactly right."

Just then my cell phone rang. I checked the caller I.D.—Blaine.

"Excuse me," I said as I flipped it open.

I listened. As I heard Blaine tell me he had my mother with him, that they were in his car and that she was fine, a sense of emotion washed over me, almost breaking my cover as a tough guy.

"Thanks," was all I could say.

Success breeds success. At least for me. My balls had instantly doubled in girth.

We had discussed what Blaine should do then, which was

get her off the radar and wait for my call, and to make sure they weren't followed. And if they were, to drive straight to the police.

I hung up and collected myself.

"You see how easy this is?" I said, speaking directly to Pascarella but making my point to all of them. "My mother's safe and sound. We're halfway home."

"I can't change what I didn't do," said Pascarella, anticipating my next move.

"Not my problem. Talk amongst yourselves. You have phones with you, I suggest you use them. I'm going into that room. I'm going to bide my time for ten minutes. If my phone doesn't ring, if I don't hear the voice of Caitlin Valentine telling me she's been left alone somewhere she can be picked up, I start telling amazing stories about dead twin sisters and blown-up airplanes and a plot on the part of one organized-crime family to extort ownership of the hotel away from the organized-crime family presently running the place. And I'll name names. I'll also touch upon the fact the Lynn Valentine murdered her husband as part of that scenario, and how I've been pressured by both families into signing over the business or the other girl will disappear."

I paused, allowing the implications to sink in, like a hail of bullets having just penetrated the skin. Merrill was shaking his head again, looking around for reinforcements. Pascarella was biting his lip to the point of blood, eyes on the floor, his brain cranking furiously. It's so much fun watching a control freak with no options. Charleen was looking directly at me, her eyes misty, easily mistaken as admiration.

"Makes for some pretty good copy, I'd say. Film at eleven, all that shit."

I waited again. There was nothing they could say.

"You have ten minutes," I said. "They're getting restless in there. You have my number. I called you this morning, in fact, so it's there."

I held up my phone for them to see.

Then I walked away, heading toward the waiting press conference with Karl at my side, walking backwards to make sure I didn't take one in the back of the head.

57

"Excuse me! Folks? If I could have your attention?"

There was no microphone, but it worked. The clamor died down as if someone had twisted the volume knob.

"My name is Wolfgang Schmitt, I am Lynn Valentine's personal assistant and hold power of attorney on all issues relative to the disposition of the Xanadu Resort and Hotel."

A mild buzz ensued. Some of the attendees had notepads open and were scribbling, probably my name. I could see Merrill, Pascarella, and Charleen in the foyer through the open double doors, hanging on my every word. Merrill was still shaking his head, and frankly I was surprise he hadn't made a stronger effort to intervene. I noted that none were on their mobile phones, though they could have made the call while I was mounting the podium. That could also be bad, but I was past the point of caring. Karl was standing to the side, and when I looked at him he grinned from ear to ear and gave me a thumbs-up. I grinned back.

"We're expecting several more people this morning, so if I could ask for your patience, I hope you will indulge the inconvenience, have some more coffee, which I hear is delicious. Thank you, it will only be a few more minutes."

I stepped to the side and was immediately mobbed. It was like a courtroom steps scene from a movie, a couple of microphones, the pushy reporters jostling for position, and my repeated response that all will be told momentarily. *Is Mrs. Valentine dead*? I will deal with that momentarily. *Is the hotel for sale*? Momentarily. *Is the rumor true that you and Mrs. Valentine were lovers, and that you were questioned in the death of Phillip Valentine*? What part of momentarily don't you understand?

They were right where I wanted them. Ravenous.

I waited five minutes. Went to the bathroom, told Karl to block the door. Sneaked back into the conference room, helped myself to a couple of cookies before they spotted me and attacked again. From my agency days I had been trained to sense a restless audience, yet while they were certainly showing signs of impatience—looking at their watches is the best clue—this was as juicy as it got here on The Strip. They'd stay here all day for a piece of the Valentines and their hotel.

Ironically, several more people arrived, including a second camera crew from a rival network affiliate. I tried to tell the press from the police, but they all looked alike to me.

I was about to again assume the podium—*mounting* it sounds too much like something from a Woody Allen flick—when my mobile rang from the vicinity of my pocket—the theme from *Raiders of the Lost Ark*. Always made people look.

"Wolf," I answered.

A young girl said, "Is this my mother's friend?"

A wave of unexpected emotion hit, the explanation for which had several levels of depth.

"Caitlin?"

"Is this Wolf?"

"It is, honey. Are you okay?"

"Yeah, we were just gonna eat. Is something wrong?"

"Who are you with, sweetheart? Who took you from the hotel?"

"Some people who work for my mom and dad. Is everything okay?"

"Everything's just fine. Where are you?"

"The mall at Caesars. In front of The Cheesecake Factory."

A girl after my own heart. These were very cool kidnapers, taking her there for lunch. It was a wrong chord, and I took note of it.

"Are they with you now?"

I could hear her hands moving on the phone, as if she might be holding it away from her ear as she looked around. Ambient noise could be heard, a public place.

"I don't know where they went."

"Are you sure? Can you see them anywhere around you?"

"No. Mike dialed the phone and handed it to me, told me to stay right here. What's going on?"

Merrill, Pascarella, and Charleen had noticed me on the phone, and had pushed their way into the room to get close. Pascarella was saying something softly to his bodyguard, so I made eye contact with Karl to put him on notice.

"Nothing's going on. Mike was right, you need to stay right there. Don't hang up, okay? Stay right where you are."

"Wolf, you're scaring me!"

"There's nothing to be scared of, sweetheart. Don't hang up, okay? I'm going to make another call, but I'll be right here. Can you do that?"

"Sure. This is kinda weird."

"I know. I'll be right back."

I held out my hand to Karl, who handed me his cell phone. He'd already called 9-1-1, as we had planned. I put it to my ear and listened. Meanwhile Karl faced away from me, right in the path of Pascarella's gorilla, who looked menacing.

"Emergency, how may I direct your call?"

"Police. Please hurry."

No response, just a static tone. Moments later a female voice answering for the Las Vegas Police Department.

"I have a kidnapping to report, and I need immediate assistance."

"Your name?"

"Wolfgang Schmitt. I'm at the Xanadu hotel."

"One moment."

It was the longest moment of my life. And I had lived through some whoppers lately.

I put my phone up to the other ear. I felt like Donald Trump closing a deal. But this was better than anything Trump could manufacture.

A man this time. "Sergeant Deshane. You are Wolfgang Schmitt?"

"I am."

"Tell me what's happening, sir."

With pleasure. And as fast as I could. My point was that the girl needed to be picked up, and fast. I was expecting a typical bureaucratic runaround, but he was surprisingly helpful. I'd been on the phone less than a minute—the crowd around me in the conference room had grown, some of the reporters have picked up on stray words, like *kidnapping*—when he suddenly put me on hold.

A few seconds later a new voice came on.

"This is Lieutenant Forbes. We have your information, and we've dispatched an officer to pick up the girl. Can you describe her, and her exact location?"

"Thirteen, looks sixteen, long dark hair, huge eyes. I don't know how she's dressed. She says she's in front of The Cheesecake Factory."

I heard him repeat this to someone within his earshot.

"We have an officer en route. Can I reach you at this number?"

"Absolutely."

"You are at the Xanadu?"

"I am."

"Please remain there. We'd like to talk to you about this."

"Just get the girl, please."

"We're on it, sir."

The line went dead. I put the other phone to my ear.

"Caitlin?"

"I'm here. I'm a little scared."

"No, honey, everything's great, don't be afraid. You'll see. In a minute a police officer will come to you. I don't want you to be scared, but I do want you to go with him. Do you understand?"

"Will he be cute like you?"

"Probably not that cute."

More ambient noise. Then voices.

"He's here, Wolf."

Now *that* was public service.

"So is he cute?"

"You were right."

"Put him on."

More rustling, then a male voice. "This is Officer Eason."

"You've got the girl? She's alone?"

"Yes sir. Who is this?"

"The guy who called it in. May I have your badge number, please?"

"Why do you want my badge number?"

"Humor me."

He covered the phone. Muffled voices again.

"Sir, detectives are on their way to the hotel to speak with you. Please remain where you are."

Then the line went dead. Another wrong note.

I handed Karl's phone back to him. I looked up to see no less than six microphones pointing at my face. Among the stares were those of Merrill, Pascarella, and Charleen, who was smiling.

I was happy to tell them that Caitlin Valentine had been found, and that she was fine. No, there had been no kidnapping, just a misunderstanding. No, the Xanadu hotel was not for sale, at least not today. Yes, I was Lynn Valentine's lover, and I was darn good at it.

There would be no more questions. They followed me to the nearest elevator, where Karl kept them at bay to ensure my privacy as I went to my room. My three duplicitous friends remained behind to lick their wounds and regroup. I had no idea which of them had made the call that freed Caitlin. And while I believed in justice, I truly didn't care a lick.

I hurried back to my room to pack. I had to get the hell out of Dodge before my luck ran out. And based on experience, luck was known to be in very short supply at Xanadu.

58

I was *so* done. By all that is good and holy and right in the universe, I *deserved* to be done. On the other hand, I probably deserved to be in custody. It was all a matter of perspective and who could afford the best lawyer.

My mother was safe. I called Blaine as soon as I got back to my room, and he already had her at a Village Inn eating waffles. Caitlin was safe and sound with the police. She had to be, as it would be virtually impossible to intercept my 4-1-1 phone call—especially if you had no forewarning that I was about to place one—and impersonate the responding officers. I wasn't sure what would become of her from there, but I was confident that they wouldn't simply leave her with Chad Merrill, whose allegiance was in grave doubt where I was concerned.

The Open Issues file, I knew, was significant. Enough to bring me back here, personal attorney in tow. But in the meantime I intended to go to Seattle and talk to Sherman Wissbaum's superiors, talk to my state's senator if I had to, whatever it took to build a base of defense against what could amount to a landslide of suspicion. Chad Merrill would be pivotal in my defense, and that remained a wild card. My leaving town in the middle of it all would be a factor. Pascarella's inevitable pack of lies would be hard to refute. And yet, I still held Lynn's power of attorney, and who knew what I might be able to trade where that was concerned.

As long as it remained off the IRS radar, the rest was something I could handle.

All of this was assimilated and churned while throwing clothes and toiletries into my suitcase. I was headed for the back stairwell and a taxi.

And then there came a loud knocking on my door. Followed by the loud pounding of my pulse against my eardrums, barely drowning out the sound of my stomach turning inside out.

It was the little bald police detective, this time with another suit and, as before, two uniforms.

"Still checking out, I see," he said, barging in.

With a pantomime he illustrated that he wanted me to offer him my wrists.

"You're under arrest, Wolf. You have the right . . ."

"Cut the shit, Sparky. What is this?"

"You are under arrest for the murders of Phillip and Lynn Valentine. And a whole bunch of other goodies."

"You're shitting me."

He was grinning ear to ear. He didn't like me much.

"I shit you not."

The cuffing went off without incident, me being a guy who knew how to pick his battles. As I was read my Miranda rights I wondered where Karl had gone, my prepaid five hundred dollars in his pocket. He'd have a great story for the locker room the next morning.

They made me wait in a squad car with one of the uniforms for thirty minutes. I had no idea why, but before the evening was over I would find out.

*　　*　　*

ON the seventeenth floor, where Bradley Pascarella kept his poster-lined office, he and Chad Merrill were engaged in a lively debate about who fucked who when there came a knocking on his door. Pascarella was irritated, since both his assistant and his bodyguard knew better than to interrupt him in this manner. Even in an emergency, buzzing in through the intercom was the safest way to keep one's job.

"What?" he screamed.

There was no answer to the question. That fact pissed him off even more than the knocking.

He stormed to the door and swung it open, ready to rip into the intruder. Maybe fire the bastard on the spot to set an example. So far it had been that kind of day.

The first thing he saw was a badge. Behind it was a short guy with no hair in a bad suit, flanked by a big guy with too much hair and a worse suit. A uniformed officer stood next to him, his uniform crisp and impressive. Behind them all stood the bodyguard, shrugging with his palms turned upward.

"Bradley Pascarella?"

"You know who I am."

"Lucky me. We'd like you to come downtown with us. Please."

"Go fuck yourself."

The shorter detective turned to his associate and smiled. "What'd I tell you."

"Asshole," replied the guy.

"Fuck you, too," said Pascarella.

"We have a warrant to search your office."

"Be my guest. Clean it up while you're at it."

"Oh yeah, I also have a warrant for your arrest."

"That's bullshit."

But the little guy was holding it in his hand, waving it in front of his face like a fan.

"You know, I'm kinda hoping you resist this. Derrick here is just dying to kick someone's ass."

Pascarella looked at Chad Merrill, who shrugged in a similar manner as the guard.

"You gonna arrest him, too?"

"Hey," said Merrill, "thanks a lot."

The cop was loving it. "Not today. Today we're just gonna arrest you."

"You got a charge?"

"Sure. A ton. You got a lawyer?"

"A whole fucking building full."

"You'll need them. You're under arrest for suspicion of murder, for starters."

The uniform was inside the office, readying the cuffs.

"You got nothin'."

"No? We got extortion, racketeering, conspiracy, tax fraud, and a whole lot more, Brad."

"Bradley."

"Whatever."

"This is bullshit."

The cuffs were going on easily.

"We got a witness, for starters. And you'll never guess who."

"I can't wait."

"Gonna have to. Don't want the witness harassed. Oh, by the way, that's on the list, too."

Pascarella didn't fight the cuffs. As they led him out of the office he turned to Merrill and said, "Call McGrath. Get me back here by noon."

Merrill watched them go. Only after the elevator door closed did he allow himself to smile.

59

The holding cell was more like an office, concrete walls, a desk, and two very hard chairs, with a little glass window in the door. Which was securely locked. I'd been there for thirty minutes, each of them eroding my confidence that this stood a chance of working.

It was then that I heard a key slide into the lock. It opened, admitting a man in a suit. He was smiling, every bit as robotically as the woman.

I gasped, unable to breath.

It was Special Agent Sherman Wissbaum, back from the dead. Behind him were two agents who immediately flanked the door, which had been pulled shut behind him.

"What?" said Sherman, mocking the fact that my mouth was gaping open and my eyes were literally popping from my skull.

"If you say I look like I've just seen a ghost," I said, "I'll kill you for real."

"Good to see you, too, Wolf."

I just shook my head. Then I put my elbows on the table and cradled my forehead in my hands, clamping my eyes closed to make it all go away.

"You did an incredible thing today," he said. "And you almost fucked it up for everyone."

I shook my head without moving my hands or opening my eyes. I'd seen it in a Christian Slater movie once, and it looked pretty cool, the very essence of disbelief.

"Start at the beginning," I said, finally coming up for air. "Where this all began."

"Great idea."

"Where's my money?"

He grinned, exchanging a glance with one of the agents, who didn't return the gesture.

"It's back in your account. Every cent."

"Was it ever gone, or was that bullshit, too?"

"Oh, it was gone, all right. I know, because I took it."

I began to breathe through tightened lips, the way pregnant women are taught for their upcoming labor. I was lightheaded, overcome with the overwhelming urge to leap over the table and create a more solid basis for my arrest.

"You're pissed," said Sherlock, his face smug. "I thought you'd be happy, getting all that money back."

"You used me," I said.

"Like an ass uses tissue," he replied.

"That's the worst analogy I've ever heard."

"True. But the sting . . . oh man. It was killer."

"Do I get to hear it? Or are you just going to sit there and gloat?"

"You not only get to hear it, you get to *star* in it, my friend."

"Can I sue you for anything? I'd like that a lot."

Sherlock again looked over at the agents, who were grinning now. "What'd I tell you? A piece of work, this guy."

And then he told me everything.

*   *   *

IT all began with Chad Merrill.

Merrill had been in trouble off and on for years, decades really, even doing time in the seventies for assault. While working security for one of the big hotels, he caught a dealer cheating, dealing winners to an associate. So he cut off the guy's thumb with a steak knife.

Did six months for that one. During his incarceration he'd built relationships that would lead him to the Nevada Gaming Commission, and eventually he became a reliable source of sensitive information from the inner circle of the gaming world. His record was expunged, allowing him to seek gainful employment wherever the Commission, and eventually the Feds, needed some knowledgeable eyes and ears.

While working at Xanadu, where he was already deeply buried as a mole, he met a woman who went by the name of Nicole. With a little digging he found out her real identity as an extension of a prominent Miami mob family that, as it turned out, had designs on Xanadu as a place to launder money. Xanadu, the Feds suspected, was already in bed with another big bad wolf named Lou Mancuso, which was the objective of Chad Merrill's assignment there, to nail down a case against the Valentines and Mancuso. But he quickly discovered that the Valentines had been victimized by Mancuso in the most horrible of ways, and they were unwilling to risk the life of their surviving daughter by going to the authorities. It was an opening they could use when the right gambit came along. Which it finally did, in the form of Nicole.

Rather than rat out Nicole, it was decided he'd give her some rope, see where it led. He was instrumental in helping her gain favor with Lynn Valentine, who the year before had lost her daughter in a disappearance that, while reported, was quickly labeled as unsolved and then shelved. Lynn, who was estranged from her husband Phillip, yet captive in the family business with him, began leaning heavily on Nicole's rock, which in turn led to a dark scheme of revenge. Not just against the people who had murdered her daughter, but against the husband whose ego and greed had caused it to happen, and who had become a pathetic lapdog to the very people who had stolen from them all that was pure in the world.

Or at least half of it. Because the dead girl had a twin sister, and she was the leverage the bad guys continued to keep in play.

Phillip Valentine, of course, had his own take on the events in question. But that was irrelevant, because it didn't suit Chad Merrill's agenda. Until one day he came forward and told a story that made even a slice of gristle like Chad Merrill hold his breath. Mancuso had shown him his daughter's body, buried and preserved in a barrel out in the desert. But it had backfired. Phillip would do anything it took to bring the man down, even if it cost him Xanadu itself.

Merrill, of course, had the entire hotel wired and was a fly on the wall for nearly every conversation the two women shared. That's when he came forward with a proposition, which Lynn accepted. They would allow the revenge scheme to progress, and Lynn would introduce Nicole to Merrill as her protector and confidant, someone who hated Phillip as much as she did. In that role Merrill told Nicole he could easily find the perfect patsy for their plan. Someone completely off the radar to both the authorities and known criminal elements, who possessed the physical attributes required to make his closeness with Lynn Valentine believable. With the help of Merrill's FBI contacts, that's when my name came up. I'd been the perfect patsy before.

Merrill hatched the entire scheme with Nicole, after first shaping it with the Feds. He told her he knew of a guy in Portland who would make the perfect shill. That, of course, would be me. She came to Portland for the express purpose of finding and then seducing me, employing a few intimate details gleaned from the FBI file, and then passed to her through Merrill. Every man has his hot buttons, and mine just happened to be on record in the Federal registry.

And that's when Sherman Wissbaum got involved.

When I first went to Seattle to ask Sherlock about the woman known to me as Renee and her friend Duncan Stevens, both of whom were representing themselves as FBI agents, he went to work on my behalf to find out what he could. What he learned was that a mole buried deeply within a suspected mob casino operation was behind sending "Renee" after me, and since Sherlock had worked with me before, he was invited in as my case officer. From that point on I was a lab rat, since the only way I'd participate in such a dangerous affair would be, once again, to serve my country. And to make a nice pile of cash in the process. Both were values I held dear, and they knew it.

The idea to make it appear that my Cayman funds had gone missing was Sherlock's. Which meant he knew about the gambit days before I came to him. It was the motivation I needed to push me over the edge—or in this case, over the state line into Nevada—to keep me in the kitchen when things heated up.

And heat up, they did. The bugged Droid phone worked fine, getting what they needed from Renee—now known as Nicole, soon to be identified as Charleen Spence—in the process. But Nicole/Charleen was only one of the fish in the pond, and we were after the big sharks. In return for helping Lynn exact a dark revenge on her husband, Nicole would be allowed to bring in her Miami people to take over the hotel from Mancuso. This, of course, was of immense interest to the FBI, and thus to Chad Merrill.

The big sharks had suddenly turned into an entire ocean of criminals.

So the plot had the green light to proceed. The scheme to switch the testosterone vials had been Merrill's, spoon-fed to Lynn, who then pitched it to Nicole, who in turn brought it to me. It was Lynn who went into Phillip's suite to switch the vials, effectively creating a safe backup against Nicole working behind the scenes on her own to plant something legitimately lethal instead.

Which she did. Or at least, I *thought* she did.

And that's when I put up my hands for Sherlock to stop.

"Come with me," he said, quick to his feet. One of the agents was already holding open the door.

60

We marched in silent single file to another room down the hall. This door was unlocked, admitting us to a more comfortable space with chairs that were actually padded.

Two people were already there when we arrived. A man and a woman. They were sitting, nursing coffee, having a nice quiet chat. When they heard the door, the man stood. Both of them greeted me with huge, enthusiastic smiles.

More ghosts. I was standing front and center before a very much alive Phillip and Lynn Valentine.

I began to laugh. It was involuntary at first, but I let it flow because it masked a rising sense of betrayal that I knew was unwarranted, and that I'd very soon have to come to terms with.

I hadn't been betrayed. I had been *used*. There was a difference. If a woman uses you for sex, that's not an altogether bad thing. If she betrays you by using someone *else* for sex, that's another story altogether.

It made sense to me.

"I was in the middle of telling Wolf the backstory," said Sherlock to the Valentines. "We got right up to the point where you both died, so I figure this was a good time for the resurrection."

I was smiling as I nodded. "I gotta say, it's very, *very* good to see you." And I meant it. At least where Lynn was concerned. I didn't exactly want Phillip dead, just on another continent.

Phillip extended his hand. "I want to thank you for what you did for Caitlin today."

What sense of celebration I had been feeling was suddenly squashed under the weight of a sudden fog. I had already assumed that Caitlin's disappearance was somehow part of the script. Phillip had too much sincerity in his eyes for that to be true.

I turned toward Sherlock. "I think I need more backstory."

"I think you do, indeed," he said.

THE entire thing had been conceived to get a reaction out of the players. To motivate them to action, and to get it all recorded as evidence. Once the fuse was lit, the fire had to be allowed to burn in a natural way, a confluence of confusion and fear and ass covering that would not alert the two parties involved—Mancuso and Germano—to the scent of a possible sting.

That's why my Droid phone was confiscated—by Thumbless Joe, who had been given employment wherever Merrill worked, a sort of karmic retribution between scumbags—so that I might be a party to the natural flow of adrenaline. They were depending on my instincts to keep the ball in play. Which I did, using my cheapo backup Verizon flip phone.

Phillip Valentine's death was staged so that I would be dealing from a defensive position, calling upon Nicole/Charleen for protection, which in turn would further gather evidence of her complicity in the bigger picture. Lynn's death was staged in order to put me in the power of attorney position, which allowed me to put pressure on the players, thus forcing their hand toward further duplicity in things dark and incriminating. And it almost worked as planned. The Germanos flew in, Pascarella panicked and arranged the hit on their airplane—all of which was captured in digital.

And of course, there was always Chad Merrill around, the puppet master to my flailing, lost self. Making course corrections that kept me on the path of their design.

I was making a "T" sign with my hands.

"You had film of someone sabotaging the Germano jet?"

"Not inside the jet, just their operative going in and out. But we have audio of the setup. Mancuso ordered the hit himself while sipping a brandy in Pascarella's suite."

"So you knew the airplane was going to go down."

Sherlock swallowed hard, swapping a quick look with the grinning agent Miranda—whose shit-eating smile had waned in this moment—and with the Valentines.

"And you let it happen."

They all looked suddenly very guilty.

"There are a couple of ways of seeing this, Wolf."

"Yeah, I can see *that*."

"A prosecution would have cost tens of millions of dollars of taxpayer's money. And there was no guarantee that what we'd gathered would stick."

I shook my head in disbelief. "So you did the taxpayers a huge favor."

"That's one way of looking at it."

"By looking the *other* way."

"These were terrible, evil people, Wolf."

"Sort of like Duncan Stevens, when he was Duncan Stevens. Rogue agents, doing the wrong things for the right reasons."

Sherlock looked away. "It's complicated."

I exhaled audibly. The entire tone of the download had changed. I had been a party to death by looking the other way. I would have to think long and hard about what to do about that.

"Tell me about Caitlin," I said.

"The natural flow of things," said Sherlock. "We wanted these people to feel the heat. You were the one with the blowtorch. With Caitlin kidnapped, we knew you'd hold the power of attorney hostage to her return. That you'd make them squirm."

I stared at Sherlock, long and hard.

"So who took the girl?"

A new voice spoke from the back of the room.

"I did."

Everyone turned and looked at Chad Merrill. He'd managed to enter through a side door, unannounced and unnoticed. He took the ball and ran with it, sensing the approaching gridlock in the room.

"Both sides were going to hardball it," he said, jumping right into the deep end of the pool. "Push on you, push on each other. We needed something to put the offense back in your court. So I took Caitlin off the property. She's been with her parents this entire time."

I winced, rolling that one over my tongue for a moment.

"What about the call today, at the press conference?"

"Legit, at least at first," Merrill continued. "I placed a call to Phillip, he coached Caitlin on what to say to you."

"But I called 9-1-1. How'd you pull that off?"

Sherlock spoke up. "This is the FBI, Wolf. We have ways to get things done. Once we knew you were on the line to the local police, we had them transfer the call to us. It was actually very easy. The lieutenant who took over from the sergeant was one of ours."

"What about the policeman who picked her up at . . ."

I allowed that one to tail off. She'd been nowhere near The Cheesecake Factory as that call was taking place.

"Again, one of ours. We had people with the Valentines all along."

I closed my eyes, cutting myself off from the many eyes that were riveted on me as I listened.

"Damn," I said softly.

Lynn Valentine came next to me and laid her hand on my shoulder. "You were a hero today. In every sense of the word."

"And you almost fucked it all up," said Merrill, smiling from ear to ear. "We were going to pull the plug this morning, there was enough evidence with the airplane thing to bring down Mancuso. And then you did your dance with the press conference, which could have gotten you killed, and us screwed."

"And given Pascarella time to leave the scene."

My eyes narrowed. "You don't know me very well if you think I was going to skip town with that little girl in the hands of . . . those people."

I just shook my head.

"I know you, Wolf." It was Sherlock, dead serious now. "That's why you were chosen for this."

Silence reigned for a moment, everyone grateful for the respite, which came in the shadow of the retribution delivered by Sherlock's words.

I was moved. But not touched.

"I have two more questions," I said.

"We arrested Pascarella today," said Sherlock, as if he hadn't heard me, or perhaps anticipating my inquiry. "We're putting together something on Mancuso, we'll have him in custody by week's end. Charleen Spence wants to cut a deal, which we're happy to do in return for what she knows about Mancuso and Pascarella. It's over, Wolf."

And then, they began to clap. It was like something out of a John Hughes movie, the guy who did *The Breakfast Club* and who was fond of peer moments that would never occur in the real world.

But it was happening now. Lynn Valentine was crying softly. Phillip Valentine's massive jaw was set firm. Chad Merrill was grinning like a photograph of an 1890 embalmer.

I hung my head. There was nothing to say, and I wasn't sure what to feel.

And then I remembered where I was.

"I still have those two questions," I said.

Sherlock just nodded his consent for me to ask.

"Why me?"

"Fair enough. Based on results, so much of this operation was off the books. Why you? Because you had proven that you could operate off the books. Because neither the Mancuso camp or the Germano camp would find out a thing about you, which made you dangerous to them. Because you could do things a federal agent couldn't, and the repercussions of those things could never come back to haunt the Agency. Frankly, that's the risk you took, that we could cut out at any time. Also, and this is huge, because I know you. What you did today is the reason your name was called for this. I knew I could count on you to do the right thing."

"Balls," I said, recalling Lou Mancuso's amused acknowledgement of what he perceived as moxie. Little did he know that I am funniest when terrified. Which I certainly was.

"What about you?" I asked, looking at the Valentines.

They responded by first looking at each other. Phillip took the first shot.

"First, we get the divorce."

"You're shitting me."

Lynn chimed in here. "It wasn't all an act, Wolf." The way her gaze bore into me let me know what she was referring to.

"Then," said Phillip, "we sell Xanadu. Get out of Nevada, let Caitlin finish school where there's still hope."

"Good luck with *that*," I said, though I regretted it immediately. Sometimes I just can't help myself.

"That's two questions," said Sherlock. "Anything else?"

"Where's my money?" I asked.

The room froze. Glances were exchanged. Watches could be heard ticking in the utter silence I had just unleashed.

"I told you," Sherlock said slowly, "your money is back in your account. Right where you left it."

I snorted a quick laugh. "I mean the *new* money. The million bucks I was promised."

Sherlock's mouth bunched into a tiny wad of pink, which in seconds turned white.

"There is no money, Wolf. I'm sorry."

I nodded. "But your country sends its most sincere gratitude."

"Sucks, don't it?" offered Chad Merrill. "I know the feeling."

"It certainly does suck," I said, noticing that nobody was making eye contact any longer. It was like someone had passed wind in the room.

As we left a few minutes later, me suddenly a free man, my eyes briefly met Lynn Valentine's. I smiled, and then she did something that would stay with me, at least for the next week, when I would find out what was behind it.

She winked. As if, after all that had transpired, she still knew something I didn't.

ONE week later, sitting in my house back in Portland, I used the commercial break from *American Idol*—which offers five full minutes of the viewer's life back to them—to check my Cayman Islands account balance on line. I'd done this several times a day since returning home—the closing on the nursing home was right around the corner—figuring that if Sherlock could snatch the funds once, he could do it again for whatever purposes suited him.

Like any deal with the devil, once you were in, you were in for life.

I thought I'd made a mistake at first. But you can't make a mistake like the one looking back at me from the screen, because no matter how badly you screw up the data entry, you simply cannot haphazardly access someone else's account. No way, no how. Which is precisely what I thought had happened.

Until, that is, I remembered Lynn Valentine's wink. Never underestimate the capacity of the heart of a mother whose child has been delivered from evil. Just as one should never underestimate the antithesis, the wrath of a woman scorned.

Both are driven by a passion men have never, since the dawn of mankind, understood.

My account balance was one million dollars higher than it had been one hour earlier.

From the soulless world that was Xanadu, one woman had spoken.

61

Six Months Later

We all have to pay the piper. Special Agent Sherman Wissbaum and his employer were about to find that out, in spades.

I marched into his office with my accountant, Big Al, at my side. He'd been researching this mission for weeks, using some contacts in the IRS to withdraw otherwise confidential information that allowed us to make our case. I love it when that happens. I'd helped out with confidential information of my own.

Sherman was all smiles and handshakes. When I introduced him to Big Al, though, he was immediately suspicious. One does not drive to Seattle with one's CPA unless one is on a mission from God. And God, as everyone knows, frowns on the Feds because of that little law about the separation of church and state.

After a round of hearty chitchat—Big Al didn't say a word—Sherlock leaned back in his chair and asked what he could do for us today.

"Actually," chimed in Big Al, a grin already beginning to form on all three of his chins, "I think you should read this first."

He withdrew a set of papers from his briefcase, and was holding them out. Sherlock took possession with a suspicious look in his eyes.

"You're gonna love this," I said.

He looked down at the paper. "What is it?"

"In essence, it's a new tax code inspired by the events of 9/11. You may have heard of it."

"Please."

"The tax code."

Sherlock read a moment, then raised his eyebrows and shook his head. "Can't say that I have."

"Allow me to paraphrase," said Big Al, totally in his element now. The guy could sing the tax code in Hebrew if asked, and he's not even Jewish. "In order to motivate people to come forward to expose the activities of criminal elements, including thieves and extortionists, as well as terrorist factions, the government has created a new regulation that provides for a twenty-five percent fee, a sort of *finder's fee*, for information that leads to the recovery of taxes otherwise due the government, but that were circumvented as part of a criminal enterprise."

Sherlock was pursing his lips, scanning the document as he listened. He had no clue where this was going.

But I did. Which was why I was smiling so hard it hurt.

Sherlock plopped the document down on his desk. "Interesting. Why are you here?"

"Frankly," I said, "we didn't know where else to take this. I was sure you'd be happy to help."

I saw the first sign of alarm on his face. Glorious.

"I'll do what I can," he said.

Big Al cleared his throat and continued.

"I've taken the liberty of studying a certain report, generated by your organization, that summarizes the financial arrangement formerly in place between the Xanadu Hotel and Casino, and one Louis Mancuso, who I believe is under indictment and in custody on a variety of federal charges."

Sherlock just nodded, otherwise frozen in place. If he leaned any further back in that chair we'd be looking at his ass any second now.

I gave a quick prayer of thanks for Lynn Valentine's sudden conversion to religion. Never mind it was Scientology. She'd sent me the report, albeit anonymously, two months after the money had mysteriously appeared in my Cayman account. Guilt being a staple of religion, I assumed the two were connected.

"According to these figures, and if my calculations are correct, Lou Mancuso took in approximately two hundred and ten million dollars in revenue from his dealings with the Xanadu Hotel over a three-year period, none of which showed up on his tax forms, either personal or for corporate holdings in which he had an interest."

Sherlock was getting the drift now. "You don't say," he muttered, beginning to rock a bit in the chair. He shot me a quick look, which was hard to read.

"Using certain assumptions, all of which are subject to audit by your people and the IRS, of course, I calculate that the government is owed about twenty-eight million dollars in back taxes on this amount, more in penalties after the fact."

"The poor bastard," said Sherlock dryly.

"Now, the penalties are not subject to the reward provision. But the twenty-eight million certainly is, and in this case there was clearly an informant responsible for the exposure of this tax fraud. If my sources are correct, collection proceedings are already underway in the form of mass liquidations of Mancuso's personal assets."

Sherlock was grinning slightly, shaking his head. "Where'd you get this guy?" he asked me, which I took as a rhetorical question.

"At a twenty-five percent finder's fee, which is clearly spelled out in the code, my client, who is the aforementioned informant, is entitled to payment in the sum of approximately seven million dollars."

Which, I didn't mention, would come in handy with the expansion plans already underway on my new nursing home empire.

Big Al sat back. His work here was done.

Sherlock was nodding again. I joined him.

"How you like them apples, Sherman?"

Then he started laughing. A true, guttural joy, unrestrained and unleashed. I couldn't tell if he was happy for me or imagining the expression on the Director's face when he got the news. It wasn't his money, after all, so I was hoping for the former.

"Very nice. Both of you. Very nice."

He cleared his throat, leaning forward before the chair gave way beneath him.

"What, pray tell, am I supposed to do with this information?"

"Actually," I said, taking over now from Big Al, who had earned his pay today, "not much. We'll be filing for the finder's fee in a few weeks. There'll be an investigation, of course, and that's where you come in."

The humor was gone from Sherlock's expression now.

"I'm assuming that you'll tell them the truth, that it was me in the middle of it all, that it was me who was the primary catalyst in Lou Mancuso's case, and because of that I'll get what the United States government intended when they drafted this law."

Sherlock worked his lower lip between his teeth, then said, "Ya think?"

"I do," I said. "So does Big Al here. We just wanted you to know."

Sherlock glanced at the door, leaning over the desk.

"There are implications if I do what you ask," he said. "This kind of thing can come back to me. On my career."

"They should give you a medal."

"Already scored a promotion, actually."

"Well there you go. You get promoted and I get . . . what? I get shit. It's all good, Sherman. Do the right thing. I know you will. You're a good man."

"We'll see."

"Or . . ." I paused to watch his heart stop for a moment, "I've been working on this article."

He glared, not happy with the implication of that.

"You write that bullshit stuff, right? *Bullshit in America.* Very cute. This fits right in."

"I agree. It's all bullshit. So does the *New Yorker.* They're offering me ten grand if I write it for them."

His eyes narrowed. "You wouldn't."

I leaned forward. "You know, Sherlock, it's like this. You get what you give. I gave, now it's my turn to get. You got, now it's your turn to give. Make sense?"

I felt for the guy. I felt for everyone these days. It's amazing what a little stroll through the fire does for one's sense of place in the world, and one's compassion for the place of others.

He sat for the longest time. Then, as if someone had thrown a switch, he grinned and slammed his hands onto the desk, standing up to signal the end of the meeting.

"Well, I wish you luck, Wolf. I have a feeling we'll be seeing each other again."

"I'll take you to lunch. That's how this all started in the first place, if you remember. It's on me."

He pointed a finger at me, gun-style. "Chicken piccata," he said.

I fired the finger-gun back at him. We were like Steve Martin and Dan Aykroyd on *Saturday Night Live,* a long, long time ago.

From the hall I heard him call out.

"You're a piece'a work, Wolf."

I pushed the elevator button, the future a blank page, full of possibilities.

A piece of work. But one that mattered. One who made a difference, however small.

I was okay with that, for now.